IMMORAL GAMES

MARISSA FARRAR

Written by Marissa Farrar

Author's Note

I'm sure if you've read book one, Immoral Steps, then you'll already have a good idea of what lies in the pages ahead. Laney, Darius, Reed, and Cade were left in a perilous situation and what happens next definitely needs a warning.

As well as there being a taboo nature with the relationships between Laney and her men, in this book you will find scenes of assault and non-con, including with a weapon. There are also scenes of choking, cock-warming, DP, and other violent and emotional moments.

If this is something you struggle with reading, then perhaps imagine they've already made it to safety, and have got their HEA. But if you love all things dark and twisted, keep reading.

Marissa.

1

laney

I'D THOUGHT THE MOMENT WHEN OUR PLANE WENT DOWN, and I'd believed we were all about to die, was the most terrifying of my life, but now I'm questioning everything.

Two armed men have emerged from the forest.

One is a match for Cade, size-wise. He has a broad nose, the bridge flattened as though it's been broken a few too many times. His head is shaved, so only a shadow of growth shows through his scalp. The other man is smaller, and slight, with brown eyes that have a dark glint to them. He has cheekbones you could slice cheese on and a thin mouth that hints at cruelty.

Everything seems to fall into sharp contrast. For the first time, I notice how the leaves on the trees have started to change color, the chlorophyll they contain breaking down and revealing the yellows, oranges and reds that the green has hidden all summer. The lullaby of the river that's accompanied us through not only our hike to this spot, but most of our time here, suddenly grows too loud, filling my ears and head.

The brightest color of all is the vivid red seeping from Cade's hairline and running down his forehead and into his eyebrow. He lies motionless on the ground. Did the blow from the gun crack his skull? An injury like that could be life threatening, and it's not as though we can call for help all the way out here.

Terror fills me at the possibility he might be dead.

My heart shatters.

I let out a scream and cover my mouth with my hands.

Automatically, Reed moves to stand in front of me to shield me with his body, but the bigger of the men swings his gun in Reed's direction.

"Stay right where you are," he commands my stepfather.

Even the woods seem to have fallen silent, the birdlife no longer filling it with their tweets and twitters, the insects no longer buzzing. Can they sense something terrible happening?

Reed speaks calmly and slowly. "Look, we don't mean you any harm. We were in a plane crash, about a month ago, I think. We're just trying to get to safety."

We've been lost out here in the wilderness for weeks now, lucky to find the cabin that's been our shelter. But with winter looming, we'd felt we had no choice but to try to hike our way to safety.

The big guy arches an eyebrow. "Is that right?"

"It is," Reed confirms. "We're not a threat to you. We'd really appreciate your help."

The man snorts laughter. "We're not the people you want to be asking for help from. In case you haven't noticed, we have guns, and we're pointing them at you."

"Yeah, I can see that," Reed says, "but there's no need. We don't mean you any harm. Like I said, we've been living out here after a plane crash."

"You found our cabin then?" the skinny one asks.

"That was your cabin?" Reed feigns innocence. "In which

case, yes, we did. Thank you. That place probably saved our lives. We're very grateful for it."

Big Guy lifts his gun. "You were poking around in there?"

Reed stiffens. "Only for supplies. We needed food and fire and water. That's all."

"You didn't find anything else?" Big Guy checks.

He's playing with us, I can tell. Toying with us like a cat with a mouse.

"No," Reed says.

I want to kick him. He shouldn't have lied. It'll only look worse for us.

"Really?" The big man bends and picks up the gun Cade dropped when he was struck. He checks the barrel. "'Cause by the way the serial number is filed off, I'd say this is one of ours. And if you found one of our guns, you not only found the rest, but you also found what else—or should I say *who* else—we left up there with them."

Reed shakes his head. "I have no idea what you're talking about. We found the gun under the sink, nothing more."

Skinny barks laughter. "Bullshit."

The men both have American accents, so I can only assume they're gun-smugglers, having brought guns in from the states to sell onto criminals across the border. Does this mean we're on the Canadian side of the border? Or not? I almost want to ask, but it's not like it's important right now.

I'm rigid with tension. How is this going to play out? There are four of us—though only three are capable of fighting. There might be only two of them, but they're armed. I'm also fully aware they're hardened criminals while we're...well...normal. I'm sure Reed could hold his own in a fight, but the person who'd be most likely to take either of these two down is currently unconscious, if not worse. I know Darius would never

3

want me to write him off because he's blind, but there's no escaping that fact.

Reed gestures toward Cade. "Please, can I check on my son? He's hurt."

The larger of the two men narrows his eyes. "Your son? He's your son?"

"Yes."

Big Guy jerks the gun toward Darius. "He your son, too?"

Reed nods.

"And what about her?"

The larger of the two men fixes his gaze on me. His eyes drop down my body and then rove back up again.

Reed gives me a look of desperation. "She's my step-daughter."

Big Guy lifts his face to the azure sky then points in our direction. "Wait one minute. I remember you. You were all over the news." He looks to his buddy. "You remember them, Zeke? This is that famous fucker. The musician. The one whose airplane crashed."

The thinner one—Zeke—drops his mouth open. "Holy shit. You're right. That's fucking insane. I can't believe you four are still alive."

I find myself glancing down to Cade and praying that Zeke's statement is still true.

"You've been all over the news," Big Guy continues. "People have been looking for you."

A flicker of hope dances inside me. Does this change things? If they realize we're not a threat against their gunrunning business, they might help us. They must have some form of transportation to have gotten here, which means they must be able to get back to civilization again.

Big Guy jerks his chin at Darius, though of course Dax can't see it.

"You're Darius Riviera, right? The blind violinist dude?"

Dax nods. "I am."

He cocks his head to one side. "And you have money. Lots of money."

Darius straightens his shoulders. "You want payment to get us out of here? I can work with that. If you get us to safety— alive and unhurt—I'll make sure you're financially rewarded for it."

Zeke purses his lips. "I'm not sure that's a good idea, Axel. If we get them to the city, they might tell the police about what they found in the roof space."

The bigger man—Axel—seems to be considering this. He nods slowly. "Good point."

My stomach drops again. Shit. If they think we're going to report them, not only will they not help us, they'll most likely decide to kill us. Assuming they're responsible for the body in the roof space, they've already proven they're capable of taking a life. It's not as though anyone is going to find our bodies out here, and the authorities most likely think we're already dead.

"We won't tell anyone," Darius says. He turns his head in our direction as though to hear us better. "Will we?"

"No," I blurt. "Absolutely not. It's none of our business. We only want to get home."

I'm telling the truth.

On the ground, Cade groans and half rolls to his side. I'm so relieved he's alive, I gulp back a sob. I didn't know if a strike to the head, like the one he took, would be enough to kill someone, but I'm sure I've read about grown men dying from only one punch, so I think it could happen.

Axel is closest to Cade, and he kicks him in the gut. "Stay down, dude."

"Leave him alone!" I cry.

He scoffs in my direction. "Or you'll what?"

I clench my jaw to prevent myself saying exactly what I'd like to do to this man—none of it good—but there's no point. My words would be empty threats.

I hate being helpless. I want to throw myself at this son of a bitch and tear at his face with my nails, and hit and kick, and bite his fucking ear off, but if I give in to this impulse, I'll either get myself or one of the guys shot. I can't stand the thought of having any of their blood on my hands.

Axel does as I ask and leaves Cade's side.

"You're a pretty little thing," he says, strolling up to me. He catches my chin in the hand not holding the gun and yanks my face up.

"Leave her alone," Reed snaps.

Axel ignores him and addresses me instead. "How old are you?"

"Eighteen." I speak from between gritted teeth.

He purses his lower lip and nods approvingly. "Eighteen, huh? Barely legal. And you've been stuck out here with your stepdaddy and two stepbrothers? How's that been for you?"

I don't meet his eye, worried he'll see the truth there. "Fine."

"Just fine, huh? I can't imagine what it would be like to be stuck out here for more than a month, never knowing if you're going to get back to civilization. It must have been intense. Going through a plane crash as well. Situations like this tend to make emotions run high. Then you've got three men, with no other women around, except for a fine piece of ass like you. Don't tell me they kept their hands to themselves?"

"I told you to leave her the fuck alone!"

Reed is raging, but Zeke aims his gun directly at his head. I'm terrified he's going to end up being shot because he's trying to protect me. I'll never forgive myself if that happens.

My cheeks burn, and I'm sure my face alone radiates the

truth, but I still manage to lie. If we survive this and get back home, this is probably going to be a question I'm asked over and over. I need to learn to be a good liar.

I lift my head and stare him in the eye. "Nothing like that happened. They're my family."

Axel gives a closed lipped smile. "Sweet."

He's clearly being sarcastic, and I return the exact same smile. To my relief, he moves away from me and joins his friend again.

"What are we going to do with them, then?" Zeke asks Axel.

Axel seems to think for a moment. "We should probably run this by Smith. He won't be happy if we don't involve him in the decision."

I don't think it's possible for my stomach to drop any farther than it already has, but the realization that there are more than two of them does it. Theoretically, we outnumber them, but one of us is blind, another is currently barely conscious, and I make up the third.

Axel sniffs. "Smith doesn't have to make all our choices for us. He's not our boss."

Zeke gives Axel a look that says this mysterious Smith most likely *is* their boss, or at least thinks he is. There's tension between them, and I wonder who the body in the roof space was. Could he have been another of their colleagues, one they fell out with for whatever reason, and decided to leave up there? If they're capable of dispatching of one of their own, then they're more than capable of killing us.

Axel lets out a huff of air. "Okay, fine. We'll take them back to the cabin, and Smith can help us decide what to do with them."

Is Smith a first name or surname? Does it even matter? I want to think there might be an opportunity one day to speak to the police and tell them about these men. I build my descriptions of them in my head, ready to report. But the truth is, if we survive this, it might end up being because we've been the ones who've been forced to kill in an 'it's us or them' situation. If we do end up killing them, are we really likely to then go to the cops to turn ourselves in?

I'm surprised how quickly my thoughts have turned to murder. I've never so much as gotten in a fist fight before, never mind take someone's life, but when I look at how badly hurt Cade is, I know I'll do it if it means we get out of here safely.

If we are forced to kill, will anyone even find the bodies? Even if we describe to the police where the plane crashed, and the location of the cabin, we still might never find it again.

I think of the pilot and copilot, and the woman who'd been cabin crew. They most likely had families and friends—people who loved them—who would be searching for their bodies, desperate to give them their final resting places and have the closure of a funeral. They'd want the plane found.

The shorter dark-haired one called Zeke stares down at Cade. "How are we going to get him back to the cabin? No way am I going to carry him all that way."

Axel shrugs. "Leave him where he is."

"What if he regains consciousness?"

"What's he going to do if he does? If he makes it back to the cabin, we'll shoot him. He's not going to be able to hike anywhere to help in that state. The cougars and bears will get him first."

Panic spikes through me as I realize they're talking about abandoning Cade out here. "No, please. We can't leave him here. He's hurt."

Axel ignores me. "We could shoot him and be done with it."

"We could shoot them all here," Zeke says.

"Wait, please. Let us live, and I'll do anything you want." I'm desperate, and I'll do anything if it means saving our lives.

He looks at me, his gaze darkening. "Anything? That's quite an offer."

Reed speaks, desperate for a different reason. "Laney, don't."

I'm talking about saving his son's life. Surely any sacrifice is worth it. Any.

"It'll be okay, Reed," I say softly.

"No, this can't happen." He addresses the men. "You already said people are looking for us. We're worth more to you alive than dead."

Axel purses his lips. "Hmm. Fans have set up GoFundMes to find proof of life of Darius Riviera. We could make bank out of this."

Zeke's gaze flicks across us. "But then we only need him. We don't need the rest of them."

Darius steps in. "If we don't all make it back to safety—each one of us, including my brother—then I'll make sure you don't get a single cent. Is that understood?"

Axel's expression grows serious. "How much are you going to grease our palms with to make sure that happens."

"Half a million," Darius says. "That must be more than whatever these fundraisers are offering. But you don't lay a finger on the girl, and you let my brother live."

Surely, these men must realize that it's a case of all of us or none. If they kill one of us, there's no way they'll be taking us back to civilization and expect us to not only keep our mouths shut but also pay them. The body in the roof space is a different matter. We don't even know what his name was. He means nothing to us. If it means us getting to safety, I'll have no problem whatsoever in forgetting I ever saw it.

"Half a million?" Axel stares at Dax. "You can do better than that, surely?"

Darius scuffs his foot against the dirt ground. "A million, then, but that's everything I have, and it's not as though I can get it straight away. You'll have to wait."

Axel bats away a fly buzzing around his head. "Bullshit. We're not waiting. Do you think we're stupid? You make us wait, and you'll go to the authorities and tell them everything. We'll never see our cash and we'll end up behind bars."

"Suit yourself." Darius remains almost supernaturally calm considering the situation. "Then you either wait, or you take the half a million—which I'll be able to do as a transfer once we get somewhere that has internet access—or you kill all of us and get nothing."

"We need to run this past Smith." Axel turns to Zeke. "Let's get back to the cabin and we'll figure out what to do with them from there."

Zeke jerks his head toward Cade. "What about the big one?"

Axel hesitates, thinking for a moment. My heart has never felt so huge, as though it's crowding out my lungs, making it hard to breathe. I'm terrified what his answer is going to be. Cade's life hangs in the balance. All it will take is a single decision to put a bullet in his head and we'll all be broken.

"If he can walk, he can come back with us," Axel says eventually.

I bark out a sob of relief.

"We need to go to him," I beg. "We need to help him up."

I wait on a knife's edge, desperate for that permission.

It feels like forever, but finally Axel lowers his gun slightly and gives a nod of consent.

I exhale a breath of relief and hurry to Cade's side. I drop to a crouch and place my hand on his shoulder. I take comfort from his warmth. I search his hairline for the injury, wanting to see how bad it is. But his hair is longer now and thick—the type of hair I'd normally long to run my fingers through—so it's hard to tell.

His eyes are shut, and blood still trickles from his hairline and catches in his eyebrow.

"Wake up, Cade," I urge him. "You need to wake up and walk."

Reed joins me, squatting on the other side of Cade, and I become aware of Darius's presence to my right. I know I'm nowhere near strong enough to lift Cade, but I can help.

"Cade," Reed says, his tone stern. "Can you open your eyes? We need you to open your eyes for us."

I hold my breath in anticipation. My heart thunders so fast, the beat of it pounds against my eardrums. How patient are Axel and Zeke going to be? How many seconds will pass before this becomes too much hassle and they decide to put bullets in the backs of our heads instead?

Darius takes over, reaching for Cade's hand. "Come on, bro. Stop messing around now. We've got to get you up."

To my relief, Cade's eyelids flutter at his brother's voice and then they open. He still seems dazed, as though he's been drugged. His eyes are open, but I'm not completely sure he sees me.

"Think you can get to your feet?" Reed asks, taking Cade's other hand.

I shift out of the way to make room.

"Hurry this shit up," Axel calls over, his tone bored. "We need to get back before dark."

Darius gets under one side of Cade, and Reed goes to the other, and between them, they manage to brace Cade enough that they're able to get him upright—first to sitting, and then to standing.

I want to weep with relief. I try not to think about the huge journey ahead of us, how difficult this is going to be. It was hard enough doing the hike when Cade was well, but now we're going to have to half carry him all the way back to the cabin. What will be waiting for us? Is it only going to be the man they call Smith, or will there be more?

Our belongings are scattered across the ground, and I gather up what I can. I can't carry everything, but I pick up my bag and Cade's, too. Darius still has his violin, but both he and Reed have left the rest of their belongings on the ground. They can't half carry Cade and all their stuff, too. It'll have to stay where it is.

I thought I was never going to see the cabin again, yet now we're going back.

2
REED

My eldest son's arm hangs loosely around my neck, and I have my shoulder wedged up under his armpit, my arm around his waist.

The skinny little asshole Zeke is leading the way, while the bigger one, Axel, is bringing up the rear, herding us like we're fucking sheep. I keep trying to think of opportunities where we can take the two of them down and make our escape, but I'd be stupid to forget that they're armed, and there's at least one more man expecting them.

Anger churns deep inside me.

I'll kill those sons of bitches. I'll fucking kill them. The first opportunity I get.

I'm fucking furious, but I'm also helpless and scared, and it's not a good combination. I don't want to do something reckless, but it's taking all my self-control not to lose my shit.

Though the situations are in no way the same, it makes me feel the way I did when Laney was sick, or when Darius lost his sight. I desperately want to do something to change our situation, but with two guns trained on us, right now, it's out of my hands.

The offer Laney made to these men reverberates around my head. These aren't the type of men who will give a shit about consent. If they want her, they'll take her. I didn't miss the way they looked at her, their eyes lighting up like they'd won the fucking lottery. I'm not sure I'll be able to control myself if they try to touch her. Even the threat of taking a bullet might not be enough.

Cade seems dazed, and he's walking with one foot dragging slightly, but at least he's walking. I pray that hit to the head with the gun hasn't given him a brain injury. If he's got any swelling on the brain, when we're this far in the wilderness, it could prove deadly. It's clear Laney is worried about him, too. She keeps watching him more than she's watching where she's going.

This is hard on Darius as well. He must want to protect us all as much as I do, but it's far more dangerous for him to be up against men with guns. I hope he did the right thing by offering these assholes money. I know it's one of the only things he has, like it's the thing that gives him power, but I'm not sure even that'll be enough to save us. It'll depend on whether they decide the money we can potentially get them is worth the risk of letting us live.

I can barely believe we're heading back to the cabin again. I'd genuinely thought, when we'd said goodbye to the place, that we'd never see it again.

The return hike takes us longer because of Cade's injury. Every step is like torture, and I'm not even the one who's hurt.

Over the past month, I'd started to look at these woods as a friend. It provided us with food, and with wood for the fire. It's been peaceful—like we've been caught up in a protective nest that's sheltered us from the rest of the world.

Now that world has caught up with us.

My neck, shoulders, and back are screaming from holding Cade upright. I groan as I try to shift his position slightly to alleviate some of the strain. It's not easy with Darius also needing me to guide him, but I haven't uttered a word of complaint. I don't dare. A simple offhand comment might be all it'll take for one of these men to decide to make us leave Cade out here in the woods. That'll be a death sentence for him.

Laney must have noted my discomfort, however.

"Let me have a turn," she offers under her breath. "I can help."

I grit my teeth and shake my head. It would have to be the largest out of the four of us who ends up being the one who's hurt. If it had been Laney, any of us could have easily carried her.

The moment the thought passes through my head, guilt stabs me. I don't wish Laney to be hurt—I would never wish that—and I hope the universe or fate or whatever other unseen force that influences our world hasn't heard me. I don't want that thought becoming true.

But then I realize how unlikely it is that we're all going to walk out of this unscathed. As though we didn't have enough to contend with after the crash and having to survive, we now have these assholes thinking they can push us around. Fuck. They *can* push us around. That's the whole fucking problem. While I have no doubt that I'd give as good as I get in a fist fight, I am helpless against men with guns, and, from the body we found, I have no doubt that they'd be willing to use them.

We slow for a moment, only to receive the jab of the end of the gun in my spine.

"Keep going. We haven't got all fucking day."

Axel is making sure we don't take any opportunity to run, though I doubt we'd get far with Cade. I want to tell Darius and

Laney to take an opportunity, if they can, to get out of here, but where would they go? Getting lost in the forest is going to kill them as easily as these armed men.

I can't help wondering if it might be a kinder way to go—especially for Laney. The possibility of them hurting her makes me want to rage, and they haven't even touched her, yet.

"Can we stop and rest?" Laney asks them. "Not for long. Just long enough to have a drink of water?"

Zeke glances over his shoulder at Axel, as though he's getting his opinion before responding, then he nods.

"Five minutes. No longer."

I close my eyes briefly in relief. My muscles are screaming, and I'm having to grit my teeth with every step.

We stop exactly where we are, and Darius and I allow Cade to sink back to the ground. We take a moment to roll out our shoulders and stretch our necks and arms. Laney still has hold of a couple of bags—we'd left the rest of our belongings back in the forest where we'd been accosted, aware we wouldn't be able to carry them as well as Cade—and she takes out the bottles of water she brought along and passes them out between us.

Before taking a drink, I hold the lip of the bottle to Cade's mouth and allow him to take a few gulps. His head wound continues to bleed, which concerns me, and he hasn't spoken. I'm not sure he understands what's going on, and if he's that out of it, it means the injury is serious. He should be resting, not being dragged for miles through the wilderness. The movement won't be helping the wound to clot either.

I take a drink as well, aware I need to stay strong for the others. All I've ever wanted is to protect them—even though I know both Cade and Darius are grown men now, that instinct never goes away—and I feel like I'm failing them at every step.

"You okay?" I ask Laney.

She sniffs and nods. She's being so brave, my perfect girl. I want to scoop her in my arms and hold her tight, to kiss the top of her head and her forehead and her neck. But I can't allow either of those two assholes to think there is anything other than her being my stepdaughter between us. Not only will they use that to their advantage, but I'm still hanging on to the hope of us making it back to the city one day. If they have that sort of information on us, it could make integrating back into society difficult.

"Time's up," Axel announces. "Back to your feet."

Darius and I get back into position and lift Cade again. I swear he's doubled in weight since I set him down. I'm worried my muscles are going to reach the point of fatigue and I physically won't be able to lift him. What will we do if that happens? We can't leave Cade out here in the open on his own. If the local wildlife don't get him, he'll die of exposure eventually.

We all make it back to our feet and keep going. How far have we come or gone now? I've completely lost track. It's like driving when you're tired and know a route too well, so you're not paying attention, and can't remember driving a chunk of it. I'm on autopilot now, focusing on putting one foot in front of the other.

The only thing that keeps me going is that we're heading back to the cabin. These men might think they know it, and the surrounding area, but we've been living there day in, day out, for the past month, and it feels like home. I'm sure even Darius will be able to find his way around both the cabin and the area surrounding it better than these men could. There's also the very likely possibility that they've arrived here via some type of transportation—most likely a boat—and if there's any way we can get ourselves to that boat, then we'll have our way out of here.

The hike back to the cabin feels ten times as long. My

concern for Cade deepens. He's barely conscious, only muttering or groaning, as though in his sleep. He's managed to walk a little, but only with the support of me and his brother.

Darius's foot hits a rock in the grass, and he stumbles. He drops to the ground, and Cade goes with him, half dragging me down, too. Laney lets out a cry of shock and immediately goes to help Darius. He's angry—I can see it in his face, angry at what's happening to us *and* his disability—and he waves her away.

"I'm fine," he says from between clenched teeth.

Tears tremble in her eyes, and I want to go to her and comfort her, but I have Cade to think about.

Axel approaches with the gun. I wonder how brave he'd be if he didn't have it. I want to tackle him, to wrench it out of his hand and jam it against his skull, but his buddy has already noticed something is going on and has turned and is covering us.

"Get the fuck up," Axel commands.

"Give me a fucking chance," Darius grinds out.

I put up my hand in a stop sign. "Just give us a minute."

Zeke shakes his head. "Slow us down any more and we might as well stop. Seems to me that we'd be better off putting a bullet in the big guy's head and be done with it."

Darius snaps toward Zeke's voice. "Then there will be zero chance of getting any fucking money out of me. Got it? This takes as long as it takes."

I stare at Zeke's face, terrified this will be enough of a reason for him to decide to kill us all, but instead a smile tweaks his lips and he chuckles.

Zeke folds his arms, so the gun is no longer pointing our way. "Fine, but we haven't got all day."

We definitely don't. Dusk is fast approaching. We've been walking all day. The sky is streaked with pink, and the trees are filled with birdsong as they settle in to roost for the night. How far are we from the cabin now? It can't be too much farther. The thought of having to hike through the forest in the dark, while holding up Cade, is not something I want to give any thought to.

We get back to our feet and set off again. Cade mutters something.

"You okay, Cade?" I ask him. "You awake?"

He says something else, but I don't understand what. He needs to rest, not be dragged for miles.

By the time I start to recognize things—a fallen log, a crop of trees, a circle of rocks—it's almost dark.

Finally, the clearing where the cabin is located appears before us. I sag in relief. Thank fuck. But then I straighten again.

Another man is waiting for us at the cabin. He's Scandinavian looking, with light blue eyes, similar to Laney's, but with almost white-blond hair.

This must be Smith.

It was two against four—though the two are armed, and the four of us aren't exactly a dangerous combination—but now they've gone one extra to evening up our number.

The man had been leaning against the porch railings but, at the sight of us, pushes himself upright.

He jerks his chin at us. "Who the fuck do we have here, then?"

Axel speaks up. "You won't believe this, but remember that plane crash with the blind violinist, the one everyone's been looking for? Well, these are the survivors."

Smith's expression remains impassive. "And what the fuck are they doing with you?"

"They've been living in the cabin all this time and found Armand and our guns."

I wonder if Armand is the body in the roof space.

Smith arches a white-blond eyebrow. "Fuck."

"Yeah, fuck. We didn't know what to do with them, but looks like there might be some money in this for us, so we've let them live, for the moment."

For the moment. Our lives hang in the balance. All it will take is a split second for them to change their minds and shoot each of us.

I can't believe we've come so far, survived for this long, and this is what will end us.

Smith folds his arms across his chest and casually leans back against the porch railings. "How much money?"

"Half a million dollars...perhaps even a million, if we decide we can trust them."

He gives a low whistle "That's not to be sniffed at."

Axel continues, "But we'll only get the money if we let them live, and that's gonna come with risks."

Smith straightens again. "We'll talk about it inside."

Zeke shoves me from behind, and I feel the solid weight of his gun again.

"Is this guy your boss?" I dare to ask.

"No. We all work together. As equals."

I'm not so sure about that. I definitely got the vibe that this new guy is the one in charge and these other two went out to do his bidding.

It feels bizarre to be back at the cabin. I mention the steps to Darius, and we both help Cade up them, Laney following close behind. The new man, Smith, pushes open the front door and we go inside.

Our mattresses are still on the floor.

I realize our mistake. These men must have arrived and immediately seen that someone had been staying here. Cade probably left tracks in the dust and dirt in the roof space that would have been easy to spot with a decent flashlight—something we'd never have been in possession of—and they probably noticed the boxes of guns had been opened, too. We must have walked along the river in the opposite direction in which they'd come. They put together that they would have seen us if we'd gone that way. They could have checked the woodstove and felt it was still warm, so they were able to infer that we hadn't been gone long.

I want to kick myself now. We'd known there was the possibility of the gunrunners coming back. Why hadn't we thought about covering our tracks better? It's too late now. As much as I wish we could go back and make different choices, that's impossible.

We lie Cade down on one of the mattresses and hunker down on the floor around him. His head is still bleeding. The red flash of blood boils mine, and I force myself to clench my fists and breathe slowly to stop myself launching at these men.

"What are we going to do with them?" Zeke asks. "Tie them up, or lock them in somewhere?"

Smith shrugs. "What's the point? Where are they going to go?"

He snorts. "Good point."

I know the reason they're not tying us up, and it isn't simply because they're armed.

We're still stuck in the middle of nowhere. That hasn't changed. If we try to run, we'd be doing so with no supplies, and they'd just track us with their guns, like they're the hunters and we're the prey.

Then there's Cade. He's not going anywhere.

The only hope I cling to is that they must have arrived here in some form of transportation, most likely a boat. If we can somehow shake these guys and reach the boat before they do, we'll not only have our freedom, we'll also have secured our way back to safety.

But right now, giving these men the slip seems near on impossible.

"We have to do what they say," I whisper to Laney. "It'll be all right."

She lifts her gaze to me, her eyebrows raised, and I can tell she's thinking 'how, *exactly*, is this going to be okay?'

"Enough talking, you two," Axel snaps.

I keep telling myself that they're not going to kill us because of Darius's offer of money, but then I glance over at Cade and think again. Jesus, he looks bad. It's almost worse that it's him who is injured. He's the tough one out of my two sons—the one who never takes any shit—and to see him like this makes me fearful.

Then I think to the revelation that he's gotten himself into trouble in Los Angeles, too, and I wonder how strong Cade really is or how much of it is a front. Are these the kinds of men he's involved with back in the city? I don't consider myself a naïve person, but even the people I came up against during my boozing, drugtaking days were lightweights compared with these men.

I haven't always been sensible. Before I had to sort myself out for the boys, I probably hadn't ever made a smart decision, but after they'd landed in my life, I changed. It wasn't until Laney came back into things that all that sensibility went out the window.

"I'm fucking starved," Axel says, rubbing his belly. "Let's get some food going."

Zeke wanders over to the kitchen area. "Yeah. I could murder a beer."

We'd left the kitchen empty; now it's stacked with coolers full of supplies.

They clearly plan on staying a while.

Zeke opens a cooler and unpacks what they've brought.

My mouth waters as he pulls out loaves of bread, blocks of cheese, and cured ham. Boxes of mac and cheese, bags of chips, and boxes of cookies follow. It feels like forever since I last ate a carb that wasn't some tasteless root we dug up from the woods. Even the packets of crackers we took from the plane feel like a lifetime ago. My body literally craves these foods, and I fight not to launch myself at them, grabbing handfuls of bread and shoving it into my mouth. I glance at Laney and can tell she's thinking the same, her gaze fixed on the bags of food. Her tongue sneaks out and licks her lower lip, which she then captures between her teeth. While we've managed to catch and scavenge enough food to keep us alive this past month, it hasn't been anywhere near the amounts we're used to, and we're all starving.

Zeke lifts a case of beer. He plucks out a bottle and cracks open the lid with a hiss.

I'm hit with the memory of sitting in the sunshine at a beach bar and taking the first icy sip of beer, and my entire body lights up with longing. I almost forget I don't even drink any more. That first sip of beer was never the last. It always went on to be multiple beers, which then became whiskey chasers. Then, inevitably, I'd black out and wake in the morning filled with a deep sense of shame and the sharp claws of anxiety digging into me, and the only thing I could numb those feelings with was another drink.

3

laney

I'M FAMISHED, AND NOW THE CABIN IS FULL OF FOOD. THE men must have a mode of transportation nearby for them to have gotten this amount of food and drink here. They wouldn't have been able to carry it all on their backs if they hiked.

If we can get down to the river, I'm sure we'll find a boat.

I have no idea how we're going to do that with three armed men standing over us, and with Cade in the mess he's in, but the knowledge that a boat is nearby seems to focus my thoughts. Yes, we might all end up dead, but we might also get to safety.

One of the men—Smith—catches me staring at the food.

He strolls over to the counter where Zeke's unpacked everything, picks up a baguette, and tears off a chunk.

"You hungry?" he asks, then takes a bite, chewing slowly.

I nod, my mouth watering. I swear I can taste that bread, the sweetness of the wheat and yeast dissolving on my tongue.

"Open your mouth then."

My heart beats harder, and though I hate myself a little for my obedience, I do as he says. He steps closer, so there's mere inches between our bodies, and breaks off another piece of the baguette. His gaze drops to my mouth and his tongue dips out to swipe across his lower lip. Slow and deliberate, he places it on my tongue, his fingers brushing my lips.

I snap my mouth shut and chew. It's as good as I imagined, and it's all I can do to prevent myself groaning like I'm having the best sex of my life. I've known hunger, especially when I'd been a child and had been less capable of providing for myself, but I'd taken for granted how easy it had been to get something as simple as bread. It had always been a good, cheap way of filling myself up—toast and butter was a favorite—and I'd missed it.

I swallow, and my face floods with heat. I'm drowning in guilt at eating when the men have been given nothing. I glance over at where Cade is lying on his back on the mattress, his eyes shut. Is he even capable of eating?

"Can the others have some, too?" I ask.

Smith smirks. "No, but you can have more. I like watching you eat."

I pinch my lips shut and shake my head. I should have said no to start with.

But Reed steps in. "It's okay, Laney. Eat, if you can."

I shoot him a desperate look. "I don't want to if you can't have any."

"You should keep up your strength. It's important."

Does he want me to keep up my strength in case we find a moment where we can escape? Is he thinking the same way I am—that there must be a boat nearby, and a boat will mean we can get away?

"Listen to *Daddy*," Smith says. "Be a good girl and do what he says. Now, open that pretty little mouth."

Well, now there's no way in hell I'm taking anything off him.

"I'd rather choke."

His expression hardens. "Then maybe you will."

Before I can cry out, he grabs me in a headlock. His big bicep tightens around my throat.

The cabin explodes with activity.

"Get the fuck off her!" Reed yells.

He lunges toward Smith, but Axel, despite his size, is fast, and places himself between Reed and his boss, his gun aimed at Reed's chest.

Darius launches toward us as well, but the press of a gun at his head halts him. Even without being able to see it, Darius knows exactly what the feel of a gun barrel is like.

I fall still, going limp in Smith's grip. I won't do anything that might see one of them quite literally losing their heads.

I'd faced my own death when I'd been in the plane and realized it was crashing, but somehow this feels so much worse. Then, I'd only been fearful for my life, but now I'm terrified for the men I love. Before now, I'd never truly understood when people said they'd die for the people they loved. I'd loved my mother, but not enough to die for her, as terrible as that sounds. She'd lived her life on borrowed time, and, deep down, I'd always believed that my life was worth more— that I would do more with my time on Earth. Now I understand the statement, because I know I'd sacrifice myself for any of these men. I'd rather die than have to face life without any of them.

Smith presses the bread to my lips, and, this time, I open my mouth. He pushes a piece of the baguette onto my tongue, but ensures his finger remains in my mouth a fraction too long. I'm tempted to bite it off. Despite myself, the pleasure sensors in my brain light up at the taste. Even these few mouthfuls give me a buzz as though I've chugged a couple of shots of espresso. It's incredible the effect food can have on the body, especially when we've been deprived of any refined carbs.

This doesn't stop me being swamped with guilt, however. I know the others must be starving while I get to eat.

Smith seems to lose interest in me and goes back to the food. I'm both relieved and disappointed that it doesn't look as though I'm going to get anything more.

Will they use food as a way of trying to control us? Or try to drive a wedge between us? Will they feed me and let the men starve? I picture how resentful they'll become of me, how they might even start to hate me. Of course, I'd refuse to eat, but how strong is my willpower? If I was truly on the verge of starving to death, would I really be able to stop myself? I want to believe I'm stronger than that, but I honestly don't know.

Smith and the others seem to have forgotten we're here for the moment. They're too busy drinking and stuffing their faces. There's no sign of them believing they'll need to ration out the helpings. The concept of being able to eat whatever and how much they want feels utterly foreign to me.

We huddle together on the mattress on the floor. Cade is still asleep—or he might be unconscious—so he's lying down, but Reed and Darius both are sitting and have their backs pressed against the cabin wall. I sit between Reed's legs, leaning against his chest for support. I hold Cade's hand in one of mine, though I have no idea if he's even aware of my touch, and Darius's in the other. We form a tight knot around each other, a defensive shield.

I watch the men getting drunk and wonder if they'll take their eyes off their weapons. How hard would it be to take one of their guns out from under their noses? The trouble with that plan is that even if we managed to get one gun, we'd still be outnumbered, and whoever tried to take the weapon would most likely end up shot.

They're a little drunk from the beer, their voices growing louder and more raucous.

This place doesn't feel like our cabin anymore. The energy is all different now these other men are here. Even the smell of the place has changed. What had once been shelter now feels like a prison. I hate that they've taken that from us. Our memories—should we live long enough to have any—will be warped by whatever these sons of bitches decide to do.

Smith finally seems to remember we're here.

"Fuck, what *are* we going to do with them?"

He tilts the neck of his beer bottle in our direction. I preferred it when they were ignoring us.

Axel shrugs. "We've got two, maybe three days before we make the exchange. We don't need to decide until then."

I don't like the sound of that. What exchange? Then the reason for them being here dawns on me. They haven't come all this way for a fun time away with the guys. They're on a job, and that job most likely has to do with the guns in the roof space.

So, someone is coming to make an exchange, and I doubt those people will be any better than the ones who are currently holding us at gunpoint. They won't be the type we can ask for help from. If Axel says they need to make a decision by then, does that mean that's all the time we have? If, when these mysterious others are due to arrive, they've decided it's not worth delivering us back to the city so they can collect on the money Darius has offered, will they then shoot us all?

Smith moves slowly, languidly, stopping right in front of us. It's almost dark outside now, but the woodstove is lit, plus they have brought a couple of small battery-powered lanterns with them, so we're able to see. His cool blue eyes appear gray in the low light, and they fix right on me.

"I think we could do with a little entertainment. What do you think, boys?"

29

Axel grins and takes another chug of his beer. "What have you got in mind?"

"A show." Smith claps once. "These two might be stepfather and stepdaughter, but I've seen the way they look at each other. They don't think of each other that way at all."

I exchange an awkward glance with Reed. What is it he's suggesting?

"I think he should fuck her for us," Smith continues with a smirk. "Eat his little stepdaughter's pussy, and then fuck her ass for us. Then afterward, we could get a go."

"No!" Reed yells, clambering to his feet.

I get up as well, and Reed grabs hold of me, angling his body in front of mine to protect me from them. I cling right back at him.

Zeke lifts his gun to remind Reed what they're holding over us. "Don't make any stupid choices, old man. If we tell you to fuck her, then you fuck her."

The muzzle of the gun feels endless, the black hole at the tip a vortex we could fall down and never be found.

"Come here, both of you," Smith commands.

Reed's grip on me tightens. "I said leave her alone."

I'm terrified he's going to end up shot, or that one of the men will shoot Cade or Darius to make a point. We don't have any choice but to do what they want. As terrible as it might be, at least we'll all still be alive.

"We have to do what they want," I tell him. "It'll be okay."

He shakes his head. "No, it's not. It's not even fucking close to okay."

"If you hurt them," Darius says, "you can kiss every cent goodbye. Lay one finger on Laney, and the deal is off."

Smith chuckles. "We haven't decided yet if it's worth keeping you alive long enough to get your money, and anyway, we're not talking about hurting anyone." He gives a smirk. "The opposite, in fact."

"I'd like to watch a father fuck his daughter," Zeke says.

"We're not even related," I tell him. His perverted little fantasy won't come true. "We didn't even know each other before the plane crash. Whatever it is you're trying to do, it won't work."

Zeke grabs his crotch. "What I'm trying to do? I'm trying to get off, sweetheart, that's what. Now, you can either put on a show for us, or you can get me off yourself."

I draw a breath. The decision between fucking this stranger and fucking Reed isn't a hard one. I don't want to do it in front of these men, but I can't see we're being given much choice.

I lean into Reed's solid body. "We need to do as he says. I'd rather it's you than him."

Reed turns and drops his forehead to my shoulder. "Fuck, Laney. How can I do that to you? Not in front of them."

I glance at the gun. "We don't have any choice."

Will they really shoot Reed if he refuses? I remember the body in the roof space and see how badly hurt Cade is. These men have no qualms in killing us if it suits them.

"Laney," Darius says, "you don't have to do this."

"It's okay, Dax. Don't do anything stupid. Just look after Cade."

I'm worried about all of us.

Darius still hasn't given up. "I meant what I said. If you hurt either of them, our deal is off the table. You won't get a fucking cent. Do you hear me?"

Smith scoffs. "There's one flaw in your deal, though. What you're saying is that if we hurt one of you, then we might as well kill the rest, because once one of you is taken out of the equation, you all are."

I watch the trouble cross Darius's handsome face.

Smith is right.

I put out my hand to take Reed's. "We can do this."

His fingers close around mine, and he gives the faintest of nods. He must realize he needs to protect his sons as well as me. His expression is a mask of pain. As a parent, I can only assume he'd always put the boys' lives before his own. He'd always choose them over himself. What about me, though? Where do I come in the level of importance? I'd never ask him to put me above Cade or Darius, and I wouldn't put myself above them either, but would he put me before himself?

My pulse is racing, but I need to stay calm, for his sake. He wants to protect me, but I need to protect him, too.

Hand in hand, we move away from Darius and Cade, giving us space.

Smith puts a gun to Reed's head. "Take off her clothes."

Reed tenses. "Fuck you."

"Don't test me. I will put a bullet in your head."

"Reed," I beg him. "Please, do what they ask."

It won't help any of us if they shoot him. It'll break me, and then I'll let these men do whatever the fuck they want to me. I won't care. If I have to stand here and watch Reed's brains be blown out because he was trying to defend me, I'll give up on living, on fighting for my life.

I tell myself it's only sex, that it doesn't mean anything. For centuries, women—and men—have spread their legs for countless reasons when they haven't wanted to. Women used to be married off to husbands thirty years older than them in order to secure alliances between families. They've fucked men they've hated for money. I'm nothing special. I haven't done anything to deserve a good man to lose his life to protect me.

"Come on." Smith sounds bored now. "I want to see those tits. Either you take off her clothes or I will."

I stare into Reed's eyes. I don't want them touching me. "Please..."

He closes his eyes briefly, and then reaches for my t-shirt. I know this must be killing him, but he catches the hem and lifts it above my head. I hadn't bothered with a bra, and the removal of the t-shirt leaves me naked from the waist up. Instinctively, I cover my bare breasts with my hands.

"Uh-uh. Hands down," Smith says.

I force them to my sides. My nipples tighten and pucker in the cool air. Reed uses his torso to block the view of my breasts from them.

I don't want to be naked in front of these men. They're standing around the room, watching the show. The biggest of our captors, Axel, points the tip of his gun to Darius's temple. My gaze lands on Cade, still lying there, semi-conscious. I hope he has no idea what's happening so close to him. He'd go crazy.

"I'm sorry," Reed tells me. "I'm so fucking sorry."

"Don't be. It's not your fault."

Reed closes his eyes and lowers his head. He doesn't want to do this, but if he doesn't, they'll shoot him, and then all that will happen is I'll end up with one of them stripping me naked and most likely raping me instead. Though even them looking at me feels like a violation, and I hate to think of them watching Reed fuck me, I'd rather it is him a million times over.

I reach up and slip my hand around the back of Reed's neck, lacing my fingers in the soft hair at his nape. "Look at me," I murmur. "It's only us."

I lift myself up slightly to brush my lips tentatively against his. This elicits a whoop of encouragement from our captors. They don't know that a kiss is the very least of the intimate contact that has happened between me and my stepfather. In their minds, me kissing him is illicit, taboo, something we should perhaps be hating.

It focuses Reed, however, and he claims my mouth, pushing his tongue between my lips. I moan, but not for the other men's benefit, but for Reed's. He needs to be able to do this, physically.

I want to cry, but I don't let myself. Just as I'm encouraging Reed to focus only on me, I'm also trying to focus only on him. I don't look at Cade, lying motionless, his head bloodied, or Darius, held at gunpoint.

"How does it feel kissing your stepdaughter?" Smith asks. "Does it feel wrong, or have you been dreaming about touching her up for years, huh?"

He clearly didn't believe me when I said we'd been strangers in each other's lives before the plane crash, or perhaps he's following the narrative that pleases him rather than the truth.

Reed doesn't answer. We stand together, our foreheads touching, Reed using his big body to block the view.

Smith waves his gun. "Move away from her. Let's see those tits."

Reed doesn't budge.

He jams the gun to Reed's head. "Do the fuck what I say."

"It's okay," I whisper to him.

I create space between us and force myself to put my shoulders back and lift my chin. I refuse to be shamed by these pricks.

Smith gives a cold chuckle. "I've got to admit, I'd been hoping for bigger."

He sounds disappointed, and I can't help but feel self-conscious. I've always wanted more curves, to be shorter with big boobs and the sort of ass that fills out a pair of jeans, instead of what I've always felt was a boyish body. Not that Reed, Cade, or Darius ever seemed to mind. They all lusted after me, no matter how I felt about my figure.

"Now the jeans and panties. Let's see her pussy."

I reach for the button and zipper myself, thinking I'll take some of Reed's pain if I do it, but Smith sees through me.

"Nope. Stepdaddy has to do it. Let's see him strip his little stepdaughter."

Reed's hands replace mine, but I squeeze the backs of them as he undoes the zipper, trying to silently tell him that I'm all right. I'll get over this—*we'll* get over this—but in order to do so, we need to survive.

He pulls the jeans and underwear down my thighs. I have to toe off my sneakers and kick the rest of the clothes away. I'm naked now, in front of armed men. Will they be satisfied if Reed and I play their little game, or will they rape me, one by one, in front of the men I've come to think of as family?

"This is all a bit dull for my liking." Smith walks a circle around us. "Let's see you fight him."

His words send a jolt through me. Fight him? How am I supposed to do that?

Smith presses the muzzle against Reed's skull, at the point right behind his ear. In my head, I see him pulling the trigger, the bullet incinerating bone and brain matter, covering me in what would remain of Reed's head.

I can't let that happen.

I'll do anything they want if it means letting him live.

"Slap her," Smith commands.

Reed presses his lips into a thin line. "No."

He jams the gun harder against Reed's head. "Slap her."

"Do it, Reed," I beg. "Please."

My heart is in my throat, and Reed's pained expression wobbles through my tear-filled eyes. The image of his head exploding plays in a loop in my mind.

"Do it!" I almost shout the two words.

His palm cracks around my cheek, my head rocking back. I

don't feel anything for a moment, but then my ear starts ringing and flares with heat, and a split second later, the side of my face burns. I gasp and lift my hand to touch the spot where he struck me.

"Not good enough," Smith says with a smug grin. "Harder."

Reed's head snaps toward him. "No."

He gives a crazed grin and lifts the butt of the gun higher. "I said harder."

I take a breath and nod. "Okay, I'm ready. Just do it."

Reed stares at me in desperation. "They're fucking with us, Laney. Can't you see that? Where is this going to stop? When they have me kill you?"

Smith butts in. "We're not going to have you kill her. At least, not yet. Where would the fun be in that? But if you don't do what I say, then *I* will kill *you*." Then he lifts the gun and aims it at me. "Or perhaps you'd prefer if I *did* kill her, right in front of you?"

Every muscle in Reed's body goes rigid. His jaw tightens, standing out in sharp contrast to his neck. When he speaks, it's with less force than before.

"No, please."

Axel chuckles. "Now it's your turn to beg. You need to learn to do what I say, *Daddy*. Hit her again, and then when she's down on the floor, you take out your cock and you fuck her, got it? And you," he angles his head in my direction, "I want you to play your part. Don't you dare just lie there and pretend nothing is happening. I want to see you fight Daddy-dearest. Punch and kick and bite. Fuck, spit in his face, if you have to. Make this entertaining for us. Got it?"

I understand what he's asking of us, and it makes me sick to my stomach.

He puts on an annoying parody of a girl's voice, making it higher pitched, as though to sound like me.

"No, Daddy, don't force your cock in my tight, virgin pussy. Don't touch my titties with your big old hands. Stop it, Daddy. Stop fucking me."

"I'm not a virgin," I spit at him.

"No? Is that because you've been a little whore for your stepfather and stepbrothers? Kept them entertained on those long, dark nights stranded in the middle of nowhere, even if you didn't want to?"

My face burns, not only from being slapped, but because this bastard has no idea how close to the truth of our relationship he's really gotten. I've never fought Reed off, though. I've always wanted him, even when it has hurt.

"Get it over with," I say, my voice breathy.

Reed's hand cracks around my face once more, and this time I deliberately go down. It's what these men want, and if it means we both get to live, then I'll put a show on for them. I cry out and clasp my hand to my face, but my eyes go straight to Reed, and I widen them, egging him on.

He drops down, planting his hands beside my head, his knees either side of my hips.

"I'm sorry, baby. I'm so fucking sorry."

I touch his cheek. "It's okay. It's not your fault."

Smith is nowhere near done with us yet.

"Spread those legs. Let's see that pretty cunt. Is it all wet for your stepdaddy, huh, slut?"

Reed looks over his shoulder at Smith. "Don't fucking call her that."

"Go on, get your cock out, Daddy. Let's see you fuck your stepdaughter, or I'll shoot her in the head. Fuck her hard enough to make her bleed."

"Ignore him," I say to Reed. "Focus on me."

Reed nods and then reaches down, flicks open his belt buckle, and undoes his button and zipper. Despite what's going on around us, he's still hard for me, and he rubs himself a couple of times until I reach down and wrap my hand around his.

"Let me," I say.

He removes his hand and lets out a breathy groan as I squeeze his length. I swipe my thumb over the head, and then circle the tip, moistening him with his precum.

"Ah, fuck, baby," Reed moans.

I shift myself beneath him, positioning his cock at my pussy.

"Yeah, do it," Zeke crows. "Fuck your stepdaughter. Give it to her good and hard."

Reed closes his eyes and sinks into me. He fills me up, driving deep, and I can't help the little cry of pleasure that escapes my lips. He pulls out a little and thrusts back in, my breasts bouncing.

The sensation of him inside me is so familiar, I can't help but take comfort in it. I close my eyes and cling to him, focusing on the movement of our bodies, how good we've always been together. I do everything I can to block out the strange men standing around us, getting off on the two of us fucking in front of them.

I hear the jangle of a buckle as one of the men opens his pants to touch himself while he's watching the show, but I try to ignore it. I'm vulnerable, exposed, but Reed's body shields me. A familiar coil of tension builds at my core, and I lift my hips, meeting Reed with every stroke, wanting more. Reed's body is curled over me, his face pressed against my shoulder, the heat of his breath against my skin. I wrap my heels around his hips and hold him close.

Smith gives a *tsk* of annoyance. "This is all too fucking sweet for me. I thought you were supposed to be fighting him."

I tense, even my inner muscles tightening around Reed's

cock. My cheek is still burning from Reed's slap, my ear still ringing. How badly does he expect us to fight? Does he actually want Reed to hurt me?

"Put your hand around her throat, choke her."

Reed sucks air in over his teeth. I can tell he doesn't want to do it, but he doesn't have a choice.

His hand wraps around my throat and he tightens his grip, hard enough that only a whistle of air gets into my lungs. I gasp and choke. Instinctively, I struggle, pushing my hands against his shoulders and then clawing at the hand around my throat.

"Keep fucking her," Smith instructs. "Good and hard."

Reed eases up on his grip on my neck, but he fucks me hard and fast. My head is dizzy from the lack of oxygen, but my pussy doesn't seem to have gotten the memo that I'm not supposed to be enjoying this. My climax builds, and the noises that strangle from my lips are a strange combination of pleasure and fear. I know Reed wouldn't kill me—he'd die himself first—but that doesn't prevent my fear of these other men breaking through.

"Fuck, I'm coming, I'm coming," Reed grunts from between clenched teeth. As he comes, slamming deep inside me, his hold tightens around my throat again, closing off my airway.

My orgasm explodes through me, and I can't even breathe through it, my toes curling, my eyes rolling. I buck and arch beneath him, my inner muscles pulsing around his cock as it floods my pussy with his cum.

Smith's voice comes from nearby. "Fuck, yeah."

I open my eyes in time to see Smith come in his hand, and I twist my face away again. I don't want to see the milky fluid spurting from his shiny cockhead, but I do, and now that image is burned on my brain.

Reed releases his hold on my throat, and I gasp in deep

lungfuls of oxygen. He slumps against me, wrapping me in his arms and holding me close.

"I'm sorry, baby. I'm so sorry. Are you okay?"

I nod against him. I'm not okay—nowhere near it—but I'm still trying to protect him. My throat is sore, my lungs burning, and I'm sure Reed's fingermarks will appear in dark bruises on the delicate skin.

It's not until he pulls away, and my neck is wet with his tears, that I realize he'd been crying. My heart tightens with pain for him. I'd never want him to feel like he's responsible for hurting me. None of this is his fault.

Reed pulls out of me and quickly covers me with a blanket.

Now Smith's come, he seems to have lost interest in me. He washes off his hand and tucks himself away.

"Well, that was fun. Let's eat."

His cronies make noises of agreement.

I aim my hatred toward Smith and his friends. Those fuckers. I hate to think about what they have planned for us next. I'm grateful they haven't touched me, but I doubt it will last.

4
DARIUS

I'VE NEVER BEEN MORE FRUSTRATED ABOUT BEING trapped in the dark.

I should be doing more. If Cade was conscious right now, he wouldn't be sitting around doing nothing. But then I remember Cade is badly hurt. If I do attempt to stop these men, that will most likely be me, as well.

I'm thankful I at least haven't been able to see what's been happening between Laney and my father—or what my father has been made to do to Laney. I've got a good idea, though. That fucking asshole, Smith, made sure he shouted enough instructions to paint a damned good picture in my mind.

Perhaps I should be grateful that they'd didn't force me to get involved, but I think it would have been preferable to being forced to stand there, utterly fucking helpless. I've never wanted to scream so much in my life, to lift my face to the ceiling and roar until my lungs burst. With the cold muzzle of the gun pressed to my temple, I barely dared to breathe.

Did that make me a coward? Should I have risked getting my brains blown out in order to step in and beat the shit out of

41

the asshole called Smith? Right now, I'd like nothing more than to smash my knuckles against his face until it becomes a wet and mushy mess, but I'm impotent in my rage.

How can we have survived so much only to be in this situation now?

I try to keep track of everyone's locations by the sounds they're making. I've taken up position back on the floor, beside my brother, my back against the wall. Cade's breathing is shallow and rapid. It concerns me. I think Reed is with Laney on the other side of the mattresses, and, as far as I'm aware, they're both sitting as well.

Heavy footsteps clomp around me, and I recognize Smith's voice.

"Well, that was fun, but now I'm bored again. Oh, wait one minute, we're in a cabin with a world-famous violinist, and he's still got his violin."

I'd left everything else behind when these men had accosted us in the forest. Maybe that made me crazy—to leave essentials like food and water and bring an instrument with me instead—but I haven't been without it since I lost my sight.

I hear the slap of one of them hitting the other's back and bellowing with laughter as though he's cracked the funniest joke ever.

"We could do with a little music around here, don't you think?"

From the direction and the sound of their voice, I assume it's Axel speaking, and he's smacked Zeke on the back.

I sense someone standing close by, and then movement stirs the air, and my violin bag is pulled from where it was wedged beside my body. I let out a yell of anger and grapple for it, hoping to yank it back down again, but it's vanished. Or at least, not vanished, but in the hands of one of those assholes now.

"Give it back," I demand.

One of the men—Axel, I think—laughs. "Or you'll what?"

I grind my teeth. "I said give it back."

"This can't be as hard as it looks," he says.

The whine of the zipper on the case meets my ears as he opens it. That son of a bitch is going to put his hands on the wood. It's like stripping a woman bare—like Reed was made to do to Laney.

No one touches my violin except me.

A painful screech rips through the air as one of the men swipes the bow across the strings. It's like the instrument is in pain, calling out for me to save it. It vibrates right down to my soul.

The two other men bellow with laughter at their buddy's attempt to play.

"Here, give it to me. I bet I can do a better job."

That's Smith's voice now.

I want to throw myself in his direction, to tackle him and wrench my violin from his hands, but I'm still conscious of the fact they're all armed. As much as I love my violin, I'm not going to risk getting myself killed for it.

I wince as another shriek fills my ears. It's like they're murdering my instrument, one draw of the bow at a time.

Smith and his friends clearly aren't impressed by the racket they're making either.

"Jesus fucking Christ," Smith says, laughter in his tone, "what's wrong with a decent guitar? Who the hell would want to play this fucking thing? It's terrible."

I speak from between gritted teeth. "It's not terrible, it's beautiful. You have no idea what the hell you're doing."

He puts on an irritating singsong voice. "Well, look at Mr. High-and-Mighty over there. I don't think you should be criticizing anyone, considering the position you're in right now. You think you're better than us 'cause you can play some stupid piece of wood and strings, do you? Because you've been on stage in concert halls and entertained all those fancy rich bastards in their suits?"

I don't reply, but yes, I do think I'm better than him. I think I'm better than all of these assholes. But I'm also smart enough to know when to keep my mouth shut, and now is one of those times.

The gentle pressure of Laney's hand finds my forearm. Without saying a word, I understand what she's trying to tell me—to breathe, to not rise to it, to be sensible. After what they made Laney and Reed do, taunting me about the damned violin is nothing. I know this, but it doesn't make me want to kill them any less.

They take it in turns, dragging the most painful sounds out of my violin, laughing at each other and mocking me.

"How about we let the expert play us a tune, then?" Smith says eventually. "He can't do any worse than us."

This elicits another volley of laughter.

My heart hitches. Does this mean they're going to give my violin back to me?

Slowly, I get to my feet. "I'll play for you," I offer. "People pay hundreds of dollars each for a ticket to watch me play. Consider this private performance a gift as thanks for getting us to safety."

They've still not said they're even going to help us, and considering the way they're treating us, I suspect that isn't going to change. If they're not going to take my offer of money to get us back to the city, what will they do with us? Have their fun and then put a bullet in each of our heads? The prospect has me vibrating with rage. We've done nothing to deserve this, other than being in the wrong place at the wrong time. That they've already hurt my brother is enough to make me want to kill them, but if they lay a finger on Laney, I'm not sure I'll be able to control myself, guns or not.

I hold out my hands for the violin.

Whoever is currently holding it seems to hesitate, but then the smooth, cool wood is placed in my open palms, shortly followed by the bow.

I run my hands over it, checking for any damage. I've always felt like the curves of the violin are like the curves of a woman. She even has ribs and a neck, and now I feel that same protectiveness rising inside me.

I'd rather destroy her than allow someone else to defile her.

"Come on, then, fiddler boy," Smith says mockingly. "Play us all a tune."

I weigh my bow in my other hand, wondering briefly if I could use it as a weapon. But I'm not naïve enough to believe that a bow could be any match against three men with guns. This isn't an action movie where the hero defeats the villain with a roundhouse kick and grabbing a gun to turn it on the others. It's real life, and I have a disability.

I need to be realistic.

"Play a tune, play a tune, play a tune," they chant, clearly enjoying themselves.

I nestle the chin rest in position, and it feels like coming home. Except this isn't home. It's so far from it right now, it's not even funny. The cabin had been starting to feel like one when it had been only us, but these assholes have destroyed that now. Whatever good memories we might have been able to take with us have been sullied.

With a roar of rage, I take hold of the ends of the bow and bring it down over my knee, snapping it clean in two. As much as I love that bow, I'd told Laney I wouldn't play again until we were somewhere safe, and I'd meant it. I have no intention of putting on a private concert for these pricks.

A gasp comes from Laney. "Dax, no!"

Will my actions get me shot? Have I been utterly reckless? Possibly. The idea that they'll punish Laney as a way of getting back at me goes through my head, and I suddenly find myself regretting my actions. I won't forgive myself if that happens. I should have just sucked it up and played for them. I don't want to keep the peace, though. I'm fully aware they have guns, but I'm sick of having to play along with their little games.

"What the actual fuck?" Smith snarls. "Think you're too good to play for us, do you? Son of a bitch. You think we'll let you get away with that? I should put you in the same state as your brother."

"No, please," Laney begs. "No one else needs to get hurt."

"You sure about that, girlie? Looks to me like this asshole is begging to get hurt. How about we take what remains of the bow and shove it down his fucking throat?"

I should have played. After what Laney and Reed were made to do, playing a fucking tune is nothing.

But I'd wanted to show the assholes that they can't just make us do everything they want. They think they're our masters and we're the puppets and they get to pull our strings. I wanted to show them we still have free will, that they can't force us to do everything they want.

"What if I choose death?" I say, bracing myself. "I guess if I do, there's no chance you'll ever see any of my money."

"Then we might as well kill all of you and be done with it," Axel snaps.

"Maybe you should."

I'm playing a dangerous game.

Smith gives a chuckle. "And where would the fun be in that?"

I'm trying to get a picture of exactly how far these men will go. What motivates them the most? Is it the thought of getting their hands on half a million bucks, or is it the sick power they have at holding us at gunpoint?

I've still got my violin in my other hand, but footsteps approach and it's wrenched out of my grip.

"How's this as punishment?" Smith says.

The crash of fragile wood hitting the floor sends shudders through me. It's better this way—better that my violin no longer exists rather than them using it as a weapon against me—but that doesn't stop it from hurting.

The crash comes again and again as my beautiful instrument is smashed into splinters.

I tell myself it doesn't matter, that, once we're out of here, buying a new violin will be like having a fresh start. It's not as though I'm the same man I was the day of the plane crash. I've been humbled, and now I'm in love. The violin was once the most important thing in my life, but now I have Laney, and she needs to come first. As long as she's okay, the rest of it can wait.

"You've made us some decent kindling there, Smith," Zeke crows.

"About all it was good for, anyway," Smith replies. "Now I'm going to get some sleep. This party fucking sucks."

"Can we use the bedroom?" Zeke asks.

Smith sniffs. "Nah, better that we all stay in here to keep an eye on them. Don't want the big one waking up and them trying to make a run for it."

Despite his words, I take a tiny amount of hope from the idea of them all sleeping. That will leave them vulnerable. I highly doubt any of us will be getting much rest tonight, though we're all exhausted after hiking for miles. We're also running on empty. I think they might have given Laney a little something to eat, but the rest of us have had nothing. Not that I resent her for it. I would give her every last mouthful if it meant her being okay.

I'm certain it's already dark outside, and, though they've most likely brought flashlights with them, their vision will still be limited in the dark. It's the one advantage I have over these men. I know this cabin, and I know the area around it as well, including the hike down to the river. It makes no difference to me whether it's light or dark.

I never want my blindness to make me feel any less of a man, and, for the most part, it hasn't. I've taken pride in my talent, in the lifestyles it's given both my father and brother, but we wouldn't be here right now if I'd never picked up a violin. They were all on that plane to accompany me—no other reason.

Perhaps I want to learn what sort of man I am without the violin. Am I any kind of man at all?

I sink back down to sitting, positioned on the other side of Cade from Laney and Reed. I like to think I'm protecting him in my own way, in the same way he's always protected me. Cade's never needed me in the same way I need him. He's always been the strong, capable one. But he's not much of a threat to anyone in the current state he's in. I'm hoping the only reason he's still asleep is that he needs the rest after both the head injury and the hike, but the worry that it's more serious continues to play on my mind. He should be in a hospital, but that is impossible.

Around us, Smith and his men have gone quiet. I hear the solid thump of the ancient sofa cushions as they crash down on them. One of the mattresses is dragged across the floor, away from us, for one of them to lie on. It means we're pretty much left with only the one mattress between us, most of which Cade is taking up.

The rest of us will be sleeping on the cold wooden floor.

5
laney

I'M DROWNING IN SADNESS.

The remains of Darius's beautiful violin lie on the floor like a pile of tinder. Cade still isn't awake and isn't showing any signs of regaining consciousness.

Though neither Smith nor either of those other two assholes touched me, I still feel exposed and violated by what they made Reed do to me. My throat is sore from where he choked me, and my face has a heated mark on it that I know will match his fingerprints. I'm glad of the darkness that surrounds us because at least it means he can't see the marks. As much as I hate what happened, the worst part was seeing the pain in Reed's eyes. Even now, when I catch sight of him in the flickering flames of the woodstove, the whites are bloodshot and his pupils are glassy. He can't look at me either, though he continues to hold me. I hate that he's been shamed while touching me. I want to do or say something that'll make things right, but I'm at a loss.

Life can be so fucking cruel. We've been through so much, and yet we're still being punished. Is it because we're bad people? We're certainly not angels, that's for sure, but do we really deserve this?

That niggling thought that this is happening because I've been sleeping with all three of them lingers in my mind. It's not that I've ever really believed that immorality is something that a god or any other higher being would punish—if that were true, there wouldn't be so many murderers and child abusers wandering around unpunished—but I still can't shake the thought.

Smith and the others have had a bellyful of beer and good food.

Now they're asleep around us, a couple of them snoring. Their guns are close at hand—Smith has his resting on his chest, his fingers still curled around the grip. Zeke is lying on his front, his head pillowed on his forearms, his weapon beneath one of his hands. I can't see what Axel has done with his, but I'm confident it won't be far from reach.

With the men asleep, the three of us huddle around Cade and speak in whispers.

"We should run," Darius says. "We're not locked in here or tied up. I'd rather take my chances with the bears than these three."

Reed shakes his head. "But what about Cade? He's not going anywhere."

Fuck, he's right.

"One of us could go for help," I suggest. "Run down to the river and try to find the boat and get to safety. They could go to the police and bring help."

We all know that person would have to be either me or Reed. Darius is capable, but sending a blind man to not only find a boat, but then navigate a river, isn't practical.

Reed would want me to go, so at least I'd be safe from these men. But he's physically stronger, and if he had to row a boat any distance, he'd be more likely to make it. Plus, I find the possibility of wild animals terrifying. I still remember how it sounded when the bear was lurking outside of the cabin, the rasp of its claws raking down the walls. If I died out there, I'd have taken the boat and left the men to their deaths. I'm not strong enough.

I tell the others my thoughts—that it should be Reed, not me, who goes.

"I can't leave you here," Reed says. "I can't. Not with these men. Not with Cade injured. The thought of leaving and not knowing what's happening to you all is too much."

I understand what he's saying. If he leaves, he doesn't know that either Darius or Cade will be able to protect me.

"But what if it's our only chance?"

I can't stand the thought of us being separated either. The idea of Reed leaving, of him vanishing into the woods, and us potentially never knowing what becomes of him, is unthinkable. It makes me want to cling to him and never let go, and I'm sure he feels the same.

He shakes his head. "No, we stick together."

I look at Darius, who nods his agreement. "If only one of us runs, they might punish the ones who are left."

Though I'm not one hundred percent sure it's the right choice, the decision calms something inside me. We're a unit, and we need to stay that way.

We could have separated and tried to go for help when we'd first been in the crash, but, other than Reed leaving to find the cabin, we'd stuck together, and we'd survived. I'd even go as far as saying we thrived. Though I'd missed the amenities of civilization—takeout, coffee, fast food, and probably most of all, hot running water—I'd found a peace out here that I'd never known back home. And it wasn't just about no longer living with my mother, though that had played its part. It was about not having to live up to social expectations. I wasn't someone who spent a lot of time living online. I'd always been too busy, but I'd had my accounts and had scrolled through, seeing how perfect everyone else's lives always seemed to be. It was about being judged because of the clothes you were wearing, or how your hair was done, or what car you drove. Even in the trailer park, we were still looked down on by our neighbors. My mom was always wasted and getting into fights with whatever current boyfriend stayed there at the time, and I was the skinny street urchin whose clothes were always dirty and too small for me. Being able to exist without the weight of those expectations has been freeing.

If we can't run, then we need a different idea.

Darius comes up with a suggestion. "Can we risk grabbing one of their guns? Or we each try to take on one, and hope we get the weapons off them before they wake up? It's got to be worth the risk, doesn't it?"

The only way we can win is if we shoot them all, and all at the same time. If one of them wakes and gets to the gun first, they'll stand a good chance of killing one of us.

I shake my head. "It's too risky. All it'll take is for one of them to wake up first and start shooting."

Dax is insistent. "What other choice do we have? If we don't kill them, they'll kill us, and we can't run because of Cade."

I turn to Reed for backup. "Tell your son it's a bad idea."

But Reed's lips are pursed, and I can tell he's thinking about it.

"I'll try to get one of their guns," Reed says. "I have to try."

"They'll shoot you." Hot tears prick against the backs of my eyes. How will we be able to keep going if Reed is dead?

"Not if I shoot them first."

He rises to his feet. I grab at his hand, but he shakes me off.

Zeke is closest, but his gun is pinned beneath his hands. Smith's weapon is most accessible, resting on his chest, so Reed approaches him.

He's only a matter of feet away, and Reed reaches out his hand. My breath is trapped in my lungs, and I squeeze Darius's fingers, terrified this is all about to go horribly wrong.

Just as Reed's hand is inches away from the gun, Smith's eyes open, fixing right on Reed.

"What the fuck are you doing?" Smith snaps, his hands tightening on his weapon.

Reed straightens. "Thought I saw a spider."

"Don't be a fucking idiot. You want to end up with a bullet in your head, old man? Now, go lie back down."

Reed has no choice but to slink back over to us. He drops to a seated position. I put my arm around him and rub his back.

"You tried," I whisper.

"It's not enough."

But it's going to have to be. For the moment, at least.

6
laney

MORNING LIGHT FILTERS THROUGH THE DIRTY GLASS OF the cabin's windows.

For one blissful moment, I'm filled with the peaceful sense of being home, but then I hear a voice I don't recognize, and it all comes flooding back.

I half sit and observe the room. I'm the first to wake.

I'm surprised I managed to sleep at all. I didn't think I would. A part of me wanted for us all to stay awake, to wait for an opportunity when we might be able to steal one of our captor's guns and make a run for it, but, because of Cade, such a plan is impossible. Besides, even if we managed to get our hands on one gun, it would still be our one weapon against theirs. One or more of us would likely end up dead.

My mouth is bone dry, my tongue sticking to the roof. My lips are cracked, and I do my best not to bite at them, knowing that when I start, I'll keep going until I make myself bleed.

How could we have slept?

We were all exhausted from the huge hike yesterday, the lack of food and water, and the emotional trauma of the day. A headache thumps behind my eyes, and my mind is foggy. A part of me wants to curl up in a ball and fall back into the oblivion of sleep, but I can't.

The memory of the previous day hits me, and I squeeze my thighs together, an uncomfortable combination of shame and arousal sweeping through me. I climaxed in front of these assholes, and they got off on it. It makes me sick, but I know worse is to come. They haven't actually touched me yet, but they will. Right now, there's a good chance they'll take turns raping me repeatedly, and then, when they've had enough, they'll kill me.

My thoughts turn to Cade. I'm filled with a blinding terror that he'll have died overnight, without any of us holding his hand or talking to comfort him. I almost don't want to look out of fear for what I'll find. I don't know how I'll cope if I discover he's died during the night. Just the expectation of grief is enough to make me want to scream and yank at my hair and beat my fists against the floor.

I've never been particularly religious, but I find myself sending up a prayer. *Please be okay.*

I'll sacrifice anything if it means he's alive.

Cade's face is pale. His eyes are closed, but his lips are parted, and as I hover my hand over the top of his mouth, the heat of his breath hits my skin. I watch his chest, studying the way it rises and falls. I take his hand and stretch out his wrist so I can feel for a pulse. For a brief moment, I can't find one, and a jolt of adrenaline goes through me, even though I can see he's breathing, but then I find it, and I exhale a shaky breath. His pulse is strong and steady. This is a good sign.

If it wasn't for the dark blood matted in his hair, it would look like he was sleeping.

Wake up, Cade, I silently beg. *We need you.*

Is he only sleeping, or is he unconscious? I'm no doctor, but

I can't help but ponder the possibilities of what this might mean if he's not just sleeping. Does he have brain damage or a bleed? What if he never wakes up?

Smith and his men begin to stir, too, scratching themselves awake, yawning, stretching. Axel gets up and then goes outside, the cabin door banging behind him. I assume he's going for a piss, and I will our local bear to eat him.

Darius and Reed both wake, too, and like me, the first thing they do is check on Cade. Darius's lips thin with worry, and Reed shoots me a look of concern, which I match with our eye contact. We don't need to say anything to understand how we all feel. Reed's gaze lands on my cheek and neck, where I'm bruised from the previous day, and he closes his eyes in dismay that he hurt me.

"I'm fucking starving," Smith announces. "What have we got?"

"What do I look like, the fucking chef?" Zeke retorts.

"You're whatever I say you are."

Zeke scowls, but he goes into the kitchen. He needs to stoke the woodstove before it'll be hot enough to put a pan on top of it to cook, but I don't bother reminding him. I doubt anything will be coming our way.

While we can manage without food, we do need water. My throat is still tender, and my headache intensifies. I'm aware it's partly from yesterday, but it's also partly dehydration.

I spot a bottle of water lying on its side beside the kitchen counter. It must have rolled out of the cooler yesterday, but they didn't notice.

I wait for a moment, until it seems everyone is distracted with their own stuff, and leave my position to scoot forward. Reed tries to stop me, but I shake him off.

Every muscle in my body screams with protest at the movement. The hike yesterday, combined with sleeping on the floor, hasn't been kind to me. My whole body is sore, and I wince and clamp the pain between my teeth as I reach for the bottle of water.

A booted foot stamps down on my wrist, and I squeal in pain.

"What the fuck do you think you're doing?"

I twist my neck enough to look up to find Axel standing there. He must have come back inside while I was focused on the bottle.

"I was getting some water."

"You ask permission, bitch."

I speak from between gritted teeth. "Fine. Can we have some water, please?"

He eases up his weight on my arm. Now my wrist is throbbing. I don't think he's broken it, but it'll definitely bruise as well.

He must be feeling generous. "Go on, then. But make it last."

Feeling like a street rat, I snatch the bottle up and scurry back to the men. I hold it out to them.

"You have some first," Reed tells me.

I want to be completely selfless and let them have a drink, but my body is shouting at me for water. I crack open the lid and take a couple of hasty gulps, careful not to spill any. I feel instant relief, and I want more, but I force myself to stop.

Reed hands the bottle to Darius before he takes a drink himself. Then we all look toward Cade.

"He's going to be dehydrated, too," I say.

Darius tears a strip from the bottom of his t-shirt. "Here, use this."

I understand what he means. If I try to pour water into Cade's mouth, it'll most likely choke him, but he should be fine with a few drips.

I dip a corner of the cloth into the water and hold it to Cade's lips, allowing some of it to trickle into his mouth. I'm worried he'll choke, but he needs to get some fluids into him, and it's not as though I can take him to hospital to hook him up to a drip. To my relief, his throat works as he swallows, so I keep going until he gives a strange gurgle and turns his head away. I take some solace in that he's conscious enough to be able to do that. He moved, and that's got to be a good sign, right? I dip the cloth back in the water, and then use it to cool his brow. It stains pink from the blood, and then turns red. My heart aches. Even hurt and unconscious, he's still beautiful to me. His jaw is covered in beard growth where he's not shaved for some time, and his long, dark lashes rest on his pale cheeks.

I lean down and place a kiss to his cheek. "Wake up, Cade. It's time to wake up now."

He doesn't react to my voice, and I try not to cry.

Darius's hand finds mine, and he squeezes my fingers. I know he feels the same way I do, and I take comfort in that. I lean into him and rest the side of my head on his shoulder.

"He's strong, Laney," Dax says. "He'll beat this."

I wish I could feel as confident as Darius sounds. Cade should have woken up by now. He is still moving slightly and making noises. Surely that means he's not completely lost to us.

The cabin fills with the scent of bacon frying, and I salivate. I haven't smelled bacon in such a long time I actually think I might weep from my desire for it. I can't help but stare at the pan it's frying in.

"Like the smell of that, do you, girl?" Smith says, his pale blue eyes glinting. "If you want some, you'll have to work for it."

I don't want anything that badly. "I don't want anything from you."

59

He jerks his chin toward my men. "What about if it's for them? What will you do then?"

"She doesn't have to do anything for us," Reed says. "Not a single fucking thing."

Smith lifts a strip of perfectly crisp bacon to his mouth and takes a bite. I can almost taste it, the saltiness of cured meat. I find myself licking my lips.

"You sure about that?" he says smugly.

We don't need the bacon that badly, but even I have to admit I'm tempted. I'm not going to prostitute myself out for food, though, no matter how good it smells.

I swallow hard. "We're sure."

Smith laughs. "It's not like you're going to have a choice, anyway, girlie. You should have taken the offer."

I shrink back, pressing myself up against Darius.

Smith takes a step closer and wrinkles his nose at me. "Though I don't want to touch you when you're filled with your stepdaddy's cum."

A spark of hope goes through me. I feel like telling him that he should have thought of that before he made my stepfather fuck me at gunpoint, but no good will come from me running my mouth. As much as it might feel good in the moment, it'll only make him angry, and when men like him get angry, they get violent.

I glance over at Cade still lying there, and my throat tightens with emotion. I hate seeing him this way, so vulnerable. He's always been the tough one, the hard one, the one who didn't take any shit. He'd hate to know what was happening to us now. It's a blessing, in a way, that he's unconscious. If he wasn't, would he try to fight these assholes? If he did, he would only end up getting himself shot.

Smith grabs my upper arm and yanks me to my feet. His

fingers dig into my skin, painful enough that I know there will be bruises tomorrow.

"Get off her," Reed says, reaching for me, too.

He grabs my other arm, and, suddenly, I'm the rope in their tug of war.

But Smith wins by using his other hand to produce the gun he must have had wedged down the back of his jeans. He presses the muzzle to my forehead, and Reed lets go as though I've burned him.

Smith curls his lip. "Or you'll what?"

I hate the helpless look on Reed's face as he releases me. I want to place my hand to his cheek and tell him I love him and that I'll be okay, but these men won't allow it.

Smith yanks me away from them. "Come on. We're going down to the river. You can clean up down there."

The river. The place where there will be a boat, assuming that's how they got here.

He jerks his chin at his men. "You two keep an eye on the others. If any of them tries something, put a bullet in their heads."

He means it, too, and the thought sickens me.

Who will we be by the time this is over? Will we get out of this with our lives, bodies, and souls still intact?

"You've got soap around here?" he asks me.

"A little," I admit. "It's in my bag."

It's only the dregs of a bottle that I have left. I've even mixed it with a little water to try to make it stretch farther. Like the rest of the toiletries we brought with us in the plane, we're down to the last few rations.

"Get it," he tells me.

He releases my arm, and I do as he says, going to my bag to retrieve my toiletries. There's a weight in my gut that tells me the only reason he wants me to look and smell nice is because he's going to rape me. What can I do, though? I can't run, because that will mean leaving the others behind, and I can't fight them. All I can do is go along with what they want, let them have their fun, and hope they leave us alone.

I hug the items to my chest, as though they can protect me in some way. Even holding the bottles feels alien. That normal part of my life, when I took getting into a shower, or being able to pop out to my local grocery store when I ran out of something, for granted.

"Let's go," Smith says.

I realize I'm going to need my towel as well, and a change of clothing. "I'll bring my whole bag," I say.

His eyes narrow. "Why? What you got in there?"

I don't have anything dangerous, but then I remember the knife I'd put in there in case we needed it for hunting or fishing, or just collecting root tubers to eat while we were on the move. The realization causes heat to flush across my face, and it dawns on me how guilty I look right now.

He snatches the bag out of my hands, opens it, and dumps the contents on the floor.

He stoops and picks up the knife. "What the fuck is this?"

Where a moment ago my face had felt hot, now all the blood drains from it, seeming to pool into my feet.

"That wasn't why I wanted to bring it. I'd forgotten it was even in there."

"Bullshit, bitch. Don't fucking try that again, or I'll use this knife to cut one of your pretty little ears off."

I draw in a breath.

"Don't you touch her," Dax snarls.

"It's okay, Dax." I want to reassure him, not wanting him to take any chances of getting shot. "It was just a misunderstanding. I'd forgotten I had a knife in my bag, that's all."

His face is rigid with fury, but he doesn't make any move to attack Smith.

I glance over at Reed, who gives me the faintest of nods. He's thinking the same way I am—that we can't risk doing anything stupid—and I hope he'll rein Darius in when I'm not around. I know this must be killing Reed, too, but he's older and not as hotheaded as his son.

"Pack the rest of it back in," Smith says. "We're going down to the river."

He keeps his hand wrapped around the softness of my upper arm, and the gun aimed at me, as we leave the cabin and step outside.

I know this route so well, I could walk it with my eyes shut. It's a beautiful day, something that feels at a complete contrast to the horror we're going through. A light breeze ruffles through the leaves overhead, and birdsong fills the air. My heart swells with emotion. I'm going to miss this place, however we end up leaving here—alive or dead.

I hear the river before I see it, the shush of water flowing, the burble as it rolls over rocks closer to the bank.

We reach the water, and I draw a breath.

There *is* a boat.

Though I'd known there was a good chance these men had one, seeing it hits me like a sledgehammer. That's our means to escape, sitting right there, bobbing on the water. They've tied it up to a boulder on the shore instead of pulling it onto the dry land. I assume that's in case they need to make a speedy escape.

The boat isn't big—far from it—but it's definitely big enough to carry the four of us to safety. We just need to figure out how the hell we can get to it without the men seeing us. I remember Cade, and my heart sinks. What I'm considering is impossible. How can we possibly get away and carry Cade as well? It's not as though Cade is a small man. Even after being out here with limited food, he's still big and muscular. If I were the one who was unconscious, perhaps it would be possible, but not him.

I blink back tears as the magnitude of our situation sinks in further. I can feel myself being pulled to a very dark place, and I try to fight it, but I don't know how long I'll be able to keep that up.

Things are only going to get worse.

"Strip," Smith says, waving his gun at me. "You can't wash properly when you've got clothes on."

Though I know it's futile, I can't help begging. "Please, let me keep my underwear on."

He snorts in derision. "No fucking chance. I want to get an eyeful of the goods."

"Please—"

"Do it!" he snaps, his voice raised.

I don't dare argue. I keep my arms folded across my body as best I can while also removing my clothes. I huddle inward, my back bowed, trying to use the rest of my body to cover my breasts and pussy. His heated stare burns through me.

"Stand straight," he demands.

Slowly, I unfold, but still I keep my arms covering me, one across my breasts, the other between my thighs.

He walks a slow circle around me, as though he's assessing cattle at a market. "Skinny thing, aren't you? Wish we'd managed to capture a girl with a bit more meat on her bones."

I don't reply, but I'm hardly going to be thick after I've spent weeks surviving in the middle of nowhere. The truth is, I've never had enough money to put on any weight. I've always had to survive on scraps. Even when I was old enough to work before and after school, the money never seemed to be enough. If I ever made the mistake of leaving my tips somewhere my mother might have found them, I was guaranteed never to see them again. She'd drink them away, or put them up her nose, or inject them into her arm. I lost count of the number of times I'd thought I'd hidden the money well, only to come home and discover it gone. I'd cry and scream, but it never did any good. She didn't care.

I experience a pang of guilt for thinking badly of my mother when she's dead, but it's not as though I'm being uncharitable. She did do those things to me. I want to tell myself that she was sick, that she was an addict, and it was the addiction that made her act that way, not her, but it's not easy. Perhaps in time, when the pain of everything is a little less raw, I'll be able to remember her with more kindness, but I struggle to do that now.

Smith swats me on the ass, and I jump.

"Get in the water."

I'm glad to be able to put some distance between me and him, though he continues to train the gun on me. He's stayed fully dressed, so I assume he has no intention of joining me in the water.

My toes find smooth pebbles, and beneath that, the slightly sludgy silt that makes up the riverbed. The water feels incredible on my skin, the cold snatching my breath. Overhead, a bird of prey circles, calling its mournful screech across the sky. I want to tilt my face up to the blueness and yell as well, letting my scream join that of the bird's. It's so empty out here, yet somehow so full, nature in every direction.

I keep going, moving deeper. Sharp stones cut and dig into the soles of my feet. The colder I get, the more it hurts, but still I ignore the pain. It's nothing compared to what could be happening to me right now. The water is at my thighs, and, after another few steps, lapping at my belly. I feel the tug of the river at my legs, a quiet insistence to let it take me away from all of this.

I could jump, I realize. Take those extra few steps to take me into the deeper, faster moving water, and leap. The current would whisk me away quickly enough, and I'd be too much of a moving target for him to shoot me—not that it would matter if he did. Would he jump in the boat and come after me, or would he decide I'd drown before he found me again?

The only thing that keeps my feet rooted to the riverbed is the thought of Cade, and Darius, and Reed. It would break their hearts if I did that, and I couldn't stand to be the cause of such pain.

"That's it," Smith calls over to me from the riverbank. "Wash that pussy nice and good. Put your hand between your legs and touch your cunt."

I hate him. Rage builds inside me like a furnace scorching through my veins. Every muscle in my body is taut and trembling. I'm vibrating from the inside out.

I refuse to give him a show. I do as he says but make it brief and perfunctory—a nurse giving a patient a bed bath. I won't make this sexy for him.

He seems disappointed, and that gladdens my heart. It's only a tiny thing, but it feels like a victory, and right now, I'll take as many of those as I can get.

I glance at the boat again. There's a motor on the back, but it's small enough to row, if necessary. The first chance I get, I'll tell the others about it. Maybe they'll be able to come up with a plan for us to reach it and get away.

"Come back to shore now," Smith shouts.

I don't want to. I want to stay out here forever. I think I know what Smith has planned for me, and the anticipation of it sickens me. I fight tears, but it's hard not to cry after everything we've gone through. I don't want him to even look at me, never mind anything more, but what I want doesn't matter.

I turn back to shore and stride through the water until I reach the bank.

My skin is goose bumped from the cold river water. My nipples are hard and tight. I catch his gaze lingering on them. His tongue flicks out and travels across his lower lip. He could easily rape me now. There's nothing I can do to stop him, but mercifully he doesn't.

I dry myself with the towel I'd taken from the hotel room all those moons ago. Once upon a time, it had been white and fluffy, and fragranced with fabric softener. Now it's a distinctly grubby gray, and is crunchy rather than soft, and smells faintly of damp. We've done our best to stay clean out here, but it's not been easy. While we've smelled fine to each other, I'm sure anyone in normal society would be grossed out.

"Get dressed then," he mutters. "But don't think for a second that you've gotten off easily. I've got plans for you yet."

My stomach unknots a fraction. Why hasn't he touched me? It's not because he thinks I'm unattractive but because he's got something else in mind.

I pull my dirty clothes back on, though I notice my underwear is missing. Gross. Did he take my panties, even though they'll have Reed's cum in them? I don't say anything. Missing underwear is the least of my problems.

We walk back up to the cabin.

"I can't believe the four of you were out here for weeks and survived," he says conversationally, as though we're friends. "That's some crazy shit. You should have all died in that plane crash."

I don't bother replying to him. What would be the point? Should I beg for our lives, plead that if fate saw to allow us to survive all of that, then shouldn't we also be allowed to survive him and his men? I know it won't work. He'll do whatever he wants, no matter what I say.

We reach the cabin, and I take the steps up to the porch. I peer through the windows, my heart in my throat in case Reed or Darius tried something to get to me and ended up shot. The river is far enough away, plus the rushing water loud enough, that it would hide the bang of a gunshot.

But, to my relief, everything seems to be the same as when we left.

Smith reaches past me to open the door and then nudges me with the barrel of the gun to get me inside.

I feel Reed's eyes on me, and Darius has turned in the direction of the door, too.

Zeke and Axel are playing cards, but both have their weapons close at hand. They barely bother glancing up as we enter.

I catch Reed's eye, but I don't know how to convey to him that I'm okay, that Smith didn't touch me. If I shake my head, will he think that it didn't go well, or if I nod, am I confirming his worst fears to him. Instead, I offer him the faintest hint of a smile and hold his gaze. I see he understands by his body language, sinking back against the wall with relief.

How long will that relief last?

"We need to go over the stash and get it ready for transporting," Smith says. "Got to make sure it's all there before the pickup."

That's the second mention of there being another party involved in all this. There's no point in hoping these other people will do anything to help us. They're clearly also going to be criminals and more worried about their guns than four strangers.

With a sigh of resignation, both Axel and Zeke throw down their cards and get to their feet.

"Bring the trunk through to the back room," Smith tells them.

The two men leave the cabin, and I wonder where they're going.

It suddenly occurs to me that we could have tried to get the guns from the roof space last night instead of trying to take the men's. Would that have been more likely to result in success? Probably not. We'd have made a lot of noise climbing up there, and they would have heard us.

Axel and Zeke return carrying a large silver trunk—like the kind musicians would use to transport instruments—between them. They must have stashed it somewhere outside. Through the hasp on the front of the trunk hangs a combination padlock. It makes sense that they'd need something more substantial than the boxes currently holding the guns. I also realize that when the guns are locked inside the trunk, the option for us to get our hands on them will be taken away from us. We missed our opportunity last night.

While the men vanish into the bedroom that has access to the roof space, I go and sit back down with the others. I don't have any underwear on, so I half cover myself with the blanket and take a new pair of panties from my bag, and quickly change. I can't look at anyone while I'm doing it. I don't want to have to tell them that Smith took my underwear.

"Are you okay?" Reed asks me when I'm done.

He still has that pained expression every time he looks at me. I wish I could make him understand that I don't blame him in any way for what happened last night.

"There is a boat," I whisper. "Tied up down by the river. If we can get to it..."

Darius has heard me, too. "How big is it?"

"Big enough."

His jaw tightens, and he nods. I know we're all thinking the same thing. What I'm suggesting is a pipedream. *How* are we going to get to it? We can barely look in the wrong direction without one of those assholes shoving a gun in our faces.

But we need to be able to hope, even if that hope is unfounded.

Without it, we might as well give up.

I turn my attention to Cade. "How has he been?"

"Much the same," Reed replies.

"Any sign of him waking up yet?"

He shakes his head, his expression a mask of pain. It's hurting me, seeing Cade so weak, but I can't imagine what it's doing to Reed, witnessing his big, strong son lying here like this.

I use a little of the water we have to dampen one side of the torn t-shirt again, gently wipe his forehead, and then dip a clean corner in the bottle to trickle more water between Cade's lips.

"I have to do something," Reed says. "We can't let these assholes do whatever they want with us."

I take his hand. "Please, don't. They'll shoot you."

He shakes his head. "It kills me looking at you right now. You have bruises on your neck and marks on your face. I did that to you."

"I don't blame you, Reed. You did what you had to do."

He can't look at me. "It's like I...forced you."

I squeeze his hand, hard enough to hurt him this time. "No. Never. I love you. I want you, no matter what the circumstances. It's in no way the same thing. Got it?"

He nods, but I'm not sure he's completely convinced.

7
CADE

I'm ready to die.

I've never felt so weak in my life, and I fucking hate it. Even after the plane crash, when the metal pole had punctured my leg and I'd walked with a limp and my teeth gritted for weeks afterward, it had been nothing compared to this.

The pain in my head is all encompassing. I've never experienced anything like it. I understand where the phrase 'blinding pain' comes from. I literally can't even open my eyes the agony is so great. I think of my brother and how this is his world, minus the pain, and my heart clenches for him.

I don't understand what happened or even where I am. One moment I was walking, the next the pain started and everything went black.

Something bad has happened, I know that much. I have a vague memory of being helped to walk—and knowing I had to —but being unable to get my legs to work properly. I think I'm back in the cabin, but I don't know why. Is it because I got sick? Did the others have to turn around and bring me back here so I can get better? Did I have a stroke or a brain hemorrhage? Or was there an accident I can't remember?

My concept of time feels all wrong. I can't tell if I've been like this for hours, or days. It seems to stretch, almost never ending, only to snap back again.

There's coolness on my forehead, and it helps, if only for a minute. Sometimes that coolness trickles across my tongue and down my throat, too. It feels so good, and I wish I could communicate to tell someone that, to encourage them to keep doing it, but my mouth won't work, and I can't rise out of the darkness.

My thoughts are hard to hold on to, to string together in a coherent line. Sometimes, I think I'm awake and that I'm able to talk and walk around, just like I always have, but then I realize I'm dreaming...or doing whatever this is.

"—can we wait until—"

A voice drifts into my consciousness, and I grasp at it, trying to hold on, but it's like trying to catch smoke with my fingers.

It's *her* voice...I struggle to remember her name. Bird? Is that it? It doesn't feel right, but something about it makes me think it must be. Bird is the only name I can think of. She's important, though—possibly the most important person in my life. There are others, I'm sure, but I can't think who they are right now. The pain is too great, and it's blocking out all my other thoughts.

Why aren't I dead already? Surely it's not possible to be in this much pain and for it not to kill you.

I distract myself with thoughts of the girl I'm thinking of as Bird. It's the only thing that makes the daggers shooting through my skull retreat. I picture my fingers lacing through her long, silky hair, of pushing my tongue between her lips. I press my nose to her forehead and inhale the scent of her skin. It's like sinking into a warm bath or getting into your own bed.

Like coming home.

Bird, Bird, Bird...Little Bird. My little Bird.

It's so close...only it's not.

Her voice penetrates the haze I'm in once more, and I cling to it to prevent myself from drowning.

8
REED

They're distracted, counting out their guns.

Zeke, the smallest of the three, is overhead, in the roof space, handing down the weapons to Smith and Axel to be stacked in the metal trunk for whoever it is they're expecting to meet here.

I glance down at my eldest son.

Come on, Cade. Wake up.

We can't run. We'd never make it any distance at all. I think of the boat. If we could carry Cade down to the river, we could put him on it and get away like that.

The only way we'll escape is if we kill Smith and his men. If even one of them is left alive, and armed, we risk one of us being shot. But how can we possibly take them down when all three of them are armed and we have nothing?

Through the open bedroom door, I eye the stack of weapons they've brought down from the roof space. Is there any way I can get my hands on one of them? Will that even be enough? Say I do manage to get hold of a gun, there are still three of them against one, and they'll likely kill me before I've even managed to fire a shot.

The only way I see this working is if we manage to separate these three, but even then, it's going to be dangerous.

While I might not be able to get my hands on the guns, there is something else I can try to steal while they're distracted.

"Wait here," I tell Laney and Dax, keeping my voice low.

Laney shoots me a stare of alarm. "What are you doing?"

I put my finger to my lips, and then check the open doorway again. The men are still distracted. I get into a crouch and then, staying low, run over to the kitchen. My heart pounds, and I imagine being back in the dark ages when people used to have their hands chopped off for stealing a loaf of bread, because that's what I'm trying to do now.

The bread has been wrapped in a cloth and left on the side. Will they notice it's missing? Or will they assume one or the other of them has eaten it? I grab the item, tuck it in close to my body, and then scoot back to the others. A quick check confirms Smith and his men are still occupied and haven't noticed.

I turn my back to the doorway, using my body as a shield, and break chunks off the loaf. I share it out equally between us and wish desperately that I could give Cade some. In case he wakes, I keep a piece wrapped in the cloth and push it under the mattress. It's not the most hygienic thing in the world, but it's better than starving.

"Thank you," Laney whispers to me.

I'm just pleased to see both her and Darius eating. If an opportunity does arise where we can make a run for it, it won't help if we're all too exhausted to move.

A bang comes from the bedroom, and we all jump guiltily.

They've closed the lid on the trunk, and I assume will have locked it as well, and are heading back into the main part of the cabin. I've eaten most of my share of the bread but slip the remaining chunk into my pocket.

"We're running low on wood for the stove," Axel says.

"Come on, you two." Zeke jerks his chin at us. "You might as well put yourselves to work instead of sitting there. Bring some wood in from the back."

I consider refusing, but what would be the point? Besides, I could do with some fresh air, and being outside might raise an opportunity that I won't necessarily have stuck in here.

I take Darius's arm. He doesn't need my help—not here—but I think we both appreciate the contact.

"You going to be all right?" I ask Laney.

She nods and then places her hand on Cade's shoulder to indicate she'll keep watch over him. I love how much she loves him. Maybe others would find that strange—that I'd want her to love another man, and my son, no less—but maybe it's because Cade *is* my son that I'm okay with it. I'd always want love in their lives, no matter where it came from, and for a while I was worried we were all incapable of it. I saw the way Cade and Darius went through women, with no attachment or even consideration that perhaps those women might want more than only sex. But it's different with Laney. She's family.

Darius and I cross the cabin and step out onto the porch.

I hate leaving Laney behind, but I'm also relieved to be out of the cabin, breathing fresh air. The whole time, I turn over possibilities of how I can get us out of this mess. It's my responsibility to take care of them all, and, right now, I'm failing them. I've never been so angry or frustrated with myself in my life. Even the times when I was trying to quit the substance abuse and kept falling off the wagon, the self-loathing and disappointment in myself was nothing compared to this.

We walk around the cabin to where the woodshed is located out back. It's definitely been depleted compared to how fully stacked it was when we'd first arrived. We'd done our best to collect wood in the forest, but with only an axe, it had been near impossible to fell anything that wasn't a younger, smaller tree, and then the wood needed to be dried out before it would burn well.

I glance over my shoulder to where Zeke has followed us out with the gun. I remember how I'd thought I needed to get them separated. My pulse picks up. I quickly scan what lies around us. The axe embedded in a tree stump. A length of wood that could be used a weapon.

What I need is a distraction, something that will take Zeke's attention away from us, so I can go for his gun.

"What are you waiting for?" the little shitbag says, motioning with his gun toward the woodpile. "Get on with it."

Darius lifts the first log, stacking it in the crook of one arm, before reaching for another. I wish I could tell him what I'm thinking, so that we could work together in some way. I've never wished for Darius to be anyone different, aware that his disability has, at least in some way, made him the man he is, but right now I'd give anything for him to be able to see. If we were able to make eye contact, perhaps he'd be able to read what I'm thinking.

Wishes are meaningless.

"We're going to need more kindling," I say, nodding to where the axe is embedded into the tree trunk. "It's going to take me a minute."

Zeke snorts. "Fine. Get on with it."

I sense Darius angling his head my way, a slight frown marking his forehead. He's clearly wondering why I'm offering to do more work, but I can't explain.

I position a larger log onto the tree trunk and get to work splitting it. *Thwack-clunk. Thwack-clunk.* It's good, steady work, but the whole time I'm thinking about how I can embed the axe into the back of Zeke's puny little head.

Darius piles the split logs high in his arms, so they're almost in front of his face. It doesn't matter. It's not as though he needs to see where he's going.

"That's enough," Zeke says to us both. "Get them all inside now."

Darius nods and turns toward the side of the cabin. As he starts to walk, his foot catches on something. While we all know not to move anything around so Darius can move unaided, these assholes haven't even thought about it. Dax stumbles and drops all the logs he'd collected.

Zeke rolls his eyes. "Oh, you fuck—"

I seize my moment. All of Zeke's attention is focused on Darius, so I lift the axe and swing it, aiming directly at this asshole's head. A blade cleanly embedded in the skull won't be loud enough to give anything away to those left inside, and Zeke will drop his gun. I'll be able to pick it up, sneak back around, and shoot the other two before they've even realized something is wrong.

Or at least that's how I picture things going down. The reality is very different.

Zeke must have sensed me swinging the axe, as he takes a step back, putting himself just out of range. The axe travels harmlessly through the air. Fuck, now I'm in trouble.

He lifts the gun and squeezes the trigger, but it's as though he doesn't completely know what he's shooting at, just a threatening movement.

The heat of the bullet burns my cheek. The crack of the gunshot sends birds exploding from the nearby trees. From inside the cabin comes Laney's cry of panic, and expletives from the two remaining men.

Darius has automatically ducked, unaware of who is shooting or why.

Zeke aims the gun at me. "Drop the fucking axe or the next one is going straight in your head."

The side of my cheek burns and something hot and wet runs down to my jaw, collecting in the beard growth and dripping off the end of my chin. Shit, that bullet got me, if only as a graze. I've been insanely lucky. If it had been a fraction of an inch to the right, Zeke would have shot me through the face. It had been more luck than judgment that he hadn't.

My fingers are wrapped tight around the handle of the axe, and I'm loath to let it go, but I have no choice. I lost my chance, and Zeke has proven he's more than willing to shoot me if he has to. Even so, I can't seem to get my fingers to relax enough to let the axe fall to the ground. Zeke senses my hesitation and swings the barrel of the gun around so that it's now aimed directly at my youngest son.

"Do you want me to shoot him, instead? Because I will fucking shoot him. Don't try me."

Movement comes from the side of the cabin, and Smith races around the corner. He's also armed.

"What the fuck is going on?" Smith demands.

Zeke responds. "That fucking prick tried to hit me with the axe."

Smith scowls at me. "Well, that was very fucking stupid. You need to know what happens when you try something stupid, only you won't be the one who ends up punished."

My blood runs cold. What the fuck does that mean?

"Get back inside, all of you." He mutters something unintelligible to himself. "Can't trust anyone to fucking behave themselves."

9

laney

I'm sick with worry.

I strain my ears, desperately trying to pick up on either Reed's or Darius's voice. Can I hope the gunshot was fired to warn off a wild animal, rather than it being aimed at one of the men I love? What if one of them is lying dead in the dirt?

I want to run out of the door and check for myself, but Axel is still here, and if I do that, I'll be leaving Cade alone and vulnerable.

More shouts come from outside. My eyes fill with tears, and I clench my fists, trying to prevent myself from screaming.

Movement comes from the porch, and I scramble to my feet, my heart pounding. In desperation, I search for them, count the number of people out there. Four. There are four, and they're all standing, which means no one is dead.

Oh, thank God.

But then they approach the cabin door, and I catch sight of Reed's face. I widen my eyes in alarm.

Fuck. What happened?

One side of his face is bright red with blood. It's all in his

81

beard growth and has run from his chin and jaw to drip down onto his t-shirt, staining the gray cotton dark.

"You're hurt!" I cry.

"I'm fine, Laney. It's only a graze."

"What happened?" Axel asks.

"The old man tried to hit me with an axe," Zeke says. "Luckily, he missed."

I'm starting to piece together the events in my head. I want to scream at Reed, to grab him by the front of his t-shirt and shake some sense into him. What the fuck had he been thinking, trying to take these men on with an axe? He's lucky he didn't get himself killed.

"Think you can try to pull that shit with us," Smith says to Reed. "Watch what happens."

Reed's head snaps in Smith's direction. "What are you talking about?"

But Smith turns to me. "Get into the bedroom."

My stomach sinks. So, Reed tried to hit one of his men with an axe, and now I'm going to be punished for his actions.

"Leave her alone," Reed snarls.

Unsurprisingly, he finds a gun in his face. "Or you'll what?"

I can't even look at the pain in his eyes. He's still bleeding, and that's not good either.

"What are they doing, Laney?" Darius asks, his expression bewildered and hurt. He turns his words toward the men. "Don't you fucking hurt her."

"It's fine. I'll be okay," I say, trying to stop my voice from breaking.

It seems crazy that I'm the one trying to comfort them when I'm the one who's about to be assaulted, but the pain on their face is worse than the one in my heart.

Smith grabs me by the back of the neck. His fingers are

hard and dig painfully into the sensitive flesh. He shoves me into the bedroom and slams the door shut behind us.

"As much as I enjoy having an audience sometimes, there are other times when I like a little privacy. Wouldn't you agree?"

I remain mute, not giving him the satisfaction of hearing me call for help or even cry.

I glance over my shoulder at the closed door and want to cry. I picture Reed and Darius on the other side, guns pointed almost lazily in their directions, preventing them from coming after me.

And I know they'll be desperate to do exactly that. It'll be killing them to think of me in here with Smith, knowing what's most likely about to happen. It's crazy that my heart is breaking for them almost as much as it is for myself. I don't want to be the cause of their pain and helplessness.

"Take off your jeans."

There's no point in arguing with Smith. It's easier to go along with what he asks. I can fight and scream and kick, but at the end of the day, he'll get what he wants. Better to be submissive and pretend none of this is happening.

I undo the button and push the jeans from my hips. They fit me perfectly when I'd first been given them in the hotel room by the personal shopper. That feels like a lifetime ago. My feet are already bare, so I kick the jeans off and leave them in a bundle on the floor.

"Lie down."

Smith jerks the barrel of his gun toward the bed. There's no mattress on it, so it's just a base of wooden slats. There's no way lying on it is going to be comfortable, but it's not as though he intends for us to sleep.

I've only been allowed to keep my t-shirt and panties on, so it's not as though I have many clothes for him to get rid of before he rapes me, but I still find myself wrapping my arms around my torso and gripping the material tightly between my fingers, as though I can hold it on.

I get on the bed and lie on my back and stare up at the ceiling. He leans over me, hooks his fingers in the sides of my panties, and yanks them down my thighs, before tossing them to one side. I clamp my thighs together, but I know it won't do any good. He's going to get what he wants, no matter what.

"Spread those legs for me, girlie." He smacks my inner thigh with the muzzle. "Let me see that pussy."

I twist my face away from him so I don't have to see the look in his eyes, and I let my thighs fall open. My cheeks burn with shame. I can feel him studying me, staring right up inside me.

"So pretty and pink."

He gets to his knees beside the bed to bring himself level with me and rubs the tip of the gun over my clit. My hips buck, and I gasp in shock. The metal is almost painfully cold against the heat of my flesh.

Despite myself, heat gathers between my thighs, and I feel myself growing wet and slippery. My clit tingles as blood rushes to the area and I become engorged.

Smith gives a cat-who's-got-the-cream smile. "You like that, huh?"

He keeps rubbing me with the muzzle of the gun. My breathing comes short and sharp, panting. He thinks it's with pleasure, but it's fear.

"You're a dirty little bitch, aren't you? A little whore who likes to get fucked. Did you like it when your stepdaddy came inside you? Filling you up with his seed? I should let each of my men take their turn with you, and then make your daddy and stepbrother fuck you as well, dipping their dicks in all our cum."

I continue to stare at the ceiling and will myself somewhere else.

He pushes the muzzle of the gun between my swollen pussy lips and probes at my entrance. The gun is a Sig Sauer and has no front sight, so at least I'm not going to get torn apart, but the metal is impossibly cold, like it's made from some other-worldly material. If that gun goes off, I'm dead. I feel sick, the room distant and spinning around me. I can't believe this is happening, but it is.

"Let's see a bit of effort on your part," he says. "You don't want my trigger finger to get all antsy."

Is he serious? He wants me to fake enjoying fucking a gun? This is insane.

A tear slips down my cheek, and I sniff. He shoots me a glare of annoyance. "That's the opposite of what I want, bitch."

He jams the gun hard up inside me, and I let out a yelp of pain.

"Now fuck it."

Feeling like I'm mimicking the few porn films I've seen, I give a moan and lift my hips.

"That's more like it."

He reaches into his pants and frees himself. Now he has one hand on the gun, and the other on his cock. I'm terrified he's going to forget which is where, and accidentally fire the weapon. I don't know if he has the safety on the gun, but that doesn't lessen my terror.

"Make it so your stepbrother and father can hear you. We need to let them know you're having a good time."

I give a moan, hoping it'll be enough to please him.

He bends down, and his mouth closes over my clit. I whimper in dismay, but my hips buck at the contact and little fireworks of arousal spark through me. My instinct is to kick and claw and scream, but there's a loaded weapon pushed up inside me, and I'm terrified if I make the wrong move, it'll blow my insides out.

I'll be having nightmares about this moment for years to come. Will I even be the same person if I manage to live through this? I'd thought I was fucked up before my mother died, but now I realize how bad things could have gotten. I want to pull away, to pretend I'm existing on another level somewhere. I even try to picture myself back in the trailer, on the foldout couch that had been my bed for so many years, but a particularly painful thrust of the gun pulls me back to reality.

Smith sucks on my clit, then laps in fast little strokes, before going back to suckling on me. I moan and twist my head, hating how my pussy responds to him, flooding with wetness. He's eating me like he's half-starved and moans his approval, the sensation buzzing through me in a way that notches up my body's arousal.

He's found a steady rhythm now, sliding the barrel in and out of me, while keeping up his attention on my clit.

Though I fight it with everything I have, my orgasm hits fast and strong, and my body jerks and shudders. I try to keep my mind and emotions detached, not wanting to think, not wanting to feel.

"Now, that was good," Smith says, nodding approvingly. "You like my mouth on you, huh? All my women say I'm good with my tongue."

He slides the gun from my body, and I snap my legs shut.

"Good girl. You did well. You're not done yet, though." He shoves his cock in my direction. Oh, God, is he going to fuck me now?

Instead, he says, "Put your hand around it."

I close my fingers around his dick and turn my head and squeeze my eyes shut. I masturbate him, my jaw tight, my lips pinched shut. I try not to think about it. It's only a dick in my hand. It's no big deal. Just skin and muscle and flesh.

His breathing comes harsher, and he thrust his hips, his cock sliding back and forth in my grip.

"Open your legs again," he commands, his voice raspy.

I let them fall apart once more. I'm sore and swollen, and I guess he likes the sight, as he groans.

"Oh, fuck."

He comes, and a hot splatter of semen hits my thighs and stomach. I snatch my hand away, try not to gag, and fail.

Smith notices.

"Ungrateful bitch," he spits. "I should have made you swallow it."

I turn my head to glare at him. "That really would have made me puke."

I hate the feel of him on my skin. I hate having the scent of his cock on my hand. I want to go down to the river and scrub my skin raw. I want to tear my skin from my body, peel it like an old bathing suit, and toss it away.

Whatever happens, I refuse to cry. He'd like that, and while he's taken so much from me, I refuse to let him see how much he's hurting me.

He throws me a wet cloth. "Clean yourself up."

I'm at least grateful for that, and I wipe down my skin, while trying not to give in to my tears.

10
REED

THE SIDE OF MY FACE FEELS LIKE IT'S ON FIRE, BUT I don't even care. All I care about is the woman behind the bedroom door and what she's going through.

"How bad is it?" Darius asks me in a low voice. "I can smell the blood."

"It's fine," I lie. "Only a scrape."

"You're not going to be any good to us if you get yourself killed."

I feel like he's shaming me.

"I had to try something."

"Just stop the bleeding," Darius tells me. "The face bleeds badly. You're probably already dehydrated, and this could put you on your back."

Axel waves a gun in our direction. "Quiet, both of you."

Darius doesn't give in. "My father's bleeding. At least give us something we can use as a bandage."

"He'll survive," Axel says.

The bedroom door opens, drawing all of our attention, and

Laney comes out of the room. She's dressed, but she doesn't look at us.

I've never wanted to kill a man as much as I want to kill Smith right now. The thought of him inside her is enough to make me want to rip his head from his shoulders and piss down his throat.

"I'm going to fucking kill you," I tell him. "If it's the last thing I do."

He laughs, infuriating me further. "Good luck with that."

I've never felt so fucking guilty about anything in my life. If I hadn't tried to attack Zeke with an axe, Smith would never have punished Laney. It's the perfect way to keep us in line. He knows none of us will try anything else now.

I need to focus on Laney. She's the one who needs me.

I reach for her. "It's okay, Laney, baby. You're still you. We love you."

Smith smirks. "Aww, how sweet."

I want to tell her that it doesn't matter, that whatever he's done to her won't change how we think or feel about her, but everything I go to say is wrong. How can I possibly say that what she's gone through doesn't matter? It will matter to her. It might matter more than anything else she's ever been through, and I can't minimize that for her. I am completely helpless, and powerless in being able to make things better.

We need to figure out how to get out of this.

I glance over at Darius. His expression is contorted with pain, and his hands are balled into fists. I can tell he feels the same way as me—wanting to tear the walls of the cabin down with his bare hands and crush these fuckers inside it.

I'm almost jealous of Cade and his not knowing. His oblivion. If—when—he wakes, however, he's going to kill every one of these bastards.

"You hurt her," Dax snarls. "If you think you're getting a fucking cent out of me now, you can think again."

"See, there's another flaw in your plan," Smith says, waving the gun in Darius's direction. "If you tell me there's not going to be any money, then I might as well shoot you now."

"No!" Laney screams. She drops to her knees in front of Smith, her fingers laced together in a prayer symbol. "Don't, please! I'll do anything you want. Just don't do that."

Laney can heal from this. It might take her a lifetime, but it is possible. Death, however...there's no coming back from that. Dead is dead.

Perhaps death would be a better option. Better than watching Laney being repeatedly raped. Does she think that way, though? Or is living—even through this— still better than whatever lies beyond death? What happens to us once we die isn't something I've given much thought to before. To me, death has always been pretty much final. One minute we exist, and the next we do not. But now I find myself longing for an after-life. I hope, if the four of us should die here, then we'll be granted the chance to be together again in whatever comes next.

Am I more accepting of this because of my age? Laney is only just an adult, and both Cade and Darius are barely into their twenties. I'm forty years old, and I've at least gotten to live half of my life. Is that why it's easier for me to accept death than any of them? It naturally feels closer for me.

I wish I could take her place, but it's not me they want.

"I'm bored, too," Zeke whines. "When do we get to have a little fun?"

Smith's lips pinch. "I'm not going to let you make a mess of her. Not until I'm done."

"How come you get to have a go and we don't," Axel says. "That's hardly fair, is it?"

"You get to have a go when I say you do."

I bristle. Are they going to hand Laney around like some sex doll? I don't know how I'm going to be able to stand by and let this happen. I'd almost rather get shot, though that's not going to do Laney any good. If I die, she'll have to deal with her grief on top of the trauma these men will be causing her.

"I'm hungry," Smith says. "I worked up a good appetite. I say we do some grilling. And where's that beer?" He claps and rubs his hands together.

He's in a good mood now, the fucker.

Laney gets up from her knees and heads over to us.

Seeing her moving so gingerly is like a stab through the heart. How could he have hurt someone as beautiful and perfect as her? I've never known pain like it. A band has formed around my chest and is pulling tighter with every second, making it hard for me to breathe. I want to soothe her, to make it all go away, but how can I?

I put out my arms, and she presses herself into my chest. I fold her into me and bury my nose in her hair.

"I'm sorry," she whispers.

"No. You don't have anything to be sorry for. I'm the one who should be sorry."

Shame and grief emanate from her, and my fury builds. How could that fucking bastard have done this to her?

I brush the tears from her cheeks with my thumbs and kiss her face, placing my lips on the red marks on her cheeks, peppering her with kisses, then down her neck to kiss the bruises on her throat.

I put those marks there, and I'll do whatever I can to soothe her pain.

She's ours, not theirs, and no matter what happens, that is never going to change.

11

laney

I LET REED HOLD ME, THOUGH I DON'T FEEL AS THOUGH I deserve his love. I climaxed with Smith. I had his mouth on me. I touched his cock. I had his cum on my skin.

Though I never wanted it, I feel as though I've cheated on them all. If we make it out of this alive, will the men I love even want me? Or will they see me as sullied goods now? Damaged and unlovable.

They're still making me feel loved right now, but what will they think of me by the time this is all over? If we ever make it back to civilization, will I even be the same person I am now? Or will the abuse change me?

I'm already sick with a shame I've never known before. It's only going to get worse.

Smith and his men have taken themselves onto the porch to carry on drinking and making themselves more food.

I don't want to think about myself or what may lay ahead for me. I'd rather focus on the others. Reed was shot—even if it wasn't a direct hit—and he must be in pain.

"How is your face?" I ask, trying to distract myself from what I've gone through.

I don't want to think about it. I never want to think about it ever again.

"I'm fine, Laney. Seriously. Don't worry about me."

"Don't ever do something like that again, okay?" I'm angry with him for being an idiot, not because I blame him for what happened. "Don't get yourself killed."

"I've already told him," Darius says. "But he's a stubborn son-of-a-bitch."

I glance down at Cade. "Reminds me of someone else I know."

"Come here." Darius reaches for me, wanting that contact.

In his dark world, with his brother unconscious, he must feel so isolated. Cade has been his eyes since he was a child, but now that's been taken from him, though hopefully only temporarily.

I leave Reed to reposition myself with Dax. He wraps his arm around my shoulder and pulls me into him. He kisses the top of my head, and I rest my temple on his shoulder.

"Are you okay?" he asks me.

"Not really. Are *you* okay?"

He seems surprised by the question. "I've been hurt less than anyone else."

"You don't have your violin anymore. That must be hard. I've never known you without it."

It's true. Even though he's refused to play the whole time we've been in the cabin, he's always had it nearby. His hands have always automatically reached for the instrument, thumbing the strings or tracing the outline of the smooth, shiny, dark wood. Seeing him without it is like bumping into someone completely out of context—a schoolteacher in a grocery store—and knowing them but being unable to place them.

"It's nothing, Laney. Nothing like what they've put you through. The violin can be replaced. I promised I wouldn't play until we made it home, and I meant it." He clenches his fists. "I wish I could do more. I feel so fucking helpless like this. What kind of man am I to sit by and allow them to do that to you?"

I cover his hand with mine. "You're alive, and that's all that matters. *We're* alive. Reed almost got killed trying to intervene. You know what would hurt me far worse than anything these men can ever do to me? Losing one of you. That's something I'll never get over, do you understand? If you want to help protect me, then you'll protect yourself."

He ducks his head, his eyes closing. "I understand, but it's still hard."

"This whole fucking thing is hard. We have to believe we're going to get through it."

He puts his hand on his brother's shoulder. "And that Cade is going to wake up."

"Yes, that, too."

I glance at Cade, and fresh tears roll down my cheeks. I miss him. Even though he's right here, I miss him. The ache in my heart is a hollowness I've never experienced before. I want him to get up and give me some attitude, to call me Cuckoo and look me up and down in that way he does that tells me he knows exactly what I need before I do.

"He's going to be so fucking mad when he wakes up," Darius says, as though he's read my thoughts. "He's going to want to burn this whole fucking place down with those pricks in it."

I find myself smiling—a tight, trapped smile that is more of a press and stretch of the lips than a real one—but I nod and squeeze Dax's hand tighter. "He really is."

The smell of steaks grilling filters through the cracks in the windows and doors. The men brought a disposable barbeque

95

with them in preparation for this meal and have set it up on the porch. My stomach gurgles and growls audibly. My mouth floods with saliva, and I swallow.

The laughter that intermingles with the clink of beer bottles and the scent of smoke makes me feel like it could be the Fourth of July. It seems crazy to think these men are gunrunners, and that they're here to do a job, not just have good time.

Axel pushes through the cabin door, carrying the leftovers of his meal on a paper plate. I can't help my heart jackhammering in my chest, or the way I rise slightly to see if there's anything for us.

He catches me looking and picks up the remains of his steak—the fat and gristle—and tosses it to me as though I'm a stray dog. I want to throw it back at him, but my body screams no. Even grilled fat is enough to give me energy. I pick it up and gnaw at it hungrily. The fat melts on my tongue, and I almost groan in pleasure. I suddenly remember the others, how they must be starving too, and am overwhelmed by guilt. I hadn't even thought about them. My body and brain had gone into survival mode, only thinking about getting sustenance inside me.

Only the inedible bits of gristle are left, and I let them drop from my fingers to the floor.

"Sorry," I whisper, my eyes filling with tears. "I should have shared."

"You don't have anything to be sorry about," Reed says.

"Stop talking!" Axel shouts over at us.

The others come back inside as well, and I cower at the sight of Smith, pushing myself into the farthest corner in case he decides he wants to have a little fun with me again. But he doesn't even look in my direction.

It's growing dark outside.

The day is almost over, and Cade hasn't woken once. Reed

was stupid and reckless for trying to attack Zeke, but if we don't do something, we're all most likely going to die here. Cade needs to be getting proper medical attention, not lying on a dirty mattress in the middle of nowhere.

I think of all the food waste they've thrown out and remember the bear. Perhaps it's crazy of me, but a part of me hopes he'll come back. That type of distraction is exactly what we need to make our escape. But then I remember the guns and realize that even a huge bear isn't strong enough to survive their bullets.

12
REED

A SMALL CRY OF ALARM COMES FROM BESIDE ME, AND instantly, I'm awake.

My heart jackhammers against my ribs. I'm so ready for fight or flight that my body immediately goes into adrenaline mode. My first thought is that someone is hurt, but as I half sit in the darkness of the cabin, everything is still.

Beside me, Laney tosses and turns, flings her hand above her head, and then lets out a similar noise to the one that woke me. In the near darkness, I can barely make out her face but sense the tension in her body.

She's having a bad dream. After everything she's gone through, it's hardly surprising. Will it pass? I don't want to wake her if I don't have to. Sometimes it feels as though sleep is our only escape from the horrors we're living through. But then her cry grows louder and she thrashes once more. Whatever respite sleep might be offering, it's definitely not helping Laney right now. I place my hand on her narrow shoulder and give her a gentle shake.

"Laney, wake up."

I have to hiss the words. The last thing I want is to wake any of those assholes.

I shake her a little harder, and she jerks awake, half-sitting, in a strange replica of how I'd woken only moments before.

"What—"

"Laney, baby, it's okay. Shh. You had a nightmare."

She lets out a shaky sigh and sinks down onto her back. "Shit."

"You okay?" I whisper.

She nods but doesn't speak.

"Come here," I tell her.

The rest of the cabin is silent around us, other than the snores of the men who've kept us captive. The flames from the woodstove have flickered down to embers, but the cabin is still warm. The side of my face where the bullet grazed me is hot and throbbing, but I try to ignore it.

I put my arms around her and draw her into me. My palm rests on her chest, above her breasts, and the fast beat of her heart pounds beneath her skin. Her breathing is rapid and shallow but is starting to slow.

The position we're in—with me spooning her—reminds me of the time she seduced me, and I took her virginity, and, despite our circumstances, I find myself getting hard. I'm ashamed of myself. I shouldn't be thinking of her that way, not after what she's been through, and I pull myself away, creating distance.

She goes stiff in my arms. "Don't do that."

For a moment, I think she means getting an erection, and my shame deepens.

"I'm sorry. It's not easy, having you so close."

We're both whispering, staying as quiet as possible.

"No, I'm not talking about that. Don't put space between

us. It makes me feel like you don't want me anymore, after what"—It's as though she can't even say his name—"he did."

I still don't know the full extent of what Smith did to her in that room. She'll talk about it when she's ready, and even though I don't want to hear it, I'll listen. I'm at least partially responsible for what he did to her, and I'll never forgive myself for it. It's the least I can do.

I hold her tighter. "Oh, baby. Of course I want you. I'll always want you."

Fuck. Is she crying? I made her cry. I've never felt like more of a bastard than I do right now.

Instantly, I curl my body back into hers, making sure she's fully aware of my cock.

"I sicken you now," she sobs quietly.

I kiss the back of her neck. "No, never. I love you. Nothing will ever change that. Nothing."

She turns her face, and we kiss, hot and urgent, our lips wet and salty with her tears. The kisses are frantic, urgent, and we breathe each other in.

She breaks the kiss and puts her hand on my jaw. "Will you just put your cock inside me, let me feel you that way as I fall asleep?"

I have to check what she's asking. "You want me to put my dick inside you?"

"Yes, I need to know how it feels without it being about you fucking me. I know that sounds a little crazy, but after..."

She doesn't need to explain.

"I'll do anything you ask of me, baby. If that's what it takes to make you feel better, then of course I'll do it."

She lifts my hand to her lips and kisses my knuckles. "Thank you."

From behind, we get into our customary position, that same one we were in the first time I fucked her. She pushes her ass out toward me. She's only wearing an oversized t-shirt and her panties, her legs bare. I'm already hard—any hint of getting to be inside her will do that to me—but that's not the problem.

I'm not sure I'm going to be able to do this. How will I be able to stay still inside her without fucking her? It's going to be insanely hard, but if it's what she wants, then I'll do it.

I pull her panties to one side. "Are you sore?" I whisper against her ear.

We're so close now, she can hear me, no matter how quiet I'm being. And we have to be quiet. We can't risk waking the others.

She nods, and it almost kills me. "Yes, a little."

"I'll be gentle."

I use my fingers on her first, touching her pussy lightly, making sure she's wet enough for me not to hurt her. She's so soft, and I'm happy to find her already wet. I want to sink my fingers deep inside her, to make her feel good, but that's not what she wants. I have to keep reminding myself this isn't about sex, no matter how the act looks on the surface. After what that bastard did to her, she needs to know she can feel safe with a man's cock inside her, that we don't all just want to take from her.

I don't want to let her down.

I crook my fingers inside her, feeling for the little pad of flesh on the inside of her walls. I apply pressure, and she lets out a breathy sigh and pushes back on me. God, she's so fucking perfect. My cock grows even harder.

"Are you ready for me, baby?" I ask her, keeping quiet. The absolute last thing I want is for Smith or any of the others to wake up and catch on to what we're doing. That might start something neither of us wants to get involved with.

"Yes, I'm ready."

Positioning the head of my cock at her pussy, I gently

nudge my hips forward. Her wet heat encases the head, and my eyes slip shut, relishing the feel of her around me.

"How does that feel?" I keep my voice to a whisper, but it's breathy now, a little ragged. "Tell me if you want me to stop."

She shakes her head. It's pillowed on my bicep. "No, don't stop."

I sink in another inch. I want to pin her down and fuck her hard, but I can't. I'm being gentle with her. Giving her what she needs. I haven't been able to save her from those assholes, but I can give her this.

Her pussy is so tight, gripping me like a hot, wet fist. I'm desperate to rock my hips, to get some movement going so I can find my release, but I don't. This isn't about me.

I stroke her hair, and her eyes slip shut. "That's right," I praise her. "That's my good baby-girl. You get some sleep now."

I'm fully inside her now, balls-deep. I hold her close, her body settling around me. The tension that knotted her up after her nightmare, and then her thinking she repulsed me in some way, seems to have flowed from her body into mine. Now she's relaxed, and I'm the one who's bunched up with pressure.

"Thank you, Daddy," she murmurs, already half asleep.

I almost explode. Fuck. I have to control my breathing. I can feel it getting faster and more desperate. In my head, I flip her onto her stomach and yank her feet either side of my legs, and press her face into the mattress while I fuck her hard from behind.

I'm trembling with want, but I have to control myself.

Her breathing grows even, and her entire body relaxes. She's asleep now, my cock is still inside her. I feel like I don't stand a chance of getting another minute's sleep tonight, but, to my surprise, when I force my breathing to grow slow and steady, and I relish the feel of her relaxed and sleeping, I do.

13
laney

WHEN I WAKE, REED IS NO LONGER INSIDE ME.

He's tucked himself away and covered me up, clearly wanting to shelter me from Smith and his men. I love him for that.

I wonder what today will bring with it. Will it be the day we finally find freedom, or will it be the day that heralds our deaths?

I take a peek at Cade. He still hasn't woken. It's been too long now. This isn't just a case of him needing extra rest. Something must be very wrong for him to have not fully regained consciousness. With every hour that passes where he's still unconscious, I become more certain he's not going to wake at all. My sense of hopelessness grows deeper.

I can't help but think back on our time in the cabin before these men found us. I remember all the times I'd believed I'd felt trapped here, how the endless trees had created a barrier between us and the real world. We'd been frightened about what our futures held, and we'd been hungry on more occasions than I can even count. I recall when I'd gotten sick and how terrified I'd been of dying, and how the men had been frightened for me, too. It had been less than perfect, but now, looking back from our current situation, it seems blissful. Though things had been hard, they'd also been peaceful. We'd had each other, and that was enough. We'd gotten off to a rocky start, but we'd found our way with each other, and I always trusted that these men would have protected me, no matter what.

Now, they've had that ability to protect me taken out of their hands, and I know they're hating themselves for it. I want to be able to tell them it's not their fault, but I know they won't believe it. I can see the pain in Reed's eyes every time one of those assholes implies they're going to hurt me. He desperately needs to be able to make them stop, but the simple fact of the matter is that he can't—not with a gun to any of our heads. All it will take is a moment, a simple, split-second decision, and one of us is dead. Then our whole worlds will be broken forever, and there will be nothing we can do to heal it again.

The cabin stirs to life around us.

We're at least allowed to use the bathroom, which I guess is something. I take as long as I can, happy to have a little privacy. I take some water in with me, and my toiletries, and wash up and brush my teeth. I'm glad there's no mirror. I can feel from the bruising on my face that I probably don't make a pretty sight. I'm still sore between my legs, but nowhere near as bad as I'd feared I'd be.

The men have made coffee, and the scent of it fills the cabin, though of course we're not offered any. They toss us literal scraps leftover from their breakfast—crusts from the bread and some bacon rind. We share it out between us. We're starving, and even though I hate eating their leftovers, the bacon and bread still tastes incredible.

I take time to drip some more water into Cade's mouth. He

swallows, and I watch his eyeballs flicker behind his lids. He even moans, and I glance over at Reed, wondering if we should take it as a good sign. To me, Cade seems to be a little more responsive, but I'm not sure if it's wishful thinking. Don't even people in a coma sometimes make noises and move? Is Cade in a coma now? I have no idea.

Smith clears his throat and gets to his feet. "Stepfather and fiddler boy, get up."

Neither of the men moves.

"Where are we going?" Darius asks.

"We need water collecting. We hadn't expected to have to keep you alive as well as us, so we've gone through our supplies quicker than we expected. I don't see why we should have to carry it when you've been drinking it all."

We've hardly drunk any of their water—surviving on the barest offerings—but there's no point in arguing.

"Two of us will take you this time," he continues, "and don't think for a moment that you'll get the better of two of us when we're armed. You'll end up with hell of a lot worse than a scraped cheek."

Reed shoots me a look. I know he won't want to leave me alone.

"I'll be fine," I tell him.

I hope that's the truth.

I'm also aware that if Reed and Darius go down to the river, then Reed will see the boat. It might give him some ideas about how we can reach it.

Could we try to slip away at night?

Even as the thought comes to me, I'm forced to push it away, my heart sinking.

Cade.

The three of us could sneak away—especially after the men have had a belly full of beer—but there's no way we could take

Cade with us. I'm terrified he's got bleeding on the brain, or swelling, or something. There is zero chance of us leaving him with those bastards, even if we thought we might be able to get help. If we left, there would be no reason for these men to keep Cade alive. I'm surprised *any* of us are still alive. The only reason we are is because they are using us as entertainment with the possibility of eventually getting money out of Darius.

And since there is no possibility of us leaving without Cade, I guess that means we're staying.

Reed and Darius both get to their feet, and they're handed a couple of plastic jerry cans—the foldable ones people use for camping. Axel shoves one unceremoniously against Darius's chest.

Dax scowls. "Watch it, asshole."

"Or you'll what?"

Darius doesn't reply.

Reed gives me a backward glance as he leaves with Smith's gun wedged against his spine. I pray he doesn't do anything stupid.

I'm left here with Zeke, but he doesn't seem too interested in me. He waits until the others are out of sight, and then steps out of the cabin, too, and finds himself a seat on the porch. I watch through the dirty window as he tilts his head back and closes his eyes against the bright morning sunshine.

With Zeke not seeming to care what I do, I take myself back to what I've started to think of as 'our corner' so I can be with Cade.

My heart is breaking, and I curl up into his inert body, pressing my nose to the bulk of his shoulder. I take some comfort that he's still warm, that his heart is beating, that his chest rises and falls with his breath.

It isn't over yet.

I don't cry for myself, but I cry for him now. My tears soak the material of his t-shirt, leaving a dark, wet patch on his sleeve.

"I'm so sorry I can't do more to help you," I tell him. "You should be in the hospital right now, not lying on this filthy mattress. You should be having scans and be hooked up to drips, and have the best doctors watching over you. You deserve that, Cade. You really do. I know you blame yourself for so much, and you're too hard on yourself, but we all make mistakes, even really stupid big ones. We're just people trying to get through this thing called life as best we can, and as long as those we love forgive us, everything will be all right again. I promise."

Cade gives a low groan in the back of his throat.

I draw a quick breath and lift my head. Is it only another one of the noises he makes? I'm not sure, something about it seemed different, but I've thought that before and he's remained unconscious.

I hold the air in my lungs, my body frozen, waiting and watching.

Cade's eyelids flicker.

I give a small cry of surprise. "Cade?"

That same flicker again, only stronger this time. He twists his head one way and then the other, and when he brings it to the center again, his eyes are open.

I don't think I've ever seen such a beautiful sight in my life.

"Oh, my God, Cade. You're awake."

"Laney?"

I burst into tears. "Yes, it's me. I'm here."

I touch his face, running my fingers over his jaw, his lips, trying to make my head believe that he's still alive and back with me. We press our foreheads, noses, and lips together in salty, tear-stained kisses.

His voice is a rasp. "Thirsty."

I'm spurred into action. "Water! I'll get you water."

I'm so thankful none of Smith's men are here to see this. What would they do? A fresh fear fills me. Will they shoot him? Cade's clearly the most physically strong out of all of us— or at least would be at full health—and so would be their biggest threat. That he's been unconscious might have been the only thing that's saved his life.

I glance out of the window. Zeke is still sitting on the porch, a gun at his side. He's working a piece of wood with a knife, carving something. He hasn't noticed the change inside the cabin, and for that, I'm grateful.

I carry a tin cup of water back over to Cade and support his head as he drinks it.

"Slowly," I tell him, keeping my voice down so I'm not overheard by the man on the porch. "I don't want it to make you sick."

Cade doesn't normally listen to me, but he does now, changing his gulps to sips.

He pushes the cup away and falls back to lie down again. "I could hear your voice," he says.

My eyes fill with fresh tears. "You could?"

"Yeah. I kept following it, like you were the sunlight and I was being held underwater. I kept trying to swim toward you."

I wrap my arms around his torso and press my cheek to his chest. I hold him tight, and then worry I'm going to hurt him and release him a fraction. "How's your head?"

"Banging." His eyes are bloodshot, and he looks like crap. "I don't really know what happened."

"The gunrunners are what happened. One of them hit you with the butt of his weapon and then brought us back to the cabin."

His face crumples as it clearly pains him to think back. "I remember glimpses of it, but it's like a dream." He tries to sit up

again, but I put my hand on his shoulder and gently press him
back down.

"Where's Darius and my father?"

"They're fine. They're out collecting water."

The way I've phrased it makes it sound as though they're
doing so willingly, as though they don't have armed men
pointing guns at their heads. I'm torn between trying to impress
just how much danger we're in on Cade and wanting to protect
him from the reality of our situation. I know if he truly understands the extent of what we've been going through, he'll want
to do something to try and save us, and currently, he's nowhere
near strong enough. All he'll do is make the situation worse.

"What about you?" he asks. "Are you okay? Did they hurt
you? Did they touch you?"

A mask of pain crosses his face that this time has nothing to
do with his head injury.

I don't want to tell him about what's happened to me. All I
want is for him to concentrate on getting better. If he knows,
he'll lose his shit and then try to kill these men. If he suffers
another blow to the head, it might kill him. I'll do anything to
protect him. He might be twice my body size, but right now he
needs taking care of.

"I'm fine," I lie. "The others kept me safe. You don't need to
worry. Please, try to rest. Get strong again."

If Cade is on the mend, we can think about trying to make
our escape. It will be dangerous, but if we stay here, I'm sure
they'll kill us. At some point, they're going to need to leave, and
we won't be going with them. Perhaps we could beg for them to
leave us here, as the winter will kill us anyway, but since we
were already trying to walk out of here when they found us, I
assume they'll think it's too much of a risk. At least if they shoot
us, they won't have to worry about us potentially reaching civilization and telling the police everything.

Cade's eyes have slipped shut, but I need him to stay awake for one more minute.

I give him a small shake. "Cade, you need to listen to me, okay? And then you can sleep."

His eyes flicker open once more. "I'm listening."

"You need to pretend you're still unconscious. These men think we won't leave you, but if they see you're awake, they might do something else to keep us here, like tie us up or lock us in or something."

"You want me to pretend?"

"It gives us an advantage, and we don't have many of those right now."

Footsteps and low voices come from outside.

"Close your eyes," I hiss at him. "Please, you need to pretend like you're still unconscious. For us."

To my great relief, he sinks back onto the mattress, and his eyes close once more. His breathing grows shallow but even. If I hadn't known he was sitting up a moment ago, talking, I'd have thought he was as sick as ever.

Movement comes from the porch, signaling their return.

I meant it when I said it might be our only advantage. Smith and his buddies need to believe we're not going to run, and if they see Cade awake, they'll know we might.

I have no idea if Cade is even strong enough to try to run. The river and the waiting boat aren't far, but they're still through rough terrain. We'd created a narrow path through the undergrowth by our constant walks back and forth over the past month, which should help.

Do any of us even know how to drive a boat? How to start one? It has an engine, and I assume there are oars somewhere onboard as well, but does it also need a key? If so, I doubt we'll be able to get our hands on it. We can still escape using the oars, though. It'll make it easier for Smith to catch up to us, but

112

the farther we get, the harder that'll become, and unless he's a really good swimmer, we'll still be able to stay out of reach.

Reed and Darius both enter carrying the water. Smith and Axel are close behind, their guns still in their hands.

I can't look at any of them, terrified they'll see in my eyes that something has changed. I'm going to need to tell Reed and Dax at some point, though. When the sun goes down and Smith and the others fall asleep, we'll be able to choose our moment and slip away.

I picture their faces as the men wake and discover not only us, but their boat, gone. They'll be the ones trapped here then. They'll be the ones who might not survive the hike back to civilization.

Anger churns and boils inside me. It's too generous to leave them alive, to even give them a chance. After what they've done to me—to us—they don't deserve to live. But we're not killers. Even Cade, as tough as he might act, hasn't murdered a man, as far as I'm aware. If they were dead, though, we'd be free. We wouldn't have to fear them coming after us.

Trying to kill them before we leave will add another layer of danger to our escape. These men sleep with their guns practically in their hands. We'd need to be certain of taking them all out quickly and cleanly, and at the same time, or there's a good chance they could end up taking one of us with them. We can't risk any of us being hurt any more than we already have. It's better if we just slip away and hope to put as much distance between us as possible before they notice we're gone.

I glance down at Cade. He's sunk back into the darkness that's cocooned him these past couple of days. I tell myself that's a good thing—hopefully, the more he rests, the stronger he'll get—but there's also that nugget of terror inside me that worries he won't wake again. What if that's the last time I ever speak to him? I think how devastated Reed and Darius will be that they weren't here for it.

We can't let Smith and his men know, but I'm bubbling with excitement to tell Reed and Darius that Cade was awake, and not only that, he was well enough to talk to me. There was no slur in his words to indicate a brain injury, and he even remembered a little of what had happened. These are all fantastic signs that he's going to make a full recovery, but I tamper my excitement because even if he gets one hundred percent better, we're still being held by armed men.

It's given me some hope, though. After everything I've been put through, how I'd felt dead inside, it's sparked that joy. A fierce protectiveness rises inside me.

Smith and his men get busy enjoying themselves, cracking the tops off beers, and deciding what they're going to eat. I'm worried they'll get drunk and decide to use us as a little entertainment, but now Cade is awake, that suddenly seems less important.

I'm bursting to tell the other two about Cade, but I need to pick my moment. I can't risk being overheard or Smith and the others thinking we're up to something. We've taken up position in the farthest corner of the cabin, huddled around Cade like his guards. I'm poised for him to wake again, to clamp my hand over his mouth in case he tries to speak. If he does, Smith and the others will find out.

And that will ruin everything..

14
DARIUS

THE MOMENT I STEPPED INTO THE CABIN I COULD TELL something had changed.

I wish I could make eye contact with Laney, at least try to find out what's happened without alerting anyone else. At least then I'd be able to get a confirmation that my instincts aren't off.

Her voice is thick, and it's clear she's been crying.

I huddle down beside her, my shoulder pressed to hers.

"Did Zeke hurt you?" I ask her, keeping my voice low.

"No," she whispers back. "He stayed on the porch the whole time. Don't worry about me."

There's something in her tone I can't quite read. It feels completely out of place. Is that...excitement? I catch her forearm in my hand, wrapping my fingers around it. She feels painfully thin, the bone not far beneath the skin.

"What is it, Laney?"

She levels her tone. "Don't you think you should check your brother?"

Cade.

What's changed suddenly hits me. Cade's breathing. It's

115

different now, not so shallow. It's more like it sounds when he's just sleeping.

Holy shit. Did Cade wake up?

I'm desperate to ask her directly, but now I understand why she's being so cagey. What will Smith do if he knows Cade has woken up? Will he see Cade as a threat and decide to put a bullet in his head?

There's something else. If Cade is awake, and the others don't know it, we finally have an advantage. Right now, they think we're tied to the cabin because we won't leave him, but if he can get up and walk away, then we won't need to stay here. I'm getting ahead of myself—I have no idea what sort of state Cade was in when he woke—but it's still something positive, and we need that.

Reed must sense something, too. I can practically feel his gaze drilling into me.

"What's going on?" he asks.

"Nothing," Laney says. "Sit with Cade awhile."

I guess she's hoping he'll notice the change, but Reed isn't as perceptive as me. Plus, his focus will be on Smith and his fellow assholes. I know his biggest fear is them hurting Laney again. I'd overheard the two of them during the night, how he'd comforted her after her nightmare. I wish it had been me she'd turned to, but I'm glad she was able to take solace from some-where. Her voice sounds lighter now, and I know that's because of Cade.

Perhaps I should feel jealous, but I don't. This is why it works between us. All any of us wants is for Laney to be happy, and she needs all of us for that to happen.

We'll each give her a little part of ourselves until she feels whole again.

15

laney

THERE'S STILL NO SIGN OF WHOEVER IT IS THEY'RE selling the guns to. I guess in a place as remote as this, it's not easy to give an estimated time of arrival. They might have gotten held up by something.

Smith, Axel, and Zeke check their phones every so often, but of course there's no service this far out.

I picture being able to grab one of their phones and calling nine-one-one, but it's not as though I'd even be able to tell anyone where we are. Telling the police we're somewhere in the Canadian wilderness isn't going to be of much help. I wonder if there's any way they'd be able to get a ping off a tower, but then I realize how ridiculous that idea is. There are no cell phone towers anywhere nearby, and I highly suspect these guys' phones will be burners anyway.

More beer is consumed, and the men grow louder, laughing raucously, smacking each other on the back. They're more focused on having a good time than paying any attention to us, so I grab my moment.

"Cade woke up," I whisper to Reed and Dax. "He spoke to me."

Reed's eyes widen, and Darius takes my hand and squeezes my fingers.

"That's the best news," Reed whispers back.

"I told him we can't let the men know he's awake, but I don't know if he's going to be able to remember that when he wakes up next."

"Someone will need to stay with him," Darius says.

I grimace. "Easier said than done."

I agree with him, but it's not as though we've been given the opportunity to make our own choices.

"Do you think he'll be able to walk?" Reed asks.

I shake my head. "I have no idea. Maybe...in time."

The trouble is that time is not on our side. These men are waiting for an event—someone coming to buy the guns—and when that happens, they'll have to decide what they're going to do with us. The easiest way to get rid of us all is to put a bullet in our heads. People already think we're dead—lost in a plane crash—so it's not as though we'll have new search parties out looking for us.

The only thing that might keep us alive is the promise of Darius's money.

The lack of the arrival of whoever it is they're meeting is clearly bothering Smith and his gang, too.

"When the fuck are the buyers supposed to get here?" Axel moans. "This is fucking ridiculous, sitting out here for days. I thought they'd be here by now."

"They might have been held up by something?" Zeke suggests.

Axel rolls his eyes. "Or they changed their minds, or the police picked them up, and they're not coming. How long are we going to wait? And what the fuck are we going to do with those four?"

I tense at the mention of us. What's it going to take for them to decide it'll be easier to shoot us than take us with them? It's not as though the boat is particularly big. Seven of us will be a squeeze.

Darius is obviously thinking the same way. "Remember the money," he says. "I'm still happy to pay you if you get us to safety. If your buyers don't turn up, it sounds like you'll need it."

I suddenly find myself praying their buyers *don't* turn up. Darius is right. It might actually give us some leverage. But if they get us to safety, what's there to stop us going straight to the police? The first thing I'd do is report the assault.

Smith doesn't dismiss Darius's offer, but he's not stupid. He must realize both Reed and Darius will happily kill him at this point. Is his greed stronger than his self-preservation? Or does he think he's indestructible?

Axel and Zeke exchange a glance.

"What if the buyers don't turn up?" Axel says. "We'll be fucked then. We might need fiddler boy's money."

"Yeah," Zeke agrees. "I can't go home with nothing. I need this cash injection."

I reach out and squeeze Dax's hand. Flutters of hope dance in my chest. We might be all right after all. We'll be able to tell them Cade is awake, and then they'll load us into the boat and drive us up the river to safety.

Smith gets to his feet. "They'll be here. They just got held up."

Axel throws back his head. "Ugh, seriously? Can't we at least put a time on it? Like if they're not here by tomorrow, then we can go and take the violinist to the city instead?"

Smith slams his hand against the wall. "Will you stop

fucking complaining? You've got food and beer, and plenty of nature—"

"I hate fucking nature," Axel snips. "I'm bored. I want the internet, and takeout, and sports."

"Why don't you put yourself to use and go collect some firewood or something?"

It's like watching siblings squabbling.

"What? By myself?"

Smith throws up his hands. "Let's all go out and collect firewood, then." He turns to us. "Come on. You can help, too."

The wood stove is kept burning right around the clock now, not only so they can cook on it, but also to keep the cabin warm. The nights, especially, are getting colder with each passing day, and it's not as though this place has any insulation to keep the chill out.

I look to Reed, and then over to Darius. I don't like the idea of us leaving Cade alone, but I don't think the men are going to give us any choice.

I'm right.

Smith waves a gun in our direction. "Come on. Up."

I consider refusing, but what would be the point? There are some things worth fighting, but we all technically benefit from there being wood, so we might as well help.

"Don't let the old man get anywhere near the axe," Zeke says. "He can't be trusted."

Reed snorts cold laughter.

We all step outside.

"Spread out," Smith says. "We'll cover more ground that way. Don't go too far away from the cabin, though."

Like we're in a sports team and each person has to mark one of the opposite team's players, Smith's men partner themselves off to cover each of us with a gun aimed as we work. Smith is with Reed. Zeke is covering Darius. I'm stuck with Axel.

I work slowly and methodically, stooping to pick up fallen branches. I snap those that are too long to carry and bundle them under one arm. Within minutes, I've lost sight of the others. I hope they'll be okay.

Axel grabs my arm, and I drop half of what I've collected. "Hey!" I protest.

"You're coming with me."

"What are you doing?" I say in alarm. "Smith said to stay near."

"I don't give a fuck what Smith said. You think he's the boss of us or something?"

I pretty much do, but I'm smart enough to know when a reply isn't necessary.

Axel continues, "And you don't belong to him, neither. The rest of us should get a go."

I don't want his hands anywhere near me. Should I scream for help? If I do, and Darius or Reed hear, they'll try to do something to prevent whatever might happen next—though I think I've got a good idea. I picture the guns aimed at them. I see the graze from the gunshot wound across Reed's cheek. If he knows Axel intends to assault me, he'll take stupid risks to try to save me. I can't let that happen, not when Cade has woken up and we might be able to run soon. As much as it sickens me, I'll go through this if it saves us all.

I realize Axel is dragging me down to the river, putting distance between us and the cabin. I want to scream and cry and fight, but I'm numb inside. A quiet acceptance of what is about to happen settles inside me, and while I'm shattering into a million pieces, it's only happening on the inside.

Axel seems to decide we're far enough away not to be over-heard by Smith as he draws to a halt. He's still got hold of my arm, his fingers digging painfully into my flesh. He spins me to face him, and then pushes a strand of my hair back and tucks it behind my ear.

"Pretty girl."

I jerk my face away, but he keeps his hold on me.

With his other hand, he pops the button on my jeans and shoves his hand down the front. I twist my face away as his hand finds its way inside my panties. Roughly, he parts my folds and pushes his finger inside me.

"Oh, yeah, nice and wet," he grunts. "Just how I like it."

He forces his mouth down on mine, and I gag as he tries to push his tongue inside my mouth. He lets go of my arm so he can find my breast, and he squeezes it hard enough to hurt. I yelp in pain, and a smile spreads across his face.

Despite my promise to myself not to fight this, I find myself begging. "No, don't, please don't."

He pushes me down to the ground and yanks off my sneakers and then my jeans. I try to fight him, to kick at him, and struggle, but he's too strong for me. He manages to get between my legs and then uses his knees to pin down my thighs. He smiles as I batter at him with my fists, and then when I try to claw at his face, he catches my wrists and pins them on the ground above my head.

He seems to be enjoying the fight. Bastard.

There's no point in wasting my breath screaming for help. We're too far away from the cabin to be heard, and no one is around who'd help me, anyway. Plus, Reed and Darius have guns to their heads. It'll break their hearts to know what I'm being subjected to.

I make a promise to myself never to tell them. Them knowing won't change what's being done to me.

Axel holds my wrists in one hand and uses the other to reach to his zipper. I go limp. There's no point in fighting. All that will happen is he'll hurt me even more. I angle my face away and close my eyes.

There's fumbling, and then pain, but I keep my eyes squeezed shut and pretend like nothing is happening. I ignore his grunts and heavy breathing, the intense pressure inside me as he takes what he wants.

I picture myself somewhere else. I'm not here anymore.

I'm with my men in the cabin, but it's only us. We're together, sitting out on the porch. I have my head in Reed's lap, and my feet on Cade's. Darius is playing for us, the mournful sound of his violin even more poignant in that he's finally playing. He always said the next time he'd play was when he made it home, and so I realize that this means he feels like he is home now. The winter is no longer a threat. We're safe and confident that we will survive. We'll create our home, and family, here, no longer having to worry about the outside world or what they'll say about us.

Smith and his men do not exist inside the world I have created in my head.

Finally, it's over, and Axel climbs off me and puts himself away. He picks up my discarded clothes and throws them at me.

"You need to wash and then get dressed," he says. "Or Smith will know."

I'm holding my panties, jeans, and sneakers in my hands. I no longer care that I'm naked from the waist down. Where only yesterday, I would have tried to cover myself with my hands or clothing, now it all seems pointless. A black weight has settled at my soul. I struggle to find any feeling inside me at all. I'm numb.

"Take off the shirt as well. You don't want it to get wet,"

Dazed, I do as he says and drop the clothes at the bank of the river and wade into the water.

"Not too deep," Axel calls after me. "I don't want to have to come in there after you."

Drowning suddenly seems like a good way to go. They say it's peaceful, for the most part. That initial struggle, but then acceptance, and the oxygen simply melts from your blood, and it's like falling asleep. Sleep sounds good. An endless sleep.

Only the thought of the others prevents me from trying something stupid. I did this for them. If I die, Smith might decide to shoot them after all.

I hold my breath and plunge beneath the icy water. My hair billows out around me, and I open my eyes. I could stay here. It's peaceful, and nobody is going to try to take anything from me. My lungs start to burn, and I wonder what will happen if I open my mouth and inhale. Will that be enough to kill me?

No matter how much I want that peace, I can't bring myself to do it. I burst from the water, gasping for air.

"Get over here, bitch."

Axel is pacing the shore, clearly anxious that I've done exactly what I was thinking, or perhaps that I'd taken the opportunity to swim away. What would I be swimming away to, though? I'd be abandoning the others, and I'd never survive out here on my own.

Reluctantly, I wade back to shore. I can't look at Axel. Every time I do, my brain tries to take me back to the moment of him forcing himself inside me, and I fight it with every-thing I have. That did not happen. It was a dream—a nightmare.

"Get dressed," he says, chucking my clothes at me again.

I'm soaking wet, and I don't have a towel. At least I'm as clean as the river can make me, though I wish I could peel off my skin and climb out of it to become someone new.

I struggle to get my jeans on over my damp skin, but the

Immoral Games

sun—while nowhere near as strong as it had been when we'd first crashed here—is still warm, and it helps to dry me.

When I'm dressed, he grabs the soft skin of my upper arm and drags me back along the little path we've created that leads between the river and the cabin. Shame sinks into me like damp into wooden walls, and I feel sick believing that Reed will take one look at me and know exactly what happened.

The men are all back inside the cabin, the work collecting wood complete.

With a fresh wave of shame and guilt, I realize I've brought nothing back with me. The bundle of sticks I'd collected is scattered across the forest floor.

Reed and Darius are sitting near Cade, and Zeke aims a gun loosely in their direction. A part of me was hoping they'd be gone. That between Reed and Darius, they'd have picked up Cade and vanished into the woods. Deep down, I know they would never do such a thing. They wouldn't abandon me to these men.

I hope that between them they've started to come up with a plan for us to escape.

Anything to make my trauma mean something.

Smith eyes us as we enter.

"Where have you been, Axel?" he asks.

"Just collecting wood, like you wanted."

"Yeah? You didn't try to get some alone time with the girl?"

I watch the exchange, wide-eyed. What's Axel going to tell him? The truth? I doubt it.

"No. We put the wood in the shed."

Smith's lips tighten. "Why the fuck is her hair wet, then?"

"She got hot and wanted to take a dip, didn't you, princess?"

I can't even look at him. Every time I do, I think I'm going to throw up. I can feel Reed's gaze on me, questioning what

125

happened. I have no intention of telling him. I'm not sure I'll ever be able to tell him, even if we survive this.

Smith picks up his beer bottle and takes a sip, his gaze locked on his colleague the entire time.

"She took a dip? You mean you got her to take her clothes off?"

"Well, she didn't go in the water fully dressed." Axel snorts, clearly not taking Smith seriously.

My heart pounds. The tension is so thick in the air I feel like I'm inhaling it. Only Axel appears to have not picked up on how much Smith is radiating with fury.

"And what else did you do while her clothes were off, Axel? Did you happen to get your dick wet?"

"So what if I did? You're not the boss of me, Smith. You're not the boss of any of us."

Smith's fingers tighten around his bottle. "Is that right, Axel?" His tone is almost jovial, but it's a stark contrast to his body language.

"Yeah, it is."

Lines appear between Smith's brows, and he beckons Axel with the finger of the hand not holding the bottle. Axel approaches and leans across the table toward Smith.

In a blur of movement and violence, Smith grabs the back of Axel's head with his free hand, holding him in position, while he drives the bottle straight into Axel's face.

I let out a scream and throw myself backward, desperate to put space between myself and the two men. My voice rises to join the yowl of agony coming from Axel's lips. He's leaning back, his hands covering his face, blood pouring between his fingers. Glass is shattered across the table and floor.

Smith sits back and casually plucks a large shard from his palm. He doesn't even wince as he pulls it free and bright red droplets run down his fingers to join Axel's on the tabletop.

"What the fuck, Smith?" Axel protests. "You could have fucking blinded me or something."

His nose is pouring with yet more blood and is at a strange angle. His lower lip is shredded, and a big chunk of glass protrudes from his cheek.

Strong arms wrap around me from behind and pull me away. Instinctively, I fight against their hold, but then Darius's face presses against the side of my head.

"It's me, it's okay, It's me."

I relax a fraction into his arms. I'm too shocked to cry. I don't think I've ever seen such violence take place right in front of me. Even the times with my mother where she brought home a man who hit her, it still never felt as shockingly violent as what just happened.

I don't know how much of what happened Darius understands. Does he know one of the men just smashed a bottle in the other one's face? He must have heard the conversation and heard the smashing glass, and the screams. I guess it wouldn't be too hard to put it together.

"Next time, you only get to fuck her if I say you can." Smith points at Zeke. "And that goes for you, too." He turns his attention back to Axel. "I should cut your fucking cock off for doing that. She's mine."

I tense at his words. Smith has claimed me. Is that a good thing? It might mean he won't let Zeke have his turn with me as well. But then I remember how he said they can only take me when he says it's their turn.

At what point will I just fade away? Draw so deep inside myself that I won't be able to find my way out? I'm fighting all I can to try to remain myself, but it's hard, and the lure of succumbing to nothingness too strong.

I wonder who the man in the roof space once was. Could he have been one of them? I want all of them dead, and it might work out well for us if they take each other down. I have no idea if there's any way to orchestrate such a thing.

Axel gets to his feet, his hands still cupped at his face. He shakes his head, sending blood spatters across the floor, and heads to the bathroom, muttering what I assume are expletives. He reaches the bathroom and enters, slamming the door behind him. It's not like they have running water in there, so I don't know what he plans on doing. I guess he wants to put a closed door between him and the man who smashed a bottle in his face.

I risk a glance over at Smith. He gets up and helps himself to another beer. He catches me looking and gives a small smile, lifting the bottle toward me in a salute.

He's proud of what he did.

"Are you okay?" Darius whispers against my ear.

I shake my head. "Not really."

I wrap my arms over the top of his and allow my back to sink into his broad chest. We hold each other tight, finding comfort in each other's presence. But I'm worried if I allow Darius to hold me for too long, Smith will do something to hurt him. I untangle myself from Darius's arms.

"Clean up that blood," Smith says to me.

I don't argue with him. The fight has gone out of me. My blood is like tar in my veins, thick and sludgy. I feel distant from my body, spaced out, somehow. I haven't cried for myself. Perhaps I never will. It's not as though I haven't suffered abuse at the hands of men before. While none of them had gone so far, it had been when I was younger and definitely more innocent. A strange acceptance settles into me that perhaps this is just my place in life. I was put on this Earth to be used and abused, and that will be my place until one of them decides to kill me.

I go to the kitchen area and find a cloth and tip some of the water brought up from the river into a separate bucket. I don't know how good a job that's going to do, but I really don't care.

A knife lying on the side catches my eye. My fingers itch to pick it up and hide it in the waistband of my jeans, but there's no point. All it will do is cause issues.

I carry the bucket and cloth over to the table and dunk the cloth in the cold water.

Then I get to scrubbing and watch impassively as the water turns red.

16
CADE

When I open my eyes again, the cabin is in near darkness.

For a flash of a moment, the idea that I'm blind, like my brother, jumps into my head. Then a flickering of light catches my attention, and I understand that it's simply nighttime.

"Cade?" Laney whispers beside me.

I turn my head. They're all here now. My whole family all looking down at me with concerned faces.

Laney puts her finger to her lips, a signal for me to stay quiet. That's how I know we're not alone.

Honestly, staying quiet isn't too hard. I'm not sure I even have the energy to speak. Laney told me I needed to pretend to still be unconscious whenever the other men were around, but I haven't had to pretend. I've been fighting to wake up, even when I want to. I've also been conscious of movement around me, of voices, some male that I don't recognize, and of Laney's, too.

The pain in my head is still blinding, but it's not as bad as it was. Before, I'd truly thought I was going to die, and if I didn't

die, then I wanted to. Though I'd struggled to regain consciousness, deep down, I'd always been aware of my family around
me. They were the only thing that kept me going—my brother,
my father, and Laney.

Except now I realize it was never just us. Other men are
here with us, and they're the ones responsible for what
happened to me.

They did something to Laney. She seems different. The
look in her eyes is haunted, and I can tell she's trying to protect
me from something. I understand—I would do the same for her
—but it's left me uneasy.

My father helps me to half sit, and Laney holds a bottle of
water to my lips to help me drink. Then they produce a piece of
stale bread and ask if I can eat.

I do, but it's mostly to please them. I have no appetite, and
though it's been a long time since I tasted bread, I struggle to
swallow.

I hate feeling this way. Physical weakness isn't something
I'm used to. I've always taken for granted that I'm physically
strong. My size and strength have gotten me where I am in life.
If I'd known how easily it could be taken away, I'd have been
more modest about it.

I wonder how Darius has been getting on without me. I've
always been there for him, but since I've been out of action,
he'll have had to find his way around without me. I know he's
far from incapable, but still the idea of him getting on with
things twists something inside me. Have I been kidding myself
all these years that he needs me as much as I've believed? Or
has he been the one taking care of me, giving me a purpose?
He's always been so driven with his music, where I've had...
what, exactly? Women, drinking, gambling...my brother?
Before Laney came into our lives, that was the sum total of my
existence.

What if they don't need me as much as I've always believed?

What if these men have done something to Laney while I've been unable to help her? The possibility makes me want to die all over again.

As Smith and the others sleep, we silently nurse Cade. Though it's been hard not to eat all of the small amount of scraps we've been given, we've hidden some from view. He's been able to eat and drink some more water. He's regaining his strength, and it's this I try to cling to. He's not strong enough to walk yet, and we have to bring him an empty plastic bottle to piss into, which he's not happy about, but he's getting better.

Our time is running out. Tomorrow, if these people Smith is here to meet haven't shown up, there's a good chance they'll decide to leave the cabin. If that happens, they might also decide they're not going to take us with them. If they continue to think Cade is unconscious, they might decide they have no choice, but if we risk letting them know he's awake now, then we'll lose any element of surprise that's on our side.

We still have the offer of Darius's money on the table. They might need it even more if their gun deal falls through.

I'm doing my best to cling to any positivity, but I'm struggling. It's like I'm trapped at the bottom of a well, and the water is nothing more than black sludge, and it's rising.

I want to strip out of my own skin and bleach my soul clean. Every time I close my eyes, I can feel Axel pushing into me, taste his tongue in my mouth, and my skin crawls with the memory of his touch.

I don't want Reed and the others to know exactly what happened with Axel. I'm filled with shame. I'm sure they've been able to work it out for themselves, but none of them has asked me directly.

Cade goes back to sleep, and the rest of us do our best to get some rest as well. Reed tries to curl himself into me in our customary position, but I'm the one who creates space between us this time. I don't want to hurt him—I'd never want that—but I just can't right now.

The third morning of our captivity dawns bright, pale sunlight slatting through the dirty windows.

I open my eyes to find Cade staring straight into them. Instantly, I'm aware of the others in the room. Have they noticed he's awake? I want to get more fluids into him and try to find him something more substantial to eat. Will he be able to stand? If he can stand, then maybe he can walk, and if he can walk, then perhaps he can run. The only thing that's been preventing our escape has been an inability to take Cade with us, but if he's mobile now, we might stand a chance.

I'm aware all of this is wishful thinking. He's still going to be incredibly weak, and attempting to make a run for it might make his injuries worse. But what choice do we have? If we don't try something, we're surely going to die.

Carefully, I reach out and run my fingers over Cade's eyes, encouraging him to shut them again. I'm hoping Smith and the others will leave the cabin for their usual morning piss and stretch, and then I can try to help Cade.

I feel like a wreck, as though I'm barely holding it together. All I want is to sleep, but I can't even find that respite. I'm terrified Smith will take me into the bedroom and finish what he started. I'm not sure I'll be able to keep functioning if that happens. I'm losing a piece of who I am with each time they assault me.

The mood in the cabin is dangerously low. Smith and his men can tell their deal is hanging in the balance and that they might have come all this way for nothing. They're bored, restless, irritable—and it's a perilous combination.

We're thrown more scraps, and each of us palms some for Cade but devour the rest. If we thought we'd been living on the barest of rations when we'd first come to the cabin, it's nothing compared to now.

I don't have much of an appetite, so I keep most of mine back for Cade. I know he'd tell me he doesn't want mine, and I should eat, but I can't bring myself to. The only reason I manage the few mouthfuls I do is because I know I need to keep my strength up if we're ever going to get out of here. No matter how it happens—whether Smith takes us with him, or if we manage to escape—we're still lost out in the middle of nowhere and have a huge journey ahead of us. Even with the boat, we have no idea what lies ahead, or how many days it'll take for us to reach a town or city.

So, I eat the stale crusts of bread and drink the lukewarm, gritty river water, and promise myself that I won't give up.

Not yet.

The morning passes. While Smith and the others are occupied, I'm able to get food and water into Cade. He's sitting up now and talking to me. He keeps staring at me, and I can tell he knows something happened while he was unconscious. I listen out for our captors, and whenever I hear them coming, I push Cade back to the mattress and tell him to sleep.

As the day heads into the afternoon, the men grow even more agitated.

Axel paces the cabin floor like a caged animal. "How long are we supposed to wait? What if they're not coming?"

Every time he comes near, I find myself rearing back, pressing myself into the wall. The fight where Smith smashed up Axel's nose seems to have been forgotten, though Axel is still sporting the injuries, his nose swollen, both eyes ringed with black and purple bruising. Though I know Smith didn't hurt him as punishment for raping me, but instead did it because Axel had gone against his wishes, I still take some pleasure in the sight.

Smith is the cool calmness among them. "Let's give it one more day. We've come all this way."

Axel shakes his head. "Then what? What do we do with the guns?"

Smith lifts his gaze to the ceiling. "We'll have to put them back in the roof and think again."

Zeke kicks out at the wall. "Fuck. What a wasted journey."

Smith looks our way. "And what are we going to do with the four of them?"

It's as though he's asking a rhetorical question or musing out loud. I don't think he's actually expecting an answer.

"I can buy the guns from you," Darius says. "You let us live, and we become business partners."

Zeke scoffs. "What would some fiddler want with a whole bunch of guns?"

"Do you even care?" Darius shrugs. "As long as you get your money, what's the difference?"

Axel and Smith exchange a glance.

"If you could get the money to us now, we might consider it," Smith says.

Darius puts his shoulders back and lifts his chin. "You know that's impossible. But get us to a town, or anywhere that has internet coverage, and I can make it happen."

This is where we're in a catch-22. If they take us some-where we can get them the money, then we can also potentially try to get help. But if we were able to get the money to them now, then there would be nothing stopping them killing us. It's a gamble on both sides. My heart still lifts with hope, however. I don't want Darius to hand all his money over to these assholes, but broke is always better than dead.

Smith sniffs. "We don't need to decide now. The original buyers still might show."

Axel flicks at a bug crawling across the kitchen counter. "Yeah, well, I'm bored as fuck. No Wi-Fi, no cable. This place sucks."

"We can make our own entertainment." Smith glances my way, and my stomach knots.

Oh, no. This can't be good.

He lifts his gun. "You know what this cabin was originally built for, don't you?"

"Hunting?" Axel takes a guess.

"Yep, hunting. I say we do a little of our own."

Axel jerks his thumb toward the coolers. "What's the point? We brought plenty of food with us."

Smith rolls his eyes. "For fun, asshole. And anyway, who says I want to eat what I catch?"

He throws me a knowing glance again, and his tongue swipes across his lower lip. "Or then again, maybe I do."

Is he talking about hunting *me*?

My blood runs cold.

Marissa Farrar

"I want to join in," Zeke says. "You two can't have all the fun."

Smith shakes his blond head. "No, someone needs to stay here and keep an eye on the men. Plus, we need someone here in case the buyers show up."

"What if the prey runs off, though?" Axel says. "What if it escapes? It might take this as an opportunity to get away from us."

I don't know why they're referring to me as an 'it' when it's clear I'm who they're talking about. Is it a way of dehumanizing me even more than they already have? My palms have grown sweaty, and my heart is racing. I'm on the edge of having a panic attack, and I force my breathing to slow, counting my inhales and exhales. I'm terrified on two levels. The first is that I don't want to have to run out into the forest alone. I've experienced for myself that there are dangerous animals in the wilderness, and I could easily end up hurt and lost. The second is that if Smith catches me, I know what he's going to do to me, and I'm not sure if I'm going to be strong enough, mentally or emotionally, to go through it again.

At some point, I'm going to break.

Smith taps his fingers to his lips, still considering Axel's comment. "Hmm, good point. Perhaps we need to give the prey a handicap." This time, his gaze flicks over to Darius. "How about him?"

Axel grins. "Yeah, that sounds like a plan."

My heart skips a beat. Are they going to send Darius out there with me? They have no idea how capable he is. They see some blind, long-haired, and now bearded musician and think he's soft, when in fact he's the opposite.

I glance back at Reed.

He shakes his head. "You don't have to do this."

"Oh, but she does," Smith says. "She has to do what I say. You all do."

"You." Smith crosses the room and kicks out at Darius. "Get to your feet."

"What the fuck?" Darius scowls. "You can't be serious?"

"I'm serious. Now, get up. Or would you prefer we send the girl out into the wilderness on her own?"

Darius stands and clenches his fists at his sides. "No, I wouldn't."

I can't believe this is happening. My head is spinning. I don't want to be separated from Reed and Cade, no matter how long, but there's still a part of me wondering if we can somehow use this to our advantage.

What would be better—staying here and potentially being raped by each of them and ending up with a bullet in my head anyway, or making a run for it, and dying of starvation or exposure out in the forest?

Of course, there's always a third option. We could find help.

The chances of that happening are so remote I don't even seriously consider it. If there was anyone out there who might be able to help us, we'd have found them by now, wouldn't we? I'm sure we've scouted every inch of these forests over the past few weeks.

"We won't survive if we get lost," I tell them. "At least let us take some water. A little food."

Reed's face is etched in terror. He doesn't know whether he should be offering to take my spot, so leaving me here with these men, or willing me to run to try to escape them.

He must know there's no point in him offering to go with us or take one of our places. He's an able-bodied, fully grown man. Sending him out into the wilderness takes the fun out of it.

It dawns on me that these men are nothing but bullies.

I glance over at Cade, and my heart clenches. I hate seeing him so fucking vulnerable. It goes against everything he stands for. He needs to be in a hospital, not lying on a bare mattress on the floor in a cabin in the middle of nowhere. Rage boils inside me at these men for doing this to us. All we wanted was to find safety. We never wanted anything to do with their fucking guns, or the body in the loft space.

Knowing that body is up there only proves what they're capable of. Who was he to them? One of their colleagues, perhaps? Someone who tried to rip them off? Or perhaps he didn't do anything nearly as bad, and they killed him for the fun of it.

The men exchange a glance.

Smith purses his lips and nods. "Okay, you can take water, but that's it."

Darius is a solid mass of tension. "You can't be fucking serious about this. Are you actually suggesting you're going to hunt Laney?"

"Sure. And you, too, just to make sure she won't get too far."

Darius bristles. "I can get around hell of a lot better than you think."

Smith chuckles. "Good. I'll look forward to seeing that."

"You're not going to shoot them?" Reed checks.

"Who says?"

Reed grits his teeth. "If you shoot them, you might as well kill me, too. Do you understand?"

"That won't be a problem."

Fuck.

As much as we might want to threaten these men, to find something we can use to bargain with, we don't have anything. The only thing they've paid any attention to is Darius's offer of money, and even then, that seemed to fail to impress. For him to get money to them means they'll have to take us back to a town or city, and, if they do that, then we'll be able to go for help. I can't see any chance of us making it out of this alive.

"What if we get lost out there?" Darius says. "You won't be able to take me up on my offer then."

Smith shrugs. "You won't get lost. It's daylight, and we're good trackers. We'll find you."

His confidence is unnerving.

"And if you lay a finger on Laney, the deal is off," Darius says.

"You don't get to decide that. I thought we'd already had that conversation. I can do whatever the fuck I want because, ultimately, you want to live. Take the deal off the table, and I might as well make you listen to me fuck her, and then shoot you the moment I come."

The worst part is that everything he's saying is true.

Darius thins his lips. "If you come straight after us, you'll catch us right away."

"Don't worry, we'll give you a head start."

"What will happen if you catch us?" I dare to ask.

"I suggest you don't let us catch you, or you'll find out."

His words are menacing. I don't know what to do for the best. Is he really giving us a chance to get away? But if we do, we'll be leaving Reed and Cade behind. I can't stand the thought of us all being separated, especially not with Cade hurt. What if he dies while we're gone? What if he dies without me or his brother beside him, holding his hand? The thought hurts like nothing else I've ever experienced, twisting inside me and making me want to scream with pain. The possibility is unbearable.

I tell myself there are things to be grateful for. At least I'll have Darius with me. Plus, we know these forests. We've walked them every day for weeks. Smith might say he's a good tracker, but he doesn't know this place in the same way we do. We've been living here; it's been our home. The forests have provided us with everything we've needed to survive.

It's the being separated from the others part that I'm finding the hardest to deal with.

Smith picks up my bag and shoves a bottle of water into the top of it before handing it to me.

"Make it last," he tells me.

I hook the bag over one shoulder and then reach out and link my fingers through Darius's. His hand is warm, his grip strong, and having that connection soothes the panic in my heart. I still feel as though I've betrayed him, and the thought is enough to bring tears to my eyes. The thought that maybe it would be easier if Smith killed me already goes through my head, but I don't allow it to linger. We have too much to live for. I'm tired, that's all. Not just tired, but exhausted, weary right down to my soul.

"Let's move out," Smith says.

I can hardly believe this is even happening.

Axel shoves Darius in the back with his gun, pushing him toward the cabin door. I have no choice but to follow. There's no way I'm letting him do this alone. We make our way onto the porch and then down the steps to the clearing. The forest surrounds us, the first few yards of trees bright and open, before growing denser and filled with shadows.

Smith lifts his gun and aims it directly at us. "Fifteen-minute head start, and then we're coming after you. On your marks, get set...Go."

What if we refuse to run? What if we say we're not going to play their sick little game? What would they do then? But I don't dare try them. They might decide that putting a bullet in one of us is payback enough for us not playing ball.

Instead, I tighten my grip on Darius's hand, send one more backward glance toward the cabin, and then we run.

I have to act like his eyes now, leading him, and warning him of dangers as we go. There's no point in us taking one of the many paths we've forged through the undergrowth during our time here. That will only make it easy for these men to catch us.

At least being away from the cabin, if only for a short time, and out of the grips of those bastards, I'll be able to breathe again. Maybe we can find somewhere to hide, and then it'll just be me and Darius together, with no threat of someone wanting to assault me for their own entertainment.

The moment the thought enters my head, I'm drowning in guilt. Yes, Darius and I might be safe and together if we found somewhere to hide, but then we'd be leaving Reed and Cade to our captors' mercies. If they can't find us, will they take their anger and frustration out on Reed and Cade? It feels as though no matter what choices we make, someone is going to get hurt. If I put the question to Reed about what we should do, he would say run and hide. He would allow himself to be harmed or even killed if it meant Darius and I were safe.

But then what would happen to Cade?

We run, our hands gripped tightly. I wish we could move faster, but that's impossible. I don't want Darius to trip and fall and hurt himself. If he twists an ankle, or worse, they'll catch us within minutes.

How much time has passed? Five minutes? Longer? Will they stay true to their word and give us the full allotted time, or did they watch us vanish out of view and then come straight after us? I shake that possibility from my head. The whole reason they're doing this is because they're bored. Where would be the fun in them catching us right away? They want to enjoy the hunt, and that means giving us enough time to get away.

My breathing grows labored, the air heaving in and out of my lungs. Though the forest is normally filled with birdsong and the buzz of insects and the scurrying of animals through the undergrowth, right now, all I can hear is the thud of my pulse racing through my ears and our gasps for air.

My throat feels as though it has closed to the width of a straw, the air whistling in and out of my tight lungs. Though all the physical activity of the last few weeks has made me lean and strong, the lack of food over the past few days has left both of us depleted in resources. I'm grateful the weather has at least turned cooler. If we were attempting this at the height of summer, I doubt we'd get far at all. My thigh muscles burn, my calves threatening to cramp, but still we go on. The canopy of branches overhead offers us shade from the sun, but sweat drips from my hairline into my eyes, stinging them.

How far have we gone now?

I don't recognize anything around me. A dart of fear stabs at my heart. What if we get lost out here? I remember the time shortly after we'd crashed where I'd walked only a short distance from the plane and hadn't been able to find my way back again. It's so easy to lose your bearings.

"I need to rest," I gasp. "Just for a minute."

We both draw to a halt. Darius stands still for a moment, his head cocked.

"I can't hear anyone coming," he says. "We're okay for the moment."

I'm not completely sure. "What if they're really stealthy?"

He huffs air through his nose. "What? Those two?"

"They caught us off guard when we were trying to hike out of here," I remind him. "We didn't hear them coming then."

"Yes, we did. We just had no idea what we were up

against."

Darius drags his hand through his long hair. "You're right, and I'm worried we still don't. I don't want us to underestimate those sons of bitches."

We sink to the ground beneath a tree and share the bottle of water, taking sips and sitting in silence while our pulses slow and our hearts stop racing. We huddle close, Darius's arm wrapped around my shoulders, our hips wedged. The sides of our heads fall together, our temples meeting.

I don't want to wallow in pity, but it's hard not to feel sorry for myself. Sometimes, I have to remind myself that it's only been a matter of a month or so—I'm no longer sure of the date—since I lost my mom. I haven't even had time to grieve for her properly, to figure out who I am without her in my life. I've been caught up in the whirlwind that's been Reed, Cade, and Darius. If I was in a different situation, I might be worrying about losing myself to them, but that's definitely the least of my concerns. Right now, I'd be happy to do that. I already feel violated and exposed by what Smith and Axel have done to me, but far worse is waiting for me if they catch us.

"Perhaps we shouldn't go back," Darius says. "We could keep going, see where we end up."

His suggestion shocks me. "You can't mean that. You can't want to leave your father and brother."

"It's what they want. Reed told me so before we left."

"And Cade?" I'm horrified. "He never got to give you his opinion."

"I know him well enough to be able to speak for him. None of us wants you to go through what those fuckers have got planned for you."

"So, we die out here in the forest instead?"

"You don't know that's going to happen. We might be able to find help."

Marissa Farrar

"We have men chasing us with guns. Think about it, Dax. If they thought we stood any chance whatsoever in running to get help, they wouldn't have let us go. They know they're going to be able to track us down and that there's no help within reach."

He sags as though the energy has been drained from every muscle in his body and covers his face with his hands. "Fuck, Laney. How are we going to get through this?"

I want to give him an answer, to tell him that everything is going to be okay. But how can I? Everything is fucked. There's a good chance we're *not* going to make it out of this alive, and, if we do, we're going to have gone through the sort of traumatic experiences that change a person.

I hate Smith and the others, I realize. I hate them with a soul consuming passion that I've never felt about any other person before. I'd thought I'd hated the men my mother brought back to the trailer, the drunk ones, the high ones, the plain evil ones who had tried to feel me up, even though they knew I was still underage, but that was nothing compared with this.

Beside me, Darius stiffens again. His spine straightens, his chin lifts.

"Can you hear something?" I hiss.

He nods and takes my hand, pulling me to my feet. The adrenaline that had abated while we rested is back in full force, surging through my veins, urging my heart to race, like a jockey with a whip.

Before I can even process what's happening, we're on the move again, hand in hand. I lead the way, jogging the best I can in the undergrowth. I want us to be silent, but I have to call out to Darius to warn him of low hanging branches or tree roots to watch out for.

The whole time, I'm braced for a gunshot to shatter the

148

relative peace of the forest. My biggest fear is that I'll hear the bang and then Darius will fall to the ground beside me, a bullet in his back. I don't think they'll shoot me—they won't get to have their fun then—but he might be an easy target.

I want to tell myself that they won't kill Dax because he's the one with the money, but I don't know how true that is. If they decide they don't need or want his money, there won't be any reason for them to keep him alive.

"Can you still hear them?" I ask after we've been running for a while. I struggle to speak, the air tight in my lungs. I'm not unfit, but running while terrified is fucking hard.

We pause once more, and I do my best to make my breathing shallower so he can hear.

"I don't know for sure it was even them," he tells me. "Just that whatever it was moving through the forest was big."

I shudder, a fresh jolt of fear going through me. Armed men aren't the only things to be afraid of out here. The wildlife can kill us just as easily. We have no means of protecting ourselves, other than making a hell of a lot of noise if something like a bear tries to approach us, and if we do that, the gunmen are more likely to find us, too. I remember the claw marks in the timber of the outside of the cabin, how huge they were. One of those paws alone would make mincemeat out of human flesh.

I tell myself there's no point in worrying about what we can't control, but it's hard not to be petrified.

We keep going. I don't know how much time has gone by, but it feels like we've been out here for ages. A different thought occurs to me. What if they don't catch us and we're still out here when it gets dark? Being out here in the middle of nowhere, with no shelter, is horrifying. I'm so thankful I'm not alone.

Eventually, we run out of steam again and are forced to stop.

I want to cry. "This is insane. What are we supposed to do —just keeping heading deeper and deeper into the forest? We're never going to find our way back again."

Darius thinks for a moment. "Listen to me. If they're coming after us, they're not going to be at the cabin, right? They'll be leaving it unmanned."

"No, they're not. Only two of them are coming after us. I overheard Smith say that Zeke needed to stand guard, to be there in case their buyers show up, and make sure Reed doesn't try anything."

Darius considers this. "Okay, but that still means their numbers are reduced. We're more likely to be able to over-power one armed man than we are three."

"But he *will* be armed," I remind him. "And one armed man can easily shoot four people before we get the chance to overpower him."

I don't want to point out that out of those four people, one is barely conscious, one is blind, and the other is a young woman. Our chances aren't looking good.

"We'll have the element of surprise on our side, though. None of them will expect us to circle back around to the cabin. They'll think we'll make a run for it."

"Will they? If we were going to leave the others behind, wouldn't we have done so by now?"

I'm starting to feel desperate. Darius is warming to his plan, but I'm terrified he's going to put us in a situation even worse than the one we're currently in.

"You're forgetting that we also have armed men tracking us," I continue. "It's not going to be that easy."

"What do you suggest, then, Laney?" he snaps.

I cringe. Darius never gets angry with me—well, rarely. I remember the time I touched his violin bow, and heat rises to my face. One thing Darius is good at is burying his emotions.

Where Cade says exactly how he feels, and Reed always considers others before he speaks, Darius doesn't speak at all.

"I don't know," I whisper.

"Because if—when—they catch us, they'll most likely take turns raping you, after they've put a bullet in my leg to make sure I can't run any farther. Is that what you want?"

Tears fill my eyes, blurring the trees into a watercolor of browns and greens around us. "No, of course not."

He must have heard the catch in my voice as I'm trying not to sob.

His shoulders sink, and he exhales a breath. He reaches out, grabs me, and yanks me into his chest.

"God, Laney. I'm so sorry. I'm so fucking sorry. I didn't mean to make you cry. None of this is your fault. I'm just angry with myself for not being more use to you—to all of you. I feel so fucking frustrated and helpless being blind right now. If I could see, I'd be able to save you."

He's holding me tight, his arms wrapped around me, his face pressed to the top of my head. I bury my nose in his t-shirt and let my tears dampen the cloth. I wish we could stay this way forever, sharing each other's body heat, feeling each other's heartbeats. I wish we didn't have two crazy armed bastards chasing us through the forest, but we can't change what's happening to us, and we can't change who we are either.

I sniff and lift my face to look at him. "You being blind makes no difference. Reed can see, and he can't save us either."

I know my words are partly to make him feel better. Would it be different if Darius could see? Would we be making different choices right now? What if it was Reed they'd sent out here with me instead of him? I picture it in my mind, but the first thing I think of is that it would have meant leaving Cade and Darius in the cabin. We would no more have abandoned them than we would abandon Reed and Cade now.

18
REED

They've been too long.

Zeke has gone outside to take up position on the porch. He's sitting back in the chair, his feet resting on the railings. It occurs to me that with Smith and Axel gone, it'll be hell of a lot easier to take down Zeke. He's smaller and lighter than I am, but he is still armed.

I think of the guns. If only they were still in those flimsy cardboard boxes that we'd first found them in, instead of the locked metal case they were moved to. I'd have been able to get one of the guns and shoot that little piss-ant Zeke in the back of the head before he even knew what was happening. But, of course, they already thought of that, which is why they moved the weapons and locked them up. What did Smith do with the key?

Taking a risk, I shake Cade awake.

"Hey, Cade. Can you open your eyes?"

His lids flutter. For a moment, I think he's going to stay asleep, but then I'm looking into his blue irises.

"Wha—"

153

His voice is too loud. I clamp my hand over his mouth and put my finger to my lips to indicate he needs to be quiet.

"Do you think you can walk?" I whisper to him.

His face creases. "I don't know."

I help him sit, and then we pause, allowing him to get his bearings. He definitely seems stronger.

It's not often that I've wished my son were smaller. I've taken pride in producing such a strapping young man. But right now, I'd give anything for him to be more like Laney's size. I might be able to get him a short distance, but much farther, and I'm going to need Darius's help. Trouble is, Darius isn't here, and I've no idea when he's coming back.

Or if he's coming back at all.

A young woman and a blind man out in the wilderness—anything could happen.

I push the thought away. Fuck that. He'll be back. They both will.

My cheek is still throbbing from the gunshot wound. It's a very real reminder of what could go wrong if I screw this up. I imagine Laney and Darius coming back to the cabin, only to find me—and possibly Cade, too—shot dead. It would absolutely destroy them.

Fuck. I need to think about this.

What if there's still a chance Smith will take Darius up on his offer? I don't want to accept help from that fucker, especially not after he hurt Laney, but there is still a possibility they'll take us to safety.

I knot my hands in my hair, unsure what to do.

I think of the boat down at the river. I'd caught sight of it during the water collection Smith made us do. It's big enough to take the four of us. Could I get Cade down to the river alone?

Before I even attempt to think about taking Zeke out, I

need to see if I can move Cade. If I can't, there's no point in doing anything more.

I check out of the window again. Zeke is still in position. Is he asleep? His limbs look loose, but I can't tell from this angle. I consider killing Zeke so that when Axel and Smith get back we'll have evened up our numbers a bit. I picture myself sneaking up behind him and wrapping a piece of wire around his scrawny little throat and garroting him to death. But then I remember the creak of the cabin door, and the way the porch floorboards squeak. I don't stand a chance of sneaking up on him. Besides, if the others come back and find I've killed him, they'll most likely kill one, or more, of us in retaliation.

"How are you feeling?" I ask my son.

Cade doesn't reply, but instead frowns and looks around the cabin. "Where is everyone?"

"Out," I tell him.

He's been lying down for days now. The muscles in his legs will have weakened. He probably won't have much balance.

He raises an eyebrow. "Out?"

"Don't worry about that now. Just listen to me. Can you wiggle your toes? Move your feet?"

He looks at me like I'm mad. "Yeah, I'm not paralyzed or anything."

"I know that. I was only making sure. Let's get you up, then." I crouch beside Cade and wrap my arm around his back, while he hooks his arm over my neck.

"I fucking hate this," he growls. "I'm pathetic."

"No, you're not," I say, as sternly as I can manage without raising my voice. "You're injured."

He spots my face. "You're hurt, too."

"It's nothing. Just a scrape." I don't tell him it hurts like a bitch, or that it was caused by a bullet. I need him to focus on himself. I'm glad he hasn't probed too deeply into the where-abouts of Laney or Darius, but I know it's coming.

I manage to get him to his feet, where we hold still once more, allowing him to get his balance. He sways, and I brace myself. It's like holding up a giant tree caught in a high wind. I'm sure if he goes down, he's going to take me with him. But I also take pride in the fact he's standing. Not long ago, I was frightened my eldest son would never wake up. I should never have doubted his strength. He's standing, and I'm about to get him to take some steps.

The whole time, I have my gaze glued on the window, never taking my eyes off the man on the porch. I'm also listening out for the return of the others. Or even the arrival of the mysterious people who were supposed to be buying the guns. I don't even want to consider how that will change things. Whoever the buyers are, they might not take too kindly on finding the four of us here. It would also mean that Smith might decide Darius's money no longer looks so attractive.

I refocus my attention on my eldest son. "Can you walk? One step at a time?"

"I'd kill to use the bathroom," he says. "I've had enough of pissing in a bottle."

I hesitate, unsure if it's the right thing to do. If Zeke finds Cade in the bathroom, they'll all know that he's awake. Fuck it. Him finding out is probably the least of our concerns right now.

He takes a few steps and then has to stop. He teeters, and I hold on, planting my feet wide to hold him up. My muscles are screaming. Fuck. I might have been strong enough to hold him upright if this were even only a week ago, but with nothing substantial to eat for days, I feel like I'm wasting away.

"Sorry," he mumbles. "Shit, fuck. Sorry."

"You don't have anything to be sorry for."

I glance back toward the window. Zeke is still in the same place.

"Ready to try again?" I ask.

"Yeah."

We keep going at our strange, shuffling pace, crossing the cabin toward the bathroom.

Cade stops outside the door and plants his hand on the wall. "Okay, I've got it from here."

"You sure?" I check.

"Yeah. I don't need my dad taking me to the fucking toilet."

I remember Laney after she'd gotten so sick, and how she hadn't wanted help either, but had eventually given in to it. She didn't have Cade's thick-headed pride, however. My heart contracts with pain at the thought of her. *Where are you, Laney-baby? Are you safe? Please be safe.*

One thing I know for sure is that I'll never be able to get Cade down to the boat on my own. If Darius was here, it would be a whole different story, but he's not. I suspect Cade and I wouldn't make it much farther than the porch and, considering we've got an armed man sitting out there, it's simply not worth the risk. I also don't want the others to come back and discover us gone. What would they think? Would they assume we've abandoned them? It doesn't matter, anyway, because that's not going to happen.

Cade finishes up and manages to get back to the bathroom door. He almost falls into my arms, and I half carry him back to the mattress. He looks exhausted from the effort it's taken to get to one side of the cabin and back. Utterly drained. I check one more time to see that Zeke is still in position and then go to the kitchen area. I rummage around in the cool boxes which aren't particularly full anymore and find some food for us. It's not much—just some crackers and cheese—but we need all the calories we can get. Cade eats slowly and deliberately. I worry every second that Zeke is going to come back inside.

As soon as he's finished, his eyes slip shut again. I tell myself it's for the best, that each time he eats and rests, he'll only get stronger. Then I glance out the window to where the sky has grown pink with the oncoming dusk, and my stomach knots again.

It's getting dark, and Laney and Darius are still out there.

19
DARIUS

More than anything, I want to protect Laney, to save her from the nightmare we've found ourselves in, but I can't.

I don't think I've ever hated my disability as much as I do now. How different would things be if I could see? Would I make different choices?

I picture myself taking down these assholes Jackie Chan style, throwing kicks and punches, sending their weapons flying. I'd be of more use to my father then, and two of us facing the three of them would be enough to take them down. But then I think of Cade, and how good he is at fighting. Cade is one of those men who will roll up his sleeves and jump into an affray that doesn't even have anything to do with him, simply because he gets off on the adrenaline of it. It's literally his job to protect me, but Axel and Zeke took him down in seconds.

Will Cade make a full recovery? How will I find my way through the world without my brother at my side?

For as long as I can remember, Cade has been my eyes. I know he blamed himself for my sight loss, though it was never his fault. We were just kids—and even if we'd been adults when it happened, it still wouldn't have been his fault. People get sick, and sometimes they don't recover, at least, not fully. It fucking sucks, but it is what it is. Besides, I might never have picked up the violin if I hadn't lost my sight.

Cade feels differently, however. He's given himself the role of my right-hand man, and I know nothing will convince him that he doesn't owe me. So, I've done what I could and ensured he was well paid for his job, that he got to live the good life, even if it was with me as a handicap at his side.

I think to Cade's confession about what he'd done with that money. How much trouble was he really in to prefer to be stranded out in the wilderness instead of having to face the loan sharks? It occurs to me that even if we do get out of this and manage to get back to civilization, we still might have a threat to deal with.

No. I shake the thought from my head. Most things can be solved with money—something I've discovered since becoming at least moderately famous. Cade might not have wanted to ask me for more, but it's not as though I don't have it. I'll pay off whatever needs paying off, and the assholes who are hassling Cade will leave him alone.

Dusk is approaching, and with it, the sounds of the forest change. Birds that had been almost silent during the day start up with their songs, calling to one another. Different insects buzz and whine around my head. Even the trees sound different, their whispers to one another growing hushed, as though the branches, too, get ready to sleep.

Laney's fingers tighten around mine. We've been holding hands for so long, I'm sure that when we do eventually let go, I'll still feel the imprint of her touch on mine, like a ghost.

"It's getting dark," she tells me. "I don't want to be stuck out here in the dark."

Darkness is all I know. It's where I'm at home.

"The dark will offer us protection," I tell her. "They won't be able to see us in the dark."

What would be better for Laney? Being in the cabin, with the warmth and light from the woodstove, but being at the mercy of those men? Or being out here, away from them, but free and untouched?

I think of my father and brother. Are they okay? Will Axel and Smith grow frustrated at their inability to find us, and take it out on them? That's my biggest fear.

"If we find the river," Laney says, "we can follow it back to the cabin."

"Is that really what you want?" I ask.

"We can't leave Reed and Cade. We just can't."

"But those men might hurt you." The thought alone kills me. How can I lead her back to that?

"Yes, they might, but if we don't go back, we'll probably die out here, and then they'll kill Reed and Cade. You know it's true."

"Fuck, Laney. It kills me to feel like I'm delivering you back into their hands."

"We don't have any choice. I want to live, Dax. I want you and the others to live, too. I'm not ready to give up yet."

She's the bravest person I know. She's willingly putting herself back into the hands of those abusive assholes for our sake.

"We don't deserve you," I tell her.

"Shh," she says.

I feel her change in position as she presses herself up against me and stands on tiptoes. Her soft, sweet mouth presses to mine—the most glorious feeling in the world—and we kiss, long and deep.

Despite our situation, I can't help but react to her proximity. Blood rushes to my cock, and I grip her around the waist, pressing her hard against me. I will never not want her, no matter what we're doing.

She senses my need and her lips part, so our tongues dance. I taste the saltiness of her sweat on her skin.

"I want to fuck you up against this tree," I tell her.

"What if they're coming? They might hear us."

"We'll be quiet."

She nods against me, giving her consent.

Still, I hesitate. "Are you sure? I mean, after—"

"Don't, Dax."

She hasn't spoken about what's happened to her. I assume she will, in time, but I don't want to hurt her or make things worse for her somehow.

"But I—" I start, but she puts her small fingers to my lips.

"You can cleanse me of them," she says, and then she kisses me again.

I nip at her lower lip, and she winds her arms around my neck and pushes her tongue into my mouth.

There's nothing elegant in our movements. We're desperate, hungry. I want to get my hands on her naked skin. It's as though knowing the danger we're in only intensifies our emotions.

We tear at each other's clothes, opening our jeans. She drags hers down her hips, but I can tell they catch on her sneakers. I can't wait for her to take off her shoes, so I just spin her around. She must plant her hands against the tree trunk, as the angle of her body changes, leaning forward slightly.

My cock is out and in my hand. It's hot and painfully hard. I don't even give the men hunting us a single thought. The only thing driving me right now is my need to be inside her.

Laney must feel the same way. "Do it, Dax. Fuck me. Make me forget." Her voice is breathy.

I understand what she's asking of me. She wants me to take her away from the horror story we've found ourselves in, if only for a short while. I reach for her, knowing exactly where she'll be, even though I can't see her. She's bent slightly at the waist, pushing her sweet little ass out toward me. I push my hand between her thighs and slide my fingers between the lips of her pussy. She's sheer perfection—slippery and wet, soft and heated. I push two fingers inside her, and she gasps then gives a little cry. I grow even harder at the sound, and I can't wait a second longer.

I remove my hand from between her legs and place the head of my cock at her entrance. I keep hold of my length, rubbing the head between her pussy lips, coating myself in her wetness. Then I ram myself inside her, hard and fast.

She lets out a cry, and I worry that I've hurt her.

"Should I stop?" I ask.

I'm not sure I can, but I have to know she's okay.

"God, no. Don't stop. I want to feel you."

I grit my teeth as I hold myself deep, bathing in the sensation of being inside her. She feels so good, her cunt tight and hot, gripped around me.

Holding back slightly, I take a little time to let her adjust to my size, then I pull out, almost to the cock head, before driving back in. I grab her hair, fisting it into a ponytail at the roots, yanking her head back like a horse in a bridle. She's completely under my control now, and I can sense how she's given herself to me. I love that trust she has in me.

My movements grow faster, building momentum. Our bodies seem made for each other, a perfect fit.

I release her hair and push my finger into her mouth. She sucks on it willingly, leaving it coated in her saliva. Then I reach down, trailing my finger between her ass cheeks until I reach her back hole. I ease the wet finger inside her, and she gives a little squeak, and her inner muscles clamp down on me.

I hold my finger deep in her ass while I fuck her hard. It's raw and primal; the noises she's making are like some wild animal. All I'm focused on is her, the way she feels, the scent of her skin, the sounds coming from her lips.

"I'm going to fill you up with my cum," I tell her.

"Yes, do it," she gasps. "I want your cum inside me."

The days of worrying about any kind of morality issues about fucking my stepsister are long gone. I like that we've corrupted her, that we've taken our sweet little Laney and shown her the pleasures of the flesh.

"I want you to come," I tell her. "Come for your stepbrother, Laney. Come around my cock."

If this is the last time we ever get to fuck, I want to make it good for her.

I've still got my finger jammed inside her ass. She needs to be quiet, so I clamp my other hand across her mouth. I hold her tight against me, her back pressed to my chest, her ass up against my hips, my hand crushed between us. We're fucking like animals, rutting in the dirt. My balls tighten, and I'm hovering on the brink, waiting to let go.

"Oh, God. Dax..." She trails off and sucks another fast breath. "Oh, fuck. I'm coming. I'm coming."

She shatters around me, her back arching, her head tilting back. I capture her mouth with mine, pushing my tongue between her lips. I explode, and we swallow each other's gasps and moans.

Finally, she grows quieter, though her chest heaves. She gives sexy little whimpers as my cock continues to jerk inside her, the fading tremors of my orgasm still running through me like an electric current.

20
laney

I wasn't sure I could handle Darius fucking me, not after what I've gone through, but it hadn't been anything like it was with them. I was sore, and it had hurt, but it was a good pain. It was as though he was washing away the touch of those other men, making me his again, even though he didn't know that I'd ever not been.

A part of me is still wrought with guilt. I still don't want to tell him, though. I'm sure they've guessed, but I'm worried about what they might do if they know the whole truth. I don't want them taking any risks and putting themselves in danger, and they might not be able to control themselves if they know the details.

By the time we come down from the high of our fucking, darkness has fallen around us.

"We should loop back around to the cabin," Darius says, planting a kiss on the sensitive spot behind my ear. "If Smith and Axel are still following us, it means only Zeke is left guarding Reed and Cade. I think it's worth the risk."

I'm still unsure. "But Zeke is still armed, and we're not."

"But it's dark now," he says. "That gives us an advantage."

"How does it give us—" The truth dawns on me. "Oh, of course."

It doesn't make any difference to Darius if it's daylight or nighttime. He'll still be able to find his way around.

I want to make sure I understand exactly what Dax is intending. "What are you saying? That we'll be able to take Zeke down, and then we'll be able to make a run for it?"

Will Cade be strong enough to run? I can't picture it, but what choice do we have?

He nods. "That's exactly what I'm saying. As long as we get away before Smith and Axel find us, we'll be fine."

"It's dangerous."

"This whole thing is dangerous."

He has a point, but even so, my stomach flips with nerves. Zeke has a gun. He won't be able to see in the dark, but that won't stop him shooting into it. And if he does shoot, it'll alert Smith and Axel that something is wrong.

"I don't know if I can even find my way back to the cabin," I say.

"Yes, you can. Think of all the nights we've spent out on the porch. You've looked at the sky on those nights, haven't you?"

"Of course."

The sky is beautiful here, especially at night. Before we came to the cabin, I had no idea how many stars there were. Or how bright they could be.

Darius continues, "Then you know where the moon is normally positioned at this time in the evening."

I close my eyes briefly, picturing it in my head. "Yes, I think so. It's normally up high, to the left of the cabin, and then creeps over the top, and goes down on the other side."

Darius lifts his face to the sky even though he can't see it. "And where is it now?" he asks.

I lift my head to join him, peering between the branches of the trees. I catch sight of the white silvery globe. "It's on my right," I tell him.

"So, we need to walk toward it."

I think I understand what he's saying. Get the moon in the position it would be if we were sitting at the cabin porch, and it will hopefully take us closer to the cabin. I have no idea how accurate that will be, but at least it's something to aim toward. Our other option is to find the river and trace it back, but finding it isn't so easy. It feels like we've been going for miles, and I've no idea what direction the river is in.

Are Smith and the others still coming after us, or have they gone back to the cabin? We're betting on us getting there before them. It's the only way we'll outnumber the one remaining at the cabin.

Trying to move at any speed in the dark is terrifying. While the moon is almost full, the thickness of the branches overhead hides it from us. I imagine this must be how Darius feels all the time. His strength and confidence mask just how fucking disorienting it is to not be able to see where you're going. I find myself doubting every footfall, expecting at any moment to be sent flying by tree roots, or to drop into a hole and turn my ankle. Another thought occurs to me. What if hunters have left traps out here? What if one of us stands on a beartrap and its metal teeth clamp around one of our legs?

I can't help but doubt every step. This feels like a completely impossible task, but still, we keep going.

I have no idea how much time has passed when Darius pulls me to a halt.

"Stop," he tells me.

Marissa Farrar

I freeze, my heart lurching. Has he heard something? Are Smith and Axel close behind us?

Instead, he reaches out a foot, touching a tree stump. Then he takes a couple of steps forward and places his hand against another tree.

"I know where we are," he tells me. "The cabin isn't far."

"Are you sure?"

In the moonlight, he nods. "Yes, it's this way."

"How is that possible?" I ask. "We've walked for miles. We should be much farther away."

"We must have inadvertently looped back on ourselves at some point. It's easily done out here. Let's go."

He sets off, but I grab at his arm, appreciating the strong muscles of his forearm, even in this situation.

"Wait. We need a plan. We can't just barge in there. Even if the others haven't gotten back, Zeke is still armed, and we're not."

"But we can take him by surprise. If we can sneak up on him, all it will take is a heavy rock or a length of wood, and we can do to him like he did to Cade."

"He'll be on edge, listening out for Smith and Axel. I don't know how easy it'll be for us to sneak up on him."

Darius thinks for a moment. "If he'll be listening out, we can use that to our advantage, make him think they're on their way back, or there's something outside the cabin that needs investigating."

I see where he's going with this. "Then when he steps outside, we take him down."

"Exactly."

I swallow my nerves. It'll still be dangerous. He'll still be armed—and, perhaps even worse than that, he'll be primed and ready to shoot. But there's no chance of us sneaking into the cabin without him noticing. Everything in that building creaks, and unless he's dead asleep, he'll hear us come in.

We have a little farther to go, but eventually the trees open up and we find ourselves back in the clearing where the cabin is located. I put out my hand to stop Darius.

"We're here," I whisper.

I have to be the eyes. I know Darius will be frustrated not to be the one who does everything—that stupid macho idea that because he's male and older meaning he has to protect the girl—but I'm not going to sit by and do nothing.

"Any sign of Smith and Axel?"

I shake my head. "No, but I can't see inside from this position. I'm going to need to look through the window."

I half expect him to give me an argument, but he knows this is something he can't do. Instead, he pulls me to him and kisses me hard on the mouth.

"Be careful."

With my heart thumping, I duck low and run to the edge of the porch. Slowly and carefully, I climb the steps.

The outer edges of the porch are the least creaky. My body-weight is the lowest it's ever been, so I use that to my advantage when it comes to being quiet. I creep around the edge, sticking close to the wooden balustrades, until I reach the cabin window.

The only light inside is from the woodstove. My eyes have been adjusted to darkness for hours now, so it's easy for me to see. I quickly spot Zeke, sitting slouched in a chair, his legs spread as though he thinks he deserves to take up more space than he does. Where is his gun? His back is to me, but I can't see it on the floor or anywhere around the chair, so I have to assume it's in his hands or rested in his lap.

I seek out Cade and Reed. When we left, we'd managed to keep up the pretense that Cade is still unconscious, but that may have changed now. I spot the shape of him lying on the mattress. Reed is sitting beside him, his back pushed up against the far wall. He has his knees bent, his arms wrapped around his shins, his head bowed.

My heart goes out to him. He looks broken, crushed.

Is he picturing us dead?

Cade and Reed have no idea where we've gone or what might have happened. The good news is that the other two aren't back. I hope those motherfuckers have gotten lost in the forest for good, or they've been eaten by a bear. I haven't heard any gunshots to signal they're in trouble, but I can always hope.

Carefully, I sneak back around the outskirts of the porch and drop to the ground where Darius is waiting.

"It's just Zeke," I whisper.

I tell him the exact positions Cade and Reed are in, using numbers on a clock face, with the front door being six.

We're going to need to move fast.

Darius has a big, heavy length of wood in his hands. He must have gotten it from the woodpile. The axe has been moved since the incident with Reed, so the wood must have been his only option. He swings it experimentally, testing the weight.

"Ready?" he asks.

I'm nervous as hell, but I nod. "Ready."

This is going to be the dangerous part. Darius needs to get up on the porch, but he's big and heavy, and it's going to creak. If Zeke gets the idea to come out and investigate before Darius is in position, then Darius is likely to end up with a bullet in his chest. The whole thing makes me sick with nerves, but this is our only opportunity, and we have to take it. What other choice do we have?

"Stick to the edges," I tell him, still whispering. "They creak less."

At a crouch, still carrying the length of wood, he climbs the few steps to the porch. He stays low, trying to make himself as small as possible, which isn't easy, given that he's not exactly a small guy. On the porch, he keeps the railings pressed to his hip, so he knows he's going the right way. One of the floorboards groans like a special effect in a horror movie, and I wince at the sound. He freezes, and we wait to see if we've been heard, but when nothing happens, he keeps going.

He ducks under the window that gives a view onto the kitchen area, and then takes a few more steps.

Darius stops right before he reaches the front door. He straightens and presses his back to the wood. He lifts the log and holds it above his shoulder, poised for action.

He'll use sound as his guide, the opening of the door, the creak of a footstep, the exhale of a breath. It's not perfect, but considering how dark it is, he has these skills to his advantage. With the cabin being more illuminated than it is outside, it'll take Zeke a moment for his eyes to adjust, and hopefully that will be all the time we need to take him down.

Now it's my turn to play my part. There's a danger that Zeke will race out and shoot wildly into the forest, but I'm hoping he won't be that dumb. There is also the possibility that Smith and Axel are somewhere nearby, and, if they are, the noises I make will bring them running. It's a gamble, but one that's worth taking if it means we get our freedom.

I suck in a breath and let out a cry as though I've been hurt. I freeze, waiting for Zeke to come rushing out, but when nothing happens, I make the same sound, only louder. He might think it's a wild animal. I wish we could see inside the cabin, to be able to tell if I've been heard and if Zeke is reacting.

I draw air into my lungs, ready to yell again, when the cabin door swings open. I have a horrible thought—what if Zeke has sent Reed out to investigate, and Darius won't know the difference, and will clobber him with the length of wood—but then I catch sight of the shape in the doorway, and the glint of the silver metal of the gun barrel and know that it's not.

Zeke takes another step, bringing himself fully onto the porch.

21
DARIUS

I know it's Zeke.

The smell of stale beer, the clink of his belt, the height at which his deep breathing emanates from, leaves no doubt in my mind.

I tighten my grip on the length of wood, brace my feet against the porch floorboards, and swing as hard as I can. In my mind, I picture the exact position of his head, and I aim the wood directly at it. A part of me is also aware that it'll only take him a fraction of a second to swing the gun and fire.

The wood meets his skull with a satisfying crunch that reverberates down my arms and into my hands. For a moment, I don't think he's going to go down, but first the gun drops to the floor with a clatter, and then he hits the deck, too.

Laney's voice captures my attention. "Oh, my God. You did it."

"We did it," I tell her.

I wish the others were here—especially Smith. I want to raise the length of wood and hit Zeke again, and again, and again, until his skull resembles a split watermelon, but we don't

have time for that. We need to get the fuck out of here before
the others come back.

Noise comes from inside the cabin. "Dax?"

It's my father.

He pulls me into a hug, smacking me on the shoulder. "I
knew you'd get back to us."

He releases me, I assume to embrace Laney as well.

"We have to go," Laney says, not taking time to explain.
"Help us get Cade up."

"Where are we going?" Reed asks.

She doesn't hesitate. "To the river. To the boat."

To my massive relief, Cade is awake, too.

"Hey, bro," I tell him, crouching at his side. "Think you can
walk if we help you?"

My hand finds his shoulder, as big and solid as ever.

"'Course I can fucking walk," he replies, ever full of his
bravado.

Despite his words, he allows Reed and me to position
ourselves either side of him, and we help him to stand.

"Laney," Reed says. "Grab whatever food and water you
can."

None of us has eaten properly for days, and it doesn't help
with our energy levels. We have no idea what kind of journey
lies ahead of us, but, even with a boat, it could be a long one.
Best to take what we can now. Deep down, I'm also thinking
that the more we take of these bastards' supplies, the less they'll
have left. We'll take their boat, and then they'll be stuck out
here with nothing, just like we were. I hope the fuckers starve
to death, slowly and painfully.

I hear the rustle and clatter of Laney grabbing a bag and
working quickly, scooping up as much as she can from around
the cabin. The coolers will be almost empty after having fed
everyone for the past few days, but I hope she grabs whatever is

left. We can't take too much, though. It'll slow us down, and we already have Cade doing that. I'd never say as much to him—he'd fucking hate the idea of being a burden to us.

I try not to think about how Smith and Axel have cell phones and can potentially call for help. I highly doubt there's any chance of them getting any service out here, but they might decide to walk to a higher spot and get it there. Of course, if they call any authorities out, they're going to have some serious questions to answer.

It's then I remember they're here to do a deal with someone. If that person shows, they'll get help no matter what.

Silently, I curse this fact. Whoever they're due to meet is bound to have some form of transportation and supplies. Fuck. Those bastards don't deserve to live. I'd like nothing more than to bash the life out of all of them, but especially Smith.

If they get out of here alive, will they come and find us? I can't worry about that now. First, we have to make sure we get away from here and survive. The rest will come later.

"Ready?" Reed says.

I'm not sure who he's directing the question toward, but I nod anyway. "Let's do this."

With Cade supported between us, we leave the cabin.

"Wait." Laney says. "The gun."

"Good thinking."

We pause as she picks it up, and then we keep going. I'm emboldened now that we have a weapon. It's not only defense against Smith and the others, but also the local wildlife.

Cade is heavy, and, in our weakened states, the going is hard. I lead the way, more capable than the others in this situation. They need the daylight to navigate their way through the forest, but that's not a problem for me. I've walked this route down to the river countless times in the past few weeks and have it mapped in my mind.

As we walk, Cade seems to grow stronger, and I find he's leaning on me less than before. He's not been on his feet in some time, and he's even weaker than the rest of us, but we're making progress. I take that as a good sign. I'd never admit it out loud, but I'd been terrified we were going to lose him. I have no idea how to find my way in the world without my big brother in it. He's been my guide—my eyes—ever since we were boys. While others in my position might have needed to employ a helper, I've always had Cade. He isn't perfect, but I trust him to have my best interests at heart.

Of course, that was before I'd learned about the money he'd gambled away. The lies he told. In the grand scheme of things, especially considering our current situation, it doesn't even matter, but if I'd learned about it when we'd been living our normal lives, I'd have been seriously pissed. I remember how Cade had also hidden his phone from us, destroying any possible opportunity for us to get rescued, but I push the thought from my mind. Now isn't the time to get pissed with my brother. If we live through this, I can deal with it then.

The forest is alive with sounds tonight. Insects buzz and chirp. An owl hoots and is replied to with a screech. Something larger rustles through the bushes. The whole time we're moving, I listen out for any sign of Smith and Axel catching up to us. We have no idea how far away they were from the cabin, and while I have the advantage of being able to move easily in the dark, we're also slow-going, and loud as hell.

When we hit the midway point on the trail, the rush of water meets my ears. I was ninety-nine percent confident I'd gone the right way, but hearing it is still a relief.

We're going to get the fuck out of here.

22
Laney

THE RIVER IS RIGHT UP AHEAD.

As well as hearing it, I catch glimpses of the moonlight reflecting off the surface between the trees.

I throw an anxious glance to Cade.

He's still being held between his father and brother, but he seems stronger. It's not easy to tell in the dark, but he's walking, and doesn't seem to be leaning on Reed and Darius so heavily. The combination of the rest he's had, plus the food and water we've been able to get into him, has definitely helped. He's going to be okay, and that lifts my heart more than anything. *We're* going to be okay.

The trees and bushes open onto the riverbank and pebbly beach where we'd skimmed stones on my birthday. That feels like a lifetime ago now. There's no way I'm the same person I was only a month ago. The old Laney is still in there some-where, the child version of me, too frightened to emerge. I won't let her out either. I need to protect that innocent version of myself. I almost laugh at that. If someone had of asked me how innocent I was at seventeen, I'd have laughed in their faces. I'd have said not innocent at all. How could I have been, growing up with my mother, and being exposed to all the men she brought back? But now I look back, I see only drunk, stupid men who made clumsy gropes or barely knew what they were doing, even when they had me pinned up against the kitchen counter and were trying to grope my young breasts or push their hands between my thighs. I'm not making excuses for them, but it was nothing like the cold, deliberate actions of Smith and his men.

Now, I wonder what kind of life lies ahead of us. I imagine I'll need to speak to a therapist sometime soon, though I can't picture telling anyone the full truth about what's happened. Just the thought of giving voice to what those men did to me sickens me. It would be like living through it all over again, and I don't think I'm strong enough for that.

There's something else I don't think I'll ever be able to tell a therapist about either, and that's the nature of my relationship with the guys, but in particular Reed. I'd be terrified it would get him in trouble, even though these things are supposed to be confidential.

I'd still have plenty to talk about, however. I could talk of the terror of the plane crash, the horror of finding the poor flight attendant's body, the hunger we suffered, and fear of the wildlife. I'd be able to talk about the kidnapping, too, how we were held at gunpoint before we managed to escape.

I can see myself suffering from nightmares for years to come.

"The boat," Reed says.

It's still there. I hadn't been totally sure it would be. I was worried Smith might have taken it for some reason or moved it to prevent us using it to escape. But he'd clearly been smug in his belief that we'd never manage such a thing, because it's right where they'd left it.

Together, we hurry toward the vessel.

The white boat is as basic as they come. It has an engine on the back, but there isn't even a proper wheelhouse, just a small central console, with a plastic awning in the middle, where the driver is supposed to stand. It's the sort of boat I'd expect to find amateur fishermen using on the river. It's only about twenty feet long, with seating for four people.

The men get there first. They help Cade in, and then Reed jumps in and checks the inside of the boat, around the central console.

He drags his hand through his hair. "Fuck. There's no key."

I get in as well, the boat moving unsettlingly beneath me. I drop the bag that contains the few items I'd managed to grab from the cabin, and then do a quick search for anything else that might be in here, but I come up empty-handed.

Whatever supplies Smith and the others brought with them, they'd moved up to the cabin. There isn't so much as a bottle of water in here. We only have what I grabbed from the cabin when we left. At least when we'd started hiking out, before we'd run into Zeke and Axel, we'd been prepared for what lay ahead. We'd brought food and water, and supplies to allow us to have a fire, and even a couple of blankets to lie on.

Now we have close to nothing.

A couple of oars are attached to the side of the boat, intended for use if something went wrong with the engine.

"We're going to have to row our way out of here," Cade croaks.

No one argues with him. It isn't as though we have much of a choice. We aren't going to risk going back to the cabin and trying to find the key, and it might be that Smith has it on him anyway.

Reed jumps back out of the boat and onto the shore to untie it from the boulder, and then plants his hands on the side of the boat to give it a solid shove into deeper water. He splashes in the shallows, getting his shoes wet, and then hauls himself back onboard.

Darius suddenly whips back around the way we'd just come. He freezes and then says, "They're coming after us."

My heart lurches into my throat. "Oh, shit."

A moment later, I hear them as well, crashing through the bushes as Smith, Zeke, and Axel give chase. They have guns, and though it's dark, it'll only take one lucky shot to kill one of us.

I'm also armed, but I'm far from being a good shot. I've handled a gun a few times in my life when my mother's sketchy boyfriends decided to show me how to shoot some cans, normally only as an excuse to get close up behind me to grab a feel while they did so. Besides, together with being a crap shot, it's also dark. I'm so scared, I'm shaking all over, and there's no way I'll be able to hold the gun steady. To add to that, I'm also standing on a boat that's now moving.

Reed yanks the oars from the sides of the boat and shoves one into Darius's hands.

"Row!" he commands.

The two men settle side by side, the oars in the water. They work in complete synchronicity, the paddles dipping into the river and pulling back, before lifting and dunking again.

A gunshot cracks through the air.

I scream, and suddenly Cade is on top of me, pressing me into the bottom of the boat. Terror that he's the one who's been shot fills me. I picture him bleeding out on top of me, and a fresh scream fills my head, but I'm unable to give it voice so it reverberates around my skull. I wriggle and squirm, trying to free myself from his weight, but then he moves, pinning me and hissing in my ear.

"Stay the fuck down, Laney."

I collapse in relief. He's not been shot. He wouldn't be speaking to me with such ferocity if he was.

Another gunshot goes off, followed in quick succession by another. I'm sick with fear, but the boat moves beneath me, and I know we're putting distance between us and the men. I have no idea what sort of range their weapons have, but it's also dark, a recent cloud blocking the moonlight, which will make their aim much harder. Shouts of anger chase us across the water, but they're growing faint now.

"Let me the fuck up," I hiss.

I want to check on Reed and Dax, make sure they're safe. Though the rhythmical splash of oars hitting the water filters through to my ears, I won't know for sure that they haven't been hit until I've seen it for myself. We came so close to losing Cade when he'd been struck by the gun that the reality that one or more of us might actually die has hit me hard.

People die. They die all the time. It seems crazy to me how someone can stop existing, but they do, and those left behind have to figure out how to carry on without them. It's only been a little over a month since I lost my mom, and there's no way I've had the time to process her death. Now I can feel that loss entwining with what I went through at the cabin, and the trauma of the plane crash, and it's pulling me down, dragging me under. I'm forcing myself to keep going right now, for the sake of all our lives, but I'm close to my breaking point. I'm not sure how much I'll be able to take. If something happens to one of the guys, it will be the end of me. I don't think I'll ever come back from that.

Cade climbs off me. "Just when I was getting comfortable," he says.

I'm relieved to hear the return of his usual snarky tone. He puts out his hand to help me up as well, but I shake my head. I don't know how strong he is yet, and I don't want to risk dragging him back down on top of me.

The boat is so small, it only takes a moment for me to fix in on the other two, sitting side by side, rowing.

Reed glances over at me. "You okay, Laney?"

"Yeah. Are you?"

He nods. "Better now we're away from them."

Have we really gotten away? We're on a boat, moving downriver. Could we be heading toward civilization?

I glance back the way we came, half expecting to see Smith and the other two running along the shoreline toward us, waving their guns around. But the effort of Reed and Dax, plus the natural flow of the river, has put enough distance between us and them that I can't even see where we pushed the boat off from.

I want to breathe a huge sigh of relief, but I don't feel as though we're in much less danger. We're now on a river, in the dark, with no idea what perils lie ahead. I'm terrified that we're going to reach a dangerous part of the river, like fast rapids, and not see it coming. I'm straining my ears to listen for a change in the river.

It's still hours until morning.

"How far away from the nearest town do you think we are?" I ask to no one in particular.

Reed replies. "As much as I want to think that we're close, I feel like we'd have been found by now if we were."

Cade agrees. "Plus, Smith and his friends wouldn't set up anywhere they think they might be found. It's impossible to say, but I reckon we're at least a day or two away from anywhere."

A day or two if we had an engine working. Right now, all we have is manpower. The magnitude of what we're trying to do is overwhelming. We have no idea if we're even heading in the right direction.

I hope a town or city is no farther than that. We don't have many supplies with us. We naturally rowed downstream, simply because it would be easier and faster, rather than trying to row against the flow, but we have no idea what lies ahead of us. We could be rowing away from civilization right now instead of toward it.

The only sounds are the grunts of Reed and Darius as they fight to keep the boat on course, and the splash of the oars against the water.

I don't want to believe that we might have actually managed to get away because I'm sure if I let myself hope, then Smith and the others will leap from the bushes on the riverside and gun us all down. But as the minutes pass, with no sign of them, that trickle of belief grows stronger.

Have we actually made it?

I glance back to where Reed and Darius are rowing.

"Are we safe?" I ask them.

From beside me, Cade says, "Well, no one's shooting at us anymore."

He's being a smartass, but I'm happy he feels well enough to be sarcastic.

Reed stops rowing. "I don't think they're coming after us now."

A bloom of relief opens up inside me. "Holy shit, we made it."

Darius holds one hand up for Reed to high-five. I reach over and hug Cade. Then we all bundle in together, half laughing, half crying. I exchange kisses with each of them, even though I'm aware of how gross we all are, and they all hug and smack each other on the back.

We're all aware of the possibility of Smith and his men

catching up with us, however, so we don't pause for too long. The natural current of the river is taking us downstream, but Reed and Darius rowing increases our pace.

The two men pick the oars back up, and we keep going.

23
laney

THOUGH WE'VE ESCAPED THE WORST DANGER, IT'S STILL not safe being on the river at night. The moonlight offers us a little illumination, but we still can't see the river ahead, and rocks and boulders loom out of the water, threatening to take the front out of the boat.

"Do you think this is the way Smith and his men came from?" I dare to ask.

Reed replies, "I have no idea, but I'd say it's unlikely they rowed a great distance upstream."

"They didn't need to row," Darius points out. "There's an engine, remember? Except we don't have the key."

Reed twists his lips. "Shit, yeah, I'd forgotten about that."

Darius continues, "Plus, we don't know for sure how they planned on getting out of here. They were waiting to meet someone, right? Perhaps that someone had a chopper or a bigger boat, or something. It would have needed to be big enough and powerful enough to carry all those guns."

I'm suddenly filled with the horror that we might come across whoever Smith and his gang were planning to meet.

I say as much to Reed.

He shakes his head. "They have no way of knowing who we are, even if they do pass us. We could be a family or group of friends out on a boat trip."

"We hardly look like we're on vacation," Cade says. "Who on vacation rows in the middle of the night and looks like us? And what if they recognize the boat?"

Darius agrees with his brother. "Yeah, we're out in the middle of nowhere. Who the hell would be this far out on a family day trip?"

Reed lifts his hand in a stop sign. "We don't know that's even going to happen. Let's not panic about something when we don't need to. We've got enough to worry about."

By 'enough,' he means the journey ahead of us. We have no idea what lies downstream, whether the river will even be passable. It's calm right now, but what if we hit rapids? How will the boat cope? We can all swim, but getting caught in something like that will be dangerous.

My stomach gurgles and growls, acid rising up the back of my throat. I can't tell if it's because I'm sick from the motion of the boat or if it's because I'm so fucking hungry. None of us has eaten properly since we were taken by the men. Both Reed and Darius must be feeling it, considering the amount of energy they're having to expend by rowing.

I make myself useful, pulling the items I'd taken from the cabin out of my bag. I have a loaf of slightly stale bread, some cold ham, a block of cheese, some crackers, and a box of cookies. I could have done with a knife, but I make do, tearing off chunks of the bread and cheese, and adding a slice of the precut ham. None of us has eaten properly in days, and we devour the food within minutes. I keep a close eye on Cade, making sure he's able to chew and swallow properly. He seems weak, but otherwise fine, but we have no idea what residual effects the head injury might have caused. I don't want him choking to death on a piece of dried bread after everything we've been through.

We pass a bottle of water around to wash the food down with. It's strange drinking bottled water after such a long time of living on only boiled water from the river. It tastes oddly chemically, though I'm not sure why. Is it the plastic of the bottle?

What else have I forgotten from normal life? I allow myself a moment of fantasy, of us finding a town or village, and people knowing who we are, and overwhelming us with their need to help. One thing I'm looking forward to more than anything is a hot shower. I swear, if I ever manage to get to live with running water again, I'll never take it for granted. I'll stand under the shower with the water as hot as I can get it and use every product I can find. While we've done our best to stay clean out here, I'm sure we probably smell. We just can't notice it about each other anymore. The other thing I'm looking forward to is the food. Being able to order whatever takeout we want, and as much as we want. I'm dying for salty, greasy fries, and a giant, juicy burger with extra pickles and the sort of mustard that hits the back of your nose.

I realize I'm daydreaming, almost half asleep, and pull myself out of my fantasy. Right now, we're a long way from reaching that goal, and I want to appreciate what we have. We have a small amount of food and our freedom, and that means a lot. It's important to count our blessings.

I share out some of the cookies, and we groan with pleasure as the sweetness of sugar bursts on our tongues. It feels like forever since I ate any form of sugar that wasn't provided by berries that we'd scavenged in the forest. It hits my bloodstream like a drug, instantly making me feel more energized. It's the middle of the night, and we all should be sleeping, but that's not going to happen.

The men don't argue when I put the other half of the food back into the bag. We need to keep our energy up, but, at the same time, we don't know how long we're going to be out here. While I want to hope that the river is going to take us straight to a community—even if it's only a small commune—there's the chance that we're heading deeper into the wilderness.

The idea sends ice water through my veins.

We could have escaped one death for another.

24

laney

It's hard to know how much time passes.

I find myself dozing, my head against Cade's shoulder. The combination of the rush of the river and the steady splash of the oars hitting the water is like a lullaby. I notice when the pace of the splashes slows and realize Darius and Reed must be exhausted.

I rouse myself to wakefulness.

"We can take over for a while," I say. "You two need to rest."

Reed shakes his head. "You're not strong enough, and Cade needs to rest."

"I'm fine," Cade insists. "I can row."

I raise my eyebrows, though Reed probably can't see me. "And I'm plenty strong enough. I'm not completely helpless. Even if it's only for half an hour, it'll let the two of you rest up."

"We could always stop," Dax suggests. "We must have put enough distance between us and them by now."

"Not yet." Reed pauses rowing. "We don't want to give them an opportunity to catch up with us while we sleep."

189

Darius isn't letting it go quite so easily. "Even if they're still coming after us, they're on foot, in the dark, trying to follow the river. They're not going to make fast progress. There's no way they can catch up with us now."

"We don't know that. It's not worth the risk. They're armed, and they won't hesitate in killing us this time."

I step in. "But we won't be able to make any progress if rowing all this way breaks you both. You're running on little food and no sleep. Let us row for a bit."

Reed finally relents. "Okay, but shout if it's too much." He looks to his son. "You, too, Cade. You've had a serious head injury. If your head starts hurting again, or your vision blurs, or anything like that, tell us. Don't try to act the hard man, okay? You won't be helping anyone."

"Yeah, I got it," Cade says with a scowl.

Darius stands and makes room for me. I settle into his place, with my back in the direction we're heading, and pick up the end of the oar. Reed also stands, the boat lurching from side to side, as he makes room for his eldest son.

Cade moves from his position to take the seat next to me—the one Reed just vacated.

I dunk the end of the oar into the water, feeling the pull and drag of it against the strained muscles in my arms. It's harder than it looks, and I glance over at Cade to make sure he's doing okay.

Because it's dark, we also have to watch out for any boulders or fallen trees that might be in our way. We're relying so much on the flow of the river to guide our path, but hitting something like that could be devastating. Anytime something emerges from the water, I use the oar to push the boat away.

It takes a minute, but then Cade and I fall into a slow and steady rhythm.

"Quit staring at me, Cuckoo," he says, his voice low.

"What? I'm not."

"Yes, you are. You keep looking over at me like you're afraid I'm going to vanish or something."

"Sorry. It's just that you gave us a scare for a while. We thought we were going to lose you."

"Well, now you know how we all felt when you were so sick."

I nod, remembering that time. It feels like a lifetime ago now.

"I don't want you to overdo it," I tell him. "If you set yourself back now..."

In the moonlight, he turns his head. "I get it, Cuckoo. I do."

If something happened that rendered him unconscious out here, it would be a massive problem. Perhaps not while we have the boat, because we'd be able to transport him in it, but if we hit rougher water, or one of the many rocks and boulders that protrude from the river, and lose the boat, we'll have an issue. There's no way we can carry Cade through the wilderness if he fell unconscious again. It would mean we'd either have to separate, and two of us keep going while someone stayed behind with Cade—though there's the possibility that we'd never be able to find them again, even if we were able to reach a town for help—or else we'd have to abandon Cade to his death in the forest.

The possibilities of both options torment me, so I decide we simply have to ensure Cade stays well.

That's going to be easier said than done out here.

While the initial euphoria of being away from Smith and the others, and of having a boat, fades, it's replaced by the understanding that we're still in an extremely perilous situation.

My muscles are burning, my biceps, across my shoulder blades, even my thighs. Because we're going downstream, the rowing is more to keep our position in the middle of the river than actually making much impact on the speed we're going. We're doing our best, but we're nowhere near as good a team as Reed and Darius.

I try to see the men's faces in the darkness. Darius has his head propped on his palm. Reed is folded over, his forehead pillowed in his arms.

It's clear we're all exhausted.

"Maybe we should stop," I say. "We can drag the boat to shore and sleep for a couple of hours."

Reed lifts his head. "What if they catch up with us?"

He doesn't need to elaborate on who 'they' are.

"I'm sure we've gone far enough now. They're not going to walk this far in the dark, especially not after they've been chasing after me and Darius for hours. They'll be exhausted as well. I'm not saying they won't come after us, but I'm sure they'll wait for morning now. We can get a few hours, at least, and then set off again at first light."

Reed looks around at the other two. "What do you think?"

"I think she's right," Darius says. "It's not safe for us on the river either. If we hit something and put a hole in the boat, we'll be screwed."

"Cade?" Reed asks.

"I don't care, man. Whatever works."

He sounds exhausted, and that's what seems to make up Reed's mind. "Okay, let's do it. If we spot a good place to stop, we'll row to shore and tie the boat up for a few hours."

It's not easy to see the shore, but we need a small cove-like area that we can row to where the current will have slowed.

There are a few things in the boat that we can use to make ourselves comfortable. Some long cushions that are on the seats, some tarpaulin. It's definitely not going to be five-star hotel standards, but I'm sure we're all so tired, it won't matter.

"What about there?" Cade points out a spot up ahead.

It's hard to make much judgement in the dark, but the bank curves inward, creating a narrow beach, and the water looks calmer. The dark hides the shore, however, so we don't really know what we're going to be heading toward.

Reed nods. "Let's do it."

Reed and Darius take our places and put their backs into rowing in the direction of the shore opposite the side we were on before. The surface is flatter, the moonlight reflecting differently than the rest of the water. For a moment, I think we're going to miss it, but then we're out of the main flow of the river and into the calm beachy area.

"Well done," I tell them.

I don't want them to think I'm not capable of helping, so I join them in jumping out of the boat and helping to pull it onto shore. The water is icy and instantly floods into my sneakers. It was already cold, but now I'm even more chilled. I'd have given anything to be back in the cabin, beside the woodstove, hands outheld to warm my palms, but then I remember the cabin isn't ours anymore—if it ever truly was—and there's no going back.

Reed glances over at me and notices me shivering. "We have to keep warm," he says. "It's important. Hypothermia can kill."

"You really think it's that cold?" I ask.

"When we're wet and rundown? Yes, it's enough to make us ill. We need to huddle together."

"My vote is that Laney goes in the middle," Cade says.

"You need to go in the middle," I throw back at him. "You need to stay warm the most."

"You and Cade in the middle," Reed says, "Darius and me on the outside."

"Are we going to have to fight over which one of us gets to go beside Laney?" Darius comments.

Reed grins at him in the darkness. "Nope, 'cause that's going to be me."

"Fucker," Darius grumbles.

Despite everything, I find myself smiling. Reed ties the boat to a tree, and then we work together to carry anything that might make our sleep a little more comfortable out of the boat onto shore. The bottom of the boat won't be comfortable, and besides, it's also wet.

"Reed, do you think you should take this?" I still have the gun I took from Zeke.

He nods and takes it from me. "Hopefully, we won't need to use it, but it's good to have."

Sleeping out in the open is going to feel strange. I've never been one for camping beneath the stars, especially somewhere as remote as this.

I hope we've pulled the boat high enough up the bank. I'm terrified that we'll turn around only to find it washed away. Reed has tied it to a tree, but a flash flood might be enough to snap the rope. Without the boat, we'd be back on foot, with no supplies. I'm terrified we'll die before we reach safety.

Are Smith and the other two still after us, or would they have given up by now? I pray they've given up. A small bloom of satisfaction swells inside me at the thought of how pissed they're going to be that we not only got away, but that we took their only chance of escape with us, too. They might have cell phones, but I can't imagine them getting any service all the way out here. If they want to get a signal, they'll have to walk, and these forests and woods aren't forgiving. It's so easy to get turned around and lose your way. I remember the first day, right after we'd crashed, when I'd wanted to get away from Cade and had gotten lost within minutes. It was only because Darius heard me crying that I found my way back again.

Smith and his men clearly know these forests a hell of a lot better than I did, however, so maybe it'll be easier for them to find help.

We bury ourselves beneath the tarpaulin. It should keep away the worst of the mosquitos. The ground is cold, and the chill soaks up through the thin cushions. I huddle into Cade. He puts his arm around me, and I put my head on his chest. I'm worried I'm going to hurt him, though he seems much better. Reed moves up behind me, spooning me. He nudges his legs and arm beneath me, so I'm as much cushioned on the men as I am on the actual cushions.

I force myself to relax, for the tension to release from my muscles. In the back of my mind, I'm still listening for Smith. The memory of what he did to me with the gun, and what Axel did to me down on the beach, tries to push into my head, and I tense up again. *No, no, no, no. Don't think, don't think.*

Reed must have picked up on my body language. "You okay, baby?"

I nod against Cade's shoulder. "Just cold."

They both huddle in closer, and I feel Darius's hand as he reaches across his brother to take mine. They're like a protective shield around me, and their love for me makes me want to cry. I don't deserve this kind of love. What would they think of me if they knew the details of what those men did to me? Would they still see me as some precious princess who needs protecting, or as something that had been spoiled—ruined. I've had another man inside me, and another's mouth on me, and the thought alone makes me sick. Though I didn't want it, I still question myself, wondering if I gave them the wrong signs. God, when Smith did that thing to me with the gun, I climaxed, didn't I? Didn't that mean I enjoyed it?

I have to hold back a sob. I don't want the men to see how devastated I am. If they notice, they'll ask questions, and I can't answer them. I don't want them to think of me any differently than they do right now. Yes, they know something happened to me, in the room, down on the beach, but they don't know the details. Without the details, they can pretend that everything is okay, just like I can.

I don't think I'm going to sleep, but finally my thoughts drift, muddling with my dreams, so I can no longer tell what is wakefulness and what is sleep.

25
CADE

Sunlight hits my face, and I screw my eyes tighter shut, fighting against the memory of where we are and the huge journey we've still got ahead of us.

I feel like shit, but it's shit that's a hundred times better than I felt only a day or two ago.

I'm also aware that it's been days since I last managed to wash, and I stink as well. I sit up and pause for a moment, listening for any change in our surroundings. Could Smith and his men have caught up to us? There's no sign of them. All I hear is the burbling of the river, the twitter of birdsong, and the buzz of insects. The sky is bright blue, the sun starting to warm the day.

It's peaceful.

The boat is still where we left it, tied up, and I find myself smiling. We're all still alive, we're together, and we finally have a mode of transportation that can get us out of here. I try not to think about what issues might be waiting for us when we get back to Los Angeles—or wherever the hell we end up—and appreciate the moment. We have a lot to be grateful for right now.

The others are all sleeping, and I don't want to wake them. Fuck knows, after everything we've been through, we need to rest when we can. Laney has shifted during the night, so she's cuddled up next to Reed now. I carefully untangle myself from the tarpaulin and wriggle out of the mass of arms and legs surrounding me.

Carefully, I get to my feet, testing my strength and balance. My head goes a little woozy for a moment but quickly clears. I'm definitely not in the same sort of pain that I was, and my arms and legs feel like they belong to me for a change.

As an experiment, I take a few cautious steps. I'm still shaky—something I hate—but I'm more like my old self. Fuck, those assholes must have seriously clobbered me to have hurt me so badly. I'm aware of how lucky I am that I don't have to live with a permanent brain injury.

I wander around a little more, feeling the strength return to my limbs with every step. I inhale the clean air of the forest, drawing it deep into my lungs, and give thanks for being alive.

The inhale reminds me of the reason I'd gotten up. I don't smell too hot.

I check the bag that Laney grabbed. I'm fucking starving as well, but I'm not going to eat without the others.

Amazingly, I find a small sliver of a bar of soap inside a plastic container in the bottom of the bag. I hadn't put any of those assholes as caring much about personal hygiene, but clearly I was wrong.

I give my armpit a sniff and wrinkle my nose. Poor Laney, having to sleep nestled into that all night. Not that she seemed to mind. She probably doesn't smell a whole lot better, but we don't notice that about each other anymore.

I strip off my shirt, and then do the same for my pants. It

feels good to be naked in the early morning sunshine. I stretch, enjoying the release of my muscles, and then stride into the river.

The water hits my thighs, so—thinking my balls will probably vanish if I dunk them right into the icy water—I stop and lean over to splash my body. I clench my teeth and shiver but get on with washing, running the sliver of soap over my skin. I duck a little lower and gasp at the chill but manage to splash water onto my face and run it through my hair. I'm distinctly beardy now, my usual stubble having grown out, and my hair has never been this long either. I'll start to look like Darius soon.

My father's raised voice comes from behind me.

"What the fuck are you doing?"

I don't bother looking over my shoulder at him to reply. "What does it look like?"

"Jesus Christ, Cade. You shouldn't be fucking swimming on your own."

I let out an irritated sigh and turn around. Maybe I should care about giving my father a full frontal, but it's not like he hasn't seen it all before.

"I wasn't swimming. I was washing. I've been lying in my own filth for days. I needed it."

He's got his arms folded over his chest, his nostrils flared, as he does when he's annoyed. "Maybe so, but you're not strong enough to be in the water on your own."

"I'm much stronger today. I wouldn't have gotten in if I didn't think I was capable."

He's not giving up. "You might have had a reaction to the cold water and had a heart attack or something."

I can't help but roll my eyes. "Seriously? I'm not a fucking invalid."

"You were unconscious for days. That's something to take seriously."

"Yeah, okay, but I feel hell of a lot better, especially after being in the water. I'm like a whole new man."

He's still giving me that disapproving stare I know so well from when I was growing up, except I'm an adult now and can do what the fuck I want.

Feeling more alive than I have in days, I stroll back out of the water. I don't have a towel, so I've got no choice but to use my t-shirt to dry off most of me and let the sun and breeze do the rest.

I catch Laney watching as I dress and throw her a wink. The corners of her lips curl, and I want to scoop her up and crush her to me. It seems crazy to me that I used to be attracted to these perfectly made-up women, with their fake nails and lashes, but here's Laney as natural as she can get, and she couldn't be more beautiful.

She still has that haunted look in her eyes, and the expression troubles me. What happened while I was unconscious?

"We should eat," Reed says, "and then keep moving. Smith and his gang are bound to be on our tail."

No one argues with him, and we share out some of the food and water.

"I'm glad you're feeling better," Darius says.

I grin. "Looking better, too. I'm lucky they didn't do permanent damage after hitting me in the head so hard."

Dax presses a smile between his lips. "I don't know...would we even be able to tell if they had?"

I punch him lightly in the shoulder. "Ha-fucking-ha. I see you didn't lose your sense of humor."

We chomp into the stale bread and share out what remains of the cold ham and cheese. It might not be Michelin star quality, but it tastes fucking amazing. I realize how much I've taken bread for granted my whole life. After living without it for weeks, it's like a food of the gods.

"We shouldn't hang around here for too long," Darius says.

I can tell by the thinning of his lips that he's anxious. He looks different, too, and at first, I can't quite put my finger on it, but then it dawns on me.

"You don't have your violin."

He shrugs. "I snapped the bow."

I can hardly believe what I'm hearing. "What? Why?"

"Those motherfuckers were trying to make me play for them."

"So you snapped your bow?"

"Yep."

I raised both my eyebrows. "Holy shit, bro."

I don't know if I should laugh or cry. I wonder what else happened while I'd been so out of it.

26
laney

Before we get back on the boat, I leave the small cove and step deeper into the forest so I can do my business without anyone watching. I don't go too far, aware there are still dangers around. I remain poised for any change in sounds surrounding me, the crack of a twig as a heavy foot lands on it, or a murmur of voices, but there is nothing. Can I bring myself to believe we're actually safe now—that Smith and the others have given up on us?

I finish up and head back to the river.

"Everything all right?" Reed asks.

He's always checking up on me.

I nod and crouch on the water's edge to wash my hands and face. "Yes, I'm fine."

I'm not, though. Not really. A tight knot of darkness swirls inside me—I'm just doing my best to ignore it. At some point in my future, if I live that long, I'll have to process what I've gone through, but first we need to make it to safety.

We work together to load everything back on the boat.

Cade is looking so much better, like his old self, and one strand of the knot inside me loosens.

He catches me watching him. "Can't take your eyes off me, can you, Cuckoo?"

I poke out my tongue. "Don't flatter yourself."

"You missed me. Admit it."

I lift my thumb and forefinger and hover them close together. "Maybe about this much."

He catches my hand and squeezes it. "Liar."

He smiles down at me and then lifts his hand and coils a strand of my hair around his finger and tucks it behind my ear.

Our position—standing down by the river—and the act of him tucking my hair behind my ear propels me right back to the moment before Axel raped me. Suddenly, I'm there again, and it isn't Cade in front of me anymore, but *him*.

I jerk away from Cade, needing to put space between us. A rush of heat floods over me, before I'm drenched in the kind of chill that sinks right down to my bones. I try to suck in oxygen, but my lungs have closed over and refuse to work.

"Laney?" Cade says, his forehead creasing in confusion. "What's wrong? What did I do...or say?"

I shake my head, though I'm not sure if I'm trying to tell him that I'm all right, or that I can't speak to tell him.

Not that I'm going to tell him.

I can't. I don't ever want to speak of what those men did to me. I want to pretend it was all some terrible nightmare, or maybe that it happened to someone else, and I only know because I'd heard about it thirdhand. I certainly don't want it to ever be something I have to relive, even if it's only in my head.

But Cade is staring at me, and even through my distress, I can tell that he knows.

His features go rigid. "What did they do to you?"

"Cade, stop," I manage to say.

"Tell me. They hurt you, didn't they? They put their hands on you. Did they rape you?"

I can't even look at him. I'm drowning in shame. I can't breathe. I can't think. I don't even want to exist.

"Fucking hell." He slams his fist against his thigh. I cower in the wake of his rage. "Those fucking bastards. We shouldn't have run. We should have stayed there and killed every goddamned one of them."

"It wasn't that easy," I say.

"Fuck, Laney. Why did you not run the very moment those men looked at you with that sort of hunger in their eyes? Why did you not run the moment one of them laid their fucking hands on you?"

"You know why."

"Yes, I do. Because of me."

I sniff. "You think it was that simple? They had guns. Smith even used his gun..." I choke on my words... "inside me. What was I supposed to do? Fight back? One slip of his finger and he literally would have blown my insides out. You think this was easy for me?"

Cade spins to his brother and father. Both their expressions are shocked at the details I've revealed.

"How the fuck did you two stand by and let it happen?"

Reed's lips thin. "They had guns to our heads, Cade. It wasn't like we had much of a choice."

"Do you think we wanted it to happen? Don't you think it fucking killed us, too?" Darius says, his expression pained.

I have to defend Reed and Darius. "It's not their fault. They did everything they could."

"They should have done more! Fuck!" He looks like he wants to tear the forest down. "Why didn't you run? You should have run sooner."

"We couldn't," Reed says. "How could we have run when

you were so sick?"

Cade spins to face him. "You didn't run because of me?"

Reed can see where this is going, and he falters. "No—not just because of that. They were armed, remember? They would have shot us."

"But you could have slipped away. You weren't tied up. The door wasn't even locked."

My heart is breaking all over again. "Cade, stop it."

He shakes his head. "You should have left me."

His words shock me. "We'd never do that."

Reed jumps in. "You're my son. I'd no more abandon you than I would cut off my own leg."

"You should have," Cade insists. "She's worth more than me, by a longshot. She shouldn't have had to go through that because of me. Do you think I'd ever want to be a burden on you? What have you been through, Laney, because of me? Because I was so fucking helpless. You should have fucking run when you had the chance."

I'm dying inside. "No, don't say that!"

He can't even look at me. "They raped you because of me."

"No, they didn't. They would have done it anyway."

I realize I've admitted what they did to me out loud. I can sense Reed staring at me, and I'm aware Darius has all his attention on me as well. Tears fill my eyes, but I blink them away. We need to be continuing our journey right now, moving forward, not looking into what's happened in the past.

"I would have died for you, Laney, but you never let me have that choice," Cade says.

I feel desperate. "If you would die for me, then why can't you understand that it goes both ways? You didn't have that choice because you were unconscious, but I wasn't. I went through what I did because I could, and I would do it all over again, if I had to."

"But I'm the one who has to live with knowing I'm the cause of them raping you. *You* did that to *me*."

I sense Cade harden, like shutters literally go down around his face, and his muscles turn to stone. The man who held me in his arms only moments before vanishes. Any vulnerability he might have shown me is washed away and replaced by the man I'd met in the hotel lobby what feels like a lifetime ago.

"You ungrateful son of a bitch," I spit. "Maybe we should have left you there to die. Do you have any idea what I've gone through? You're feeling sorry for yourself after I was—" I cut myself off, knowing what I'd been about to say. Sexually assaulted. With a fucking gun. And then raped by a different man. That he even dares feeling sorry for himself after what I've been through makes me rage.

He slowly shakes his head, his lips pinching. "That's exactly what I'm talking about, Cuckoo. I'm not feeling sorry for myself. Not in the slightest. I'm fucking furious that you went through something so fucking abhorrent. Am I grateful to you? No. Fuck no. I would rather be dead. Now I have to live with the fact you were assaulted because of me." He thumps himself in the chest. "Because of me!"

"And *I* have to live with what happened to *me*."

He glares at me. "So, which of us is the winner in this situation? You should have left me and run."

Angry, frustrated tears fill my eyes. "What about Reed and Darius? Do you think they could have left you, even if I'd said we should? They love you, too."

"They'd have been all right without me. I never wanted to be a burden."

I gesture toward his brother. "What about Dax? He's blind. Do you think he sees himself as a burden?"

"No, because he's not one. He's the one who's provided us with our lifestyle for the past however many years. He's the talent. What the fuck am I? Some dumbass meathead who's only ever gotten in trouble. First the gambling debt, and now this."

"You've always been there for Darius. He'd want to be there for you, too."

Cade shakes his head. "I haven't always been there. If I had, he'd never have been threatened by those loan sharks back home. I'd have called for help the moment we crashed instead of using this as a way to escape. I'd thought us being stranded out here was bad enough, but now you've been raped, and it's all my fault." His whole face is pinched with pain. "You should have fucking left me, Laney. I'm not worth staying for."

My heart breaks for him, but at the same time, I want to punch some goddamned sense into him. He might be saying that he's not feeling sorry for himself, but that's sure as hell what it looks like to me.

I fold my arms across my chest. "Well, you know what, I'm not giving up on you. Say whatever the hell you like, push me away if that's what makes you feel better, but you're not getting rid of me that easily."

He purses his lips and shakes his head. "Give up, Laney. It's time you start learning when people don't want you around."

"Fuck you, Cade."

His words are like a blade to my heart. Though I know he's only saying it to hurt me, it works. It's the one thing I've always feared in my life. I never felt like people wanted me around. I definitely never thought my mom wanted me around. I only got in the way of her partying and was in the way when she brought men home, or, even worse, drew their attention away from her. Even when I'd made the occasional friend at school, I'd always thought they were only tolerating me, and same for people I worked with. In my head, they rolled their eyes when I walked away and talked about me behind my back. I never once felt confident or comfortable in any type of relationship until I ended up with Reed and his sons. That I could have gotten that wrong makes it hard for me to breathe.

Reed steps in. "That's enough, both of you. We need to leave. We can't stand out here fighting forever. None of us wanted what happened, but it did, and now we need to move on."

I want to hug him. Instead, I just nod.

Cade scowls and storms off to the boat. How did everything turn to shit so quickly?

"You okay, Laney?" Reed asks.

"Don't be nice to me, okay?" If he is, I'll only cry.

"Let's get moving," he says instead.

"We weren't wrong, were we, not to leave Cade?"

"No, we weren't wrong, but I understand why he's so upset. He's blaming himself. I blame myself, too. There were things I could have done differently."

"The only people to blame are...them." I don't even want to say their names. "None of you did that to me."

"I know, baby."

He pulls me into a hug, and I let him hold me. I squeeze my eyes shut and bury my nose in his chest. Fucking Cade. Why does he have to be such a fucking idiot at times?

Reed releases me, and we head to the boat. I climb onboard, joining the brothers, and Reed pushes us away from the bank and jumps in as well.

We set off down the river again, Reed and Darius both back on the oars.

The bright morning sunshine has vanished, and chilled wind funnels across the water, whipping around our heads and shoulders. I shiver violently, my arms wrapped around my torso. Cade sits at the front of the boat, watching out for any hazards in our path. I want to go to him and wrap myself around him for warmth, but he's still pissed at me, and now I'm pissed at him, and neither of us wants to be the one who breaks.

How can he not see how much he's hurting me by his behavior? He tries to make out like he's going to do better, but then he pulls this shit. I would never have left him to die, and neither would his father or brother. That doesn't mean the assaults I went through are his fault, no matter how much he's trying to twist things in his head.

In the distance, the sky is darkening as storm clouds roll in.

"That doesn't look good," Reed comments.

Darius nods. "I can smell rain."

A heavy raindrop strikes my forehead, large enough to make me flinch as it splatters. A second hits my nose, and then a third taps me on the head. Shit.

The rain grows heavier.

"Quick, get under shelter," Reed commands.

The tiny awning isn't going to do much to keep us dry. The rain is almost sideways now, and I'm already soaked through. My jeans are heavy and cling to my legs, and my t-shirt does nothing to offer me any protection against the cold. A deep sense of doom settles into my soul. Is this our punishment?

The rain drums onto the awning overhead. A couple of fat droplets slip off the canopy and run down my back. It thrums on the river around us, each raindrop creating a tiny crater in the surface. It shows no sign of abating. Will the river burst its bank?

With the amount of rain entering the river, the speed and pace of the water flow is only going to increase. It could get dangerous. All it would take is a rocky area and the boat could end up dashed to pieces, and we'd drown with it.

Water can be deadly.

27
DARIUS

The rain doesn't last long, but it's heavy enough to soak us all through, and to swell the river.

The boat bobs and bounces across the rapids, hopefully taking us closer to a society we've managed to live without for the past month.

We're going to need to find civilization soon. We're almost out of food and water. We can drink the river water, but we'll be taking the chance, hoping it doesn't make us sick.

I hear it before anything else, though at first I can't place it. It's like a distant roar, as though we're near a busy freeway. Crazily, hope lurches inside me, thinking we might finally have found civilization, but then I realize how insane that is. We haven't seen so much as a dirt track, so it's not like we're going to suddenly hit the interstate.

Beneath me, the boat bobs and bounces, and we seem to pick up speed. The pressure against the oar in my hands increases, the water dragging against it, trying to pull out of my grip.

"Have we hit rapids?" I ask, aiming the question to no one in particular.

My father replies. "Yeah, but they don't look too bad. I'll let you know if they get any worse."

I hesitate and then say, "I think we need to get off the river."

"What? Why?"

"I can hear something. It doesn't sound good."

Reed hesitates and then says, "You think the rapids are going to get worse?"

"Yeah. Much worse."

I don't want to frighten them, but what had sounded like the freeway only moments earlier now sounds like thunder.

"Can you hear that?" Laney asks. "Is that what I think it is?"

"A waterfall." I could punch myself for not speaking up sooner.

I sense Cade rise.

"Oh, fuck."

The front of the boat rises and slaps down again, and cold spray hits the back of my head and soaks into my t-shirt. Laney gasps, and Cade lets out a yell of dismay.

In only moments, we've gone from riding a reasonably calm river, to feeling as though we're being tossed around in a tumble dryer.

"We need to get to shore!" Reed shouts above the roar of the water.

"How?" Laney cries.

We can no longer control the direction the boat is going. My oar hits something solid and hard—a boulder or fallen tree trunk, most likely—and it tears from my hands, taking off a layer of skin at the same time. I'm too worried about what lies ahead to worry about a little friction burn.

"Row to the right bank," Reed tells me.

It's not that easy, though.

There are rocks and boulders everywhere, and I cringe each time the boat smacks up against one. If we're not careful, we're going to end up with a hole in the hull, but what can we do?

"Row!" Reed yells.

I put my back into it, ignoring the pain in my hands, keeping the oar at an angle to try to drive the boat toward the shore on the right-hand side of the river. With every stroke of my oar, I'm battling the power of the river. It's getting stronger, more powerful, and I feel like we might as well be four ants floating on a leaf. That's the amount of impact we're having on our direction.

"Should we jump?" Laney asks, her tone high-pitched with panic. "Try to swim to the shore?"

"That would be suicide," Cade replies. "We have to hang on and hope we get through this in one piece."

"And if we don't?"

"Then we don't."

She barks out a sob. "Oh, my God."

"Sit down, Cade!" my father yells.

"I'm trying to see what's up ahead."

I picture Cade standing up in the bow, craning his neck. The river can be deceptive. With all its curves, it's not always easy to see what's coming, and it's hard to tell what's calm and what's rough when at a distance.

"You'll end up tossed out of the damned boat if you're not more careful," he throws back.

I want to grab my brother and drag him down myself, and then take hold of Laney and hold her tight to me, as well. But my hands are occupied with the oar, and though I can't see what's coming, I do my best to sense the flow of water and keep us away from the bigger boulders. I wonder if it would be better for Cade to have the oar instead of me, but with his injury, I don't know if he'll do any better. For once, I'm stronger than he is. Instead, he shouts out to me, telling when we're approaching something we need to avoid. When to slow and when to lift the oar from the water completely.

Once more, he is my eyes.

The distant thunder turns to a roar.

Surely this isn't going to be how we lose our lives, not after everything we've survived?

"Oh, God, the waterfall," Laney gasps.

"How big is it?" I ask.

"It's impossible to tell," Reed says. "All we can see is the drop where the water ends."

My heart thumps, and every muscle in my body is rigid with tension.

"Pull your oar in," my father instructs. "We can't do anything more. We're just going to have to hold on."

If there are rocks at the bottom of the waterfall, we're going to be dashed to pieces. Even if we survive, we might be injured, and, without a boat, we're never going to make it out of the forest.

But I pull in my oar and place it into the bottom of the boat. I jam both my feet on top of it, holding it in place. If, by some miracle, we get through this, we're going to need the oars. I hear the clatter of my father doing the same.

"I love you," Laney cries, her voice thick with tears. "I love all of you."

"We love you, too, baby," Reed tells her, though he has to shout to be heard above the rush of the river and the roar of the waterfall. "We're going to be okay. Come here."

Movement brushes beside me as she hunkers down on the

bottom of the boat. Her hand finds my knee, and I cover her fingers with mine, squeezing tight.

Cade comes to join us, cramming himself in next to Laney, so all four of us are a tight knot together in the middle of the boat. I hold on to Laney with one hand and the side of the boat with the other.

My heart is in my throat. This moment takes me back to the seconds before the plane went down, the knowledge that I'm facing my death. I'm more worried about losing one of my family than I am about my own demise, but only a fool wouldn't be completely shit scared.

Is it better that I can't see what's coming, or worse? I can imagine it, though, and from the noise of the water hitting the bottom, it sounds big.

I can tell by the change in volume and the tightening of Laney's hand on my knee and the way Reed and Cade tense that we're almost there.

And then the world drops right out from under us.

28
laney

WATER SURROUNDS ME.

Up, down, left, and right...a churning, boiling mass of water. I have no idea which way is up, and I'm tumbling over and over. I kick out and try to push with my arms, desperate to break free. My lungs burn and I'm desperate for air, but if I let myself inhale, I'm dead.

Where are the others? I have no idea. It all happened so fast. When the boat went over the edge of the waterfall, we all fell. I remember losing my grip on everyone and everything. It was as though they all vanished, as did the boat beneath us. The sense of weightlessness was almost like flying for a fraction of a second, but then I hit the water.

I remember the smack of the impact, and then being caught beneath the fall. Now I'm trapped under the water like I'm in a spin-cycle.

I'm going to die, I'm sure of it. I'm not going to find the surface, and any second now I'll be forced to breathe in, and then I'll drown. I almost feel a strange acceptance at the thought. At least then I can stop fighting. I'll no longer have to be in so much pain.

Something grabs the back of my t-shirt and yanks me through the water.

Suddenly, I'm on the surface, my face out of the water, and I gasp huge lungfuls of air. I cough and splutter and try to get my bearings, but I'm completely disoriented and still panicking.

"Quit it, Laney!" a stern voice commands me. "You're going to drown us both."

It's Cade.

Knowing he's there calms me enough to take in my surroundings. We're in a large pool of water. The waterfall is to my left, white, churning foam on the surface where the fall hits, and then the river continues downstream.

I cough again. "Reed? Dax?"

"I haven't seen them."

"Oh, God."

I've only been in the water a matter of minutes, but I'm already exhausted. My toes find purchase on the riverbed, and I realize I've lost one of my sneakers. I don't even care that it's cold and sludgy. I'm just relieved to not have to swim any more.

With our arms around each other, we splash our way out of the pool and toward the riverbank where we both collapse.

"Are you okay?" he asks.

"Yeah. I'm all right." I cough again. My lungs are still burning and my throat hurts. My neck is sore, most likely from whiplash from hitting the water, and will probably get worse over the next few days, but it's not like I can't handle that. I'm more worried about the others.

"What about you?"

Cade already has a head injury. Going through that can't have been good for him.

"Don't worry about me. We need to find the other two."

We look around, searching desperately.

Pieces of the boat are continuing to float down the river, carried by the flow of water. If the boat could end up that far downstream, there's no reason Darius or Reed wouldn't be that way, too. Maybe one of them even managed to keep hold of part of the boat when we went over the edge?

I cast my gaze back over the surface of the pool. While they might have been washed downriver, there's also a chance they're somewhere beneath the water, drowning while we just stand here.

Cade clearly has the same thought, as he leaves me on the side of the bank and strides back in.

"Dad?" he calls. "Darius?"

If they're beneath the surface, they're not going to respond.

He lifts his arms above his head and dives back under the water. I don't know how much he'll be able to see under there. The churning of the waterfall stirs up all the silt, so visibility can't be good.

I'm holding back tears. We can't have lost them; we just can't. I want to make myself useful, and while I can't bring myself to go back in the water, I can still look. I run down the riverbank, ignoring my one bare foot, following the trail of destruction that is the remains of our boat. There's no way we'll be traveling any farther in it. It wasn't a big boat, anyway, and the force of hitting the water has destroyed it.

My limbs don't feel like they belong to me. I'm soaked down to the skin and shaking all over. I force them to move, though, urging myself on. This could literally mean the difference in finding Reed and Darius alive or dead.

I scramble and stumble and half fall. I search frantically, my heart lifting each time I think I catch sight of something, and then dropping again as I realize the thing I think is a man's arm or leg is actually part of a cushion or a length of wood. My heart is breaking with every step, and I'm convinced it's only going to be Cade and me left.

I glance back over my shoulder to where Cade continues to search the pool. He dives beneath the surface and swims underwater, trying to find his father and brother, then runs out of air and gulps down another lungful, before repeating the process all over again. He seems as desperate as I am, and I have a horrible feeling that if one of them is still beneath the water, it will be too late.

I'm also worried about Cade's head injury. He's going without oxygen for long periods of time, which can't be good after what he's already been through. What if I lose him, too? The idea of being lost out here on my own strikes cold terror into my heart. I'll never make it. What would be the point, anyway, if I didn't have them? I'd give up, find a tree or a bush to curl up underneath, and wait to be killed by the cold or maybe a wild animal.

On the other side of the bank, I catch sight of something. For a moment, I think my eyes are playing cruel tricks on me again, but then the shape morphs into that of Darius. It's definitely him.

"Cade!" I scream. "Dax is here!"

Is he alive or dead? I can't tell, and I can't risk going back into the water to try to cross to the other side. The rush of the water is still too strong, and it's carrying with it all the debris from the waterfall. If I try to get in to cross, I have no doubt that I'll be swept away.

"Darius!" I yell across the water. "Can you hear me? Please be okay!"

He lets out a groan and half pushes himself up on his forearms before breaking into a volley of coughing.

My legs give way beneath me, and I crumple to the ground, tears streaming down my face. He's alive.

But Reed is still missing.

Something wet and cold touches my shoulder and I jump, but it's only Cade.

"How the fuck are we going to get over there?" he wonders out loud.

I don't know if he's actually expecting a reply, but I have no suggestions, so I shake my head.

Darius is still coughing, but he's sitting up on his haunches now. His face is grazed, but he seems unharmed. Other than a few bumps and bruises, we've miraculously escaped unscathed. That's all except Reed, of course, who could be dead, his body drifting down the river, tangled in with the remains of the boat.

We can't expect Darius to navigate that side of the river alone. We're going to have to figure out how to reach each other.

"Who's over there?" Darius shouts, when he's finally caught his breath. "Is everyone all right?"

"It's me, Laney," I say, "and Cade. We don't know where Reed is."

"Fuck," Darius curses. He shakes his head at himself. "I should have warned you all about the waterfall sooner. I heard it but didn't know what it was. If only I'd said something as soon as I heard it."

"This isn't your fault, bro," Cade calls back.

I can't imagine how frustrated Darius must be knowing that his father is missing and being unable to do anything to search for him. At least Cade and I can look for him, but Darius can't even do that. I tell myself that Reed must be here somewhere. He can't have just vanished.

I can't picture the three of us existing without him. While Cade might act like the alpha male, Reed is our patriarch. He's the one we all turn to.

I miss him already.

Cade shouts across the water. "Dax, you need to stay put while me and Laney keep searching. Okay?"

He shakes his head. "Not okay. I feel fucking useless."

"Listen out for him. He might be hurt and unable to get to us, but he still might be able to call for us."

Darius nods.

I know Cade is only trying to make Dax feel better by giving him something to do. We're not giving up on Reed yet. I wipe the tears from my face and force myself to standing once more. I exchange a glance with Cade.

"We keep looking," he says.

I nod in agreement. We've already searched the pool and this part of the river, so we have no other choice but to head downstream and pray he's been washed up on the bank like Darius was.

Pieces of the boat are everywhere.

"I think it's safe to say that we're going to be traveling on foot from here on out," Cade says.

I can't bring myself to speak; grief has clogged up my throat. I'm barely holding back the panic threatening to engulf me. All Reed has ever done is try to watch out for us all. My mind keeps trying to take me to a place where he is no longer in this world, and I can't handle it.

With every passing minute, I become more convinced we're not going to find Reed alive. I'm terrified I'll spot his body floating face down in the river.

Cade's voice tears me from my maudlin thoughts.

"Look! Over there!"

I follow his line of sight to where he's pointing.

It's the front of the boat, caught on a tangle of logs and sticks in the middle of the river. Miraculously, Reed is lying half in the boat, half in the water. Relief that his top half is in the boat, not face down in the river, sweeps through me.

We both break into a run.

With his longer legs, Cade gets there first. He splashes into the water.

"Dad!"

"Cade, be careful," I call after him, but he ignores me and keeps going.

He's chest deep in the river now, and I'm terrified he's going to be swept away. But, somehow, he stays on his feet.

Cade has almost reached the boat, and he grabs a fallen tree trunk and hangs on to it. I'm terrified the wood will dislodge and sweep them both downriver. He must be exhausted after trying to find his brother and father in the pool.

"Is he alive?" I shout.

Cade twists slightly to look over his shoulder at me. "I'm not sure."

"Oh, God." I find myself praying. *I'll do anything if he's still alive. Anything.*

How many times have I done that now, as though God would pay any special attention to the four of us? I've been sleeping with my two stepbrothers and my stepfather. At this point, I'm pretty sure I'll be heading down instead of up, if that's what happens to us once we're gone. I might not be innocent now, but I had been once upon a time, and then I had a drug addict who liked to bring sketchy boyfriends home for a mother. Before I was barely old enough to have breast buds, I'd learned the world was not a kind place, and that no one out there was going to watch out for me. I certainly don't feel like I've ever had any god or even a guardian angel looking after me.

"I'm going to bring him over," Cade shouts back.

Does that mean Reed is alive?

"Tell me, please. Is he breathing?"

"I—I can't tell."

My stomach drops, my heart twisting into a knot. My chest

is heavy and painful with grief. We'd have been too lucky for us all to survive. I knew it. We were going to lose one of us at some point.

I'm crying again, this time silently, the tears pouring down my cheeks. I'm struggling to see, my vision is so blurred. But I can make out Cade half climbing onto what remains of the boat. I remind myself that Reed is Cade's father, and this must be killing Cade, too. I'm worried Cade is going to take a risk that he wouldn't for anyone other than his family, to put himself in danger.

I'm still angry with him at how he treated me, but I can be angry with him and love him at the same time. I can't handle losing him, too.

Cade manages to get his arm underneath Reed and half lifts, half pulls him from the remains of the boat. My heart is in my throat as they both hit the water. Cade is a big guy, but Reed isn't exactly small, and after Cade's injury, I'm still worried about him.

The water's too strong, dragging them downstream.

"Fuck," Cade gasps, struggling.

"No!"

I'm not going to stand here and watch them drown.

Cade must sense what I'm planning.

"Stay on the bank, Laney."

"Fuck that."

I jump into the water and head straight for them. There's a branch that's half on the bank, the end trailing in the river. I don't know if it's attached to anything, but it's all I've got, so I grab it anyway. I give it an experimental tug and it seems to hold, but that's with only my weight, and I weigh a fraction of what Cade plus Reed do.

The water pummels at my legs, threatening to tear my feet out from under me. I keep going, one hand wrapped around the tree branch, the other reaching for Cade and Reed.

"Take my hand," I shout to Cade.

"Fuck, Laney. I told you to stay on the bank."

"Just fucking do it."

He's hanging on to Reed, doing his best to keep Reed's head above water. I don't dare to look at Reed too hard, still terrified Cade is wasting his time and is only bringing Reed's body back to us.

Cade lets go of Reed with one hand and grabs mine. His fingers are freezing, but I squeeze them tight. I dig my heels into the sludgy riverbed and hang on. There's no way I'm strong enough to pull the two of them onto shore, but what I offer them is a lifeline, a way of connecting to the shore, like rope across a river. I pray the branch will hold. My muscles strain, and the pressure on my shoulder joint is intense, but it allows Cade to get out of the fastest point of the river and, together, we fall into the shallows, an exhausted, desperate mess.

Cade lifts me, and together we get Reed onto dry land. Darius is still on the other side of the river, anxious for news.

I press my fingers to the side of Reed's neck. His skin is horrifyingly cool to the touch. Is he dead? But then I feel it, his pulse faint but definitely present.

"He's alive," I say, "but I don't think he's breathing."

"Give me some space."

Cade leans over and pinches his father's nose with one hand and tilts his chin with the other. He covers Reed's mouth with his own and blows before releasing his grip on his nose and starting chest compressions. They seem too much—hard and violent—and I'm sure Cade will be hurting him.

I can barely see, I'm crying so hard. In my head, I repeat *please, please, please, please.*

Cade goes back to Reed's mouth, but before he gets the chance to exhale, a thin trickle of water runs from the corner of Reed's lips. Then, from out of nowhere, Reed lurches to one side, coughing hard, and more water bursts from his mouth.

I fall back on the ground, my hands shaking hard, my chin trembling so much my teeth chatter. It's the shock. I'd genuinely thought we were going to lose him. I don't know how much more of this I can take. It feels like my heart is being stretched in every direction, and at any moment, it's going to tear in two.

"He's breathing," Cade says. Then he raises his voice for his brother's benefit and shouts, "He's breathing, Dax! He's going to be okay."

I cover my face with my hands and sob in relief, my shoulders heaving. I can hardly believe it. I'd convinced myself he was dead. I don't know how badly injured he is, but, for the moment, he's alive, and that's all that matters.

We've still got the difficult situation of Darius being stuck on the opposite side of the river, however. If it was any of the rest of us, perhaps it wouldn't be such a problem, but we can't expect Darius to navigate a strange riverbank alone. No matter how capable he is, he has no idea what lies ahead of him.

Cade rubs his father's back as Reed coughs up more water and sucks in air.

"You're okay," Cade reassures him. "You're going to be fine."

I pray he's right.

The minutes tick past, but finally, Reed can talk. He looks around and realizes his youngest son is missing.

"Dax?" he croaks.

Cade squeezes his shoulder. "He's fine. He's just stuck on the other side of the river."

"We all made it," Reed says.

I pull him into a hug, not caring that he's soaking wet. He feels so good, and I want to hold him forever.

He hugs me back, one of those big bear hugs that completely envelops me. "It's okay, Laney. We're going to be okay."

I wish I could believe him, but what the fuck are we going to do now? We've got no boat, no food, no way of building a fire and getting dry and warm. I don't even have two sneakers.

How are we supposed to get to safety like this?

29
DARIUS

BEING SEPARATED FROM THE OTHERS AND HAVING NO IDEA of my surroundings unnerves me.

I don't want to move. A step in any direction could be perilous. I could end up back in the river, or falling down the bank, or walking into a goddamned tree. I'm not sure I've ever been so disoriented in my life, and I fucking hate it.

Thank God we've all survived. There was more than one moment where I'd believed we'd lost my dad. I genuinely hadn't expected to get good news.

I feel around on the ground and find a decent sized stick. It's not perfect, but it'll stop me walking into anything. I need to find a way across the river, but it's not as though we're going to come across a bridge anywhere nearby.

Cade's shout comes from the other side. "We're going to rest for a while and then try to make our way downstream. There might be somewhere shallower where we can cross."

"Is everyone all right?" I call back.

"Yes, just exhausted."

I know how they feel. We're all coming to the end of our

resources. I don't want to give up hope, but despair is creeping in. We've been incredibly lucky to survive the waterfall, but how can we make it much farther? I don't know what sort of condition my father is in now, but we have no food or water—unless we take the risk of getting sick and drinking the river water—and tonight it's going to get cold. We're all soaked, and while it might not be freezing yet, spending a night out here while wet through could easily bring on hypothermia.

I find a tree to wedge my back against and wait until the others say they're ready to move. I close my eyes, allowing the sun to warm me. I doze, drifting between conscious thought and a kind of dream state. In my dream, I can see again. I'm standing on stage, my beloved violin in my hands. I position the chin rest and brandish the bow. I gaze out into the audience, but my eyes are only drawn to one person. Laney. I realize what this means. I'm going to play for her, and that must mean we've made it home...

I lurch into wakefulness. Instinctively, I reach for Laney, wanting to reassure myself she's close, but then I remember a whole river separates us. Fuck. Why couldn't we have washed up on the same side? I want my brother and father with me, too, but in a different kind of way. My chest aches for her. We haven't been apart ever since she came into our lives, and I'm not sure how to function without her.

I need her.

I try to convince myself that this is only temporary and we'll be reunited soon, but how the fuck is that going to happen? I don't know what sort of condition my father is in, but is he really going to be well enough to try to cross the river? No, I can't ask that of him. I can't—and won't—ask it of Laney, either. I won't let her put herself in more danger for me.

"You okay over there, Dax?"

My brother's voice shouts over to me. I scramble to my feet

and then remember the stick. It's not much, but I'm going to need it.

"Yeah, I'm okay."

As okay as someone in my position can be...which right now is not fucking okay at all. Maybe they should leave me. I'm only going to slow them down. They could find help and come back for me. As long as they stick to the river, they should find their way back again.

It's the sensible option, but I don't bother suggesting it. They won't abandon me, just like I'd never abandon them.

"Is Dad all right to walk?" I call over.

Reed is the one who replies. "I can walk."

I'm resigned to what needs to happen. "We'd better keep going, then."

"Are you sure you're going to be all right?" Cade is clearly worried about how this is going to work.

"I'm going to have to be. Let me know if I'm going to walk off the side of a cliff or something, okay?" I keep my tone dry. I might be joking, but many a true word is said in jest. The way our luck has been going, it wouldn't surprise me.

Then I force myself to reframe my thoughts. We have been lucky. In some ways, we've been insanely lucky. We survived a fucking plane crash and over a month in the wilderness. We got away from armed men and lived through going over a waterfall.

I find myself smiling. Not many people can say that.

I know which side of me the river needs to be on to make sure I'm at least walking in the right direction. The sun on my face also helps. It makes the darkness not so absolute.

With the stick in my hand, I take the first few tentative steps. The stick hits something hard—a rock, perhaps, or a fallen tree trunk—and I shuffle sideways to get around it. My path is clear again, so I keep going. I'm aware of how slowly I'm moving, but it can't be helped. Falling and breaking a limb right now would be signing my death warrant. Besides, I can't imagine my father is in any state to move quickly either, and Cade and Laney must be exhausted.

Every so often, their voices drift over to me from the other side of the river. Cade calls out if he spots me veering off course, or if he sees an obstacle in my way.

I appreciate the help, but it's hard not to feel alone and isolated.

I miss Laney's company the most.

I keep thinking she's near me. I turn to tell her something, only to remember she's not there. I have a constant sense that something is missing, like someone has carved out my heart and left only a hole there and is expecting me to live just the same. There is no part of me that doesn't miss her. My brain wants to talk to her. My hands need to touch her. My heart tries to reach out to hers.

Each part of me keeps forgetting that she's out of reach.

30
laney

I HATE TO SEE DARIUS STRUGGLE. IT BREAKS MY HEART. He's so vulnerable over there. He's using a stick he's found to help him navigate, but it's slow going. I know how mad he'll be as well, how frustrated.

We have no choice but to keep going. The whole way, we watch the river, trying to find a spot where it might be easier and safer to cross so we can all be reunited again. The river is wide, however, and for the most part it's deep. When we do reach shallower parts, its full of rocks and the water churns and roils over the tops of them.

It doesn't take long before I'm limping. I lost one of my sneakers, so now every time my socked foot lands on a rock or spikey twig, it pierces straight into my sole. I do my best not to wince or suck air over my teeth, not wanting to make a fuss. Walking with only one shoe is hardly a big deal after everything else. It's not easy going, though.

I watch the riverbank, hoping my sneaker might have washed up somewhere downriver, but there's no sign of it. I still spot the odd piece of the broken-up boat, however, so I haven't completely given up hope.

Cade frowns at me, as though he's only just noticed I've lost a shoe. "Fuck, Laney. You can't keep walking like that."

I grit my teeth. "I don't have much choice."

"Yes, you do. Take my boots."

"I'm not taking your boots, Cade. They'll be huge on me, anyway."

"Still better than you being bare-footed."

He drops to the ground and starts yanking off his boots.

"I'm not wearing them," I insist.

"Yes, you fucking well are." He pulls the other one from his foot and shoves them at me. "Now, put them on."

I fold my arms over my chest, refusing to take them. "No."

"Laney," his tone is cold, "put on the boots or I will put you over my knee. I swear I will."

I widen my eyes, and glance to Reed for some backup, but he only shrugs.

"I don't think he's messing around," Reed says.

"Okay, fine."

I take them from him and pull off my one remaining sneaker, and then slip my feet into the boots. They're huge, as I'd expected, and they'll probably give me blisters, but at least my soles are protected.

"Thanks," I tell him.

He smiles at me and puts out his hand. I take it and pretend to help him to his feet, though we both know he could pull me straight down if he wanted.

We keep going for a while, Cade bare-footed now, me slopping around in his boots.

Cade slows and then stops. "What about here? Does it look shallower?"

I study the water for a moment. It does look shallower, though the water is still moving at a fast pace.

Darius hasn't noticed we've stopped, so Reed calls over to him. "Wait up, Dax. We're checking out this part of the river."

The shout elicits a fresh volley of coughing, and I frown over at him in concern. Could he still have water in his lungs? I read once about something called dry drowning, where someone unknowingly inhales water into their lungs, only it doesn't affect them right away, but it can kill them later.

Darius has drawn to a halt as well.

"It makes more sense for Darius to come to us than the three of us go to him," Cade says.

I shake my head. "No. He can't see where he's going."

Cade's tone is hard. "I'm aware of that, Laney, but Reed is still weak, and Darius is stronger than you. It's better that we risk one of us than three."

I bristle. I'm still angry at Cade for his reaction to what Smith and Axel did to me, and this comment only riles me further.

"Risk one of us? Is that how you're thinking of this? If it's a risk, we shouldn't attempt it at all."

He shakes his head. "Jesus Christ, Laney, every single step we take in this place is a risk." He gestures to the other side of the river. "Dax being over there by himself is a risk. He could fall or be attacked by a bear. The river might change again so his side turns into a cliff. What the fuck are we going to do then?"

I do see his point, but I still think we're in a better position than Darius.

If we had a rope, we could throw it across and help him that way, but we have nothing. Only the clothes we're standing in.

I'm not giving up yet. "We could hold each other's hands,

make a kind of human rope. The three of us are more likely to be more stable in the water than Dax on his own."

Reed looks between us. "Laney's got a point, Cade."

Cade's lips thin. "You shouldn't go back in the water."

"That's not your choice to make," Reed continues. "Darius is my son, and I'll give my life for him in an instant."

I believe him, too.

"And Laney's life?" Cade insists. "Would you give her life, too?"

"You don't get to make that decision for me," I say. "Neither of you does. If I want to try it, that's my choice."

Cade's shoulders sink. He can see he's been defeated. He turns back to his brother.

"We can try to make it over to you to help," Cade shouts.

Darius straightens his shoulders. "I don't want any of you putting yourselves at risk for my sake."

"But it makes—"

Cade doesn't get the chance to finish. Darius has already turned to face the river and is walking straight toward it.

I realize what he's about to do. He's coming over.

"Darius, no!"

The look of determination on his face isn't to be argued with. He's crossing the river so we don't have to. I'm betting that he thinks if he gets swept away and drowns, then at least it's him and not one of us. What he hasn't considered is that if he gets into trouble, we'll end up coming after him anyway.

He splashes into the water, looking sure-footed and resolved. He still has the stick, but I can't see what use it's going to be.

"Fuck," Cade curses. Then he turns to me and Reed. "Stay here."

The water is chest deep now, and Darius lets go of the stick. It's not much use when he needs to swim.

"Don't come over, Cade!" Dax yells. He must have heard what his brother said.

The rush of the river is already pushing Darius father downstream. The worst part is that Darius probably doesn't even know the extent to which he's being pushed off course. My heart is racing, and I run down the side of the bank, trying to stay in line with Darius. I picture him running out of strength, his head sinking beneath the surface, and his body being dragged away from us. But he keeps going, his strong arms striking out against the water, propelling him across. Cade is also being pushed downriver, but he's closer to Darius now.

He shouts for his brother. "Dax! I'm over here."

Darius turns his head and renews his efforts.

I clamp my hand to my mouth. I sense Reed watching with the same horror.

I don't think it's going to happen, but Cade reaches him, and they cling to each other. Cade turns back in our direction, and they both half swim, half crawl back to shore.

They climb up onto the bank and fall onto their backs, both breathing hard.

Cade finally half-sits.

"Jesus, bro. You're a fucking idiot. Did I ever tell you that?"

Dax sits up as well. "I'm sure you have, plenty of times."

Cade smacks him on the shoulder. "Well, here I am, telling you again. You could have gotten yourself killed."

"Better me than one of you."

I hear the pain in his voice and go to him. I drop to the ground and wrap my arms around his neck and bury my face in his chest. He folds into me, holding me tight.

"It's okay," he says against my skin. "We're together again now. I just couldn't take another step without having you beside me."

My tears wet my cheeks, and I hold him tighter.

It's getting dark. I can't believe we're going to be spending another night out here. This time we don't even have the cushions from the boat or the tarpaulin. It's only us and the forest.

We all need to rest, and we don't even need to say it out loud for us all to come to the same conclusion. We head toward a small copse of trees and drop to the ground. Poor Darius and Cade are wet again, but they strip out of their sodden clothes and hang them on the tree branches to dry out. It's probably better to be naked and huddled up to us than it is to try to sleep in wet clothes that will only get colder during the night.

Cade props himself up against the tree, and I lie with my head rested on his lap.

"You know that's a dangerous position for you to be in," he jokes.

We both know there won't be anything like that going on tonight. We can have physical intimacy without it needing to be about sex.

Reed lies behind me, my back pressed to his chest, his knees tucked in behind mine. The weight of his arm falls around my waist, and I can't help but be taken back to the early days when we would lie like this, and I'd wake to find his erection digging into my spine. I'd known he'd wanted me, even back then, and I'd used this position to my advantage. I'm tempted to do it again, but I know Reed won't fuck me with his sons watching, and vice-versa. While they seem happy enough to share me—and Cade and Darius have often fucked me at the same time—it feels weird for Reed to get involved in that way. He's always kept himself separate from the boys, which I completely understand.

Darius lies on the other side of me, pillowing his head on his bicep. He reaches out and touches my face, stroking my cheeks, my eyelids, my lips, as though he's trying to visualize me. His touch is so familiar, and, despite everything, I let out a sigh and sink deeper into relaxation. I'm completely exhausted, and the heat of their bodies surrounding me is already warming me up. I've been shivering for what feels like forever, but one by one, each of my muscles eases and I drift off to sleep.

31
CADE

I STILL DON'T AGREE WITH THE CHOICES LANEY, MY brother, and my father made, for not leaving me when they had the chance, but looking down into her sleeping face now, it's hard to stay angry with her.

In the fading light, I study her features. The gentle upward slope of her nose. Her long lashes resting against her cheeks. The Cupid's bow of her lips. My hands hover above her head, and my palms itch to stroke her hair.

She's so fucking perfect, it makes my chest ache.

But even as the thought goes through my head, the dangerous combination of pain and anger rises inside me. I clench my teeth and fists and try to push the thoughts away.

I don't want to think about it too deeply, but there's jealousy there, too. I hate that another man has been inside her, that they touched her in that way. That they forced her legs apart and took her and took her and took her. Every time I look at her, it's all I can see. I didn't witness what happened, but I can still see it. Did they come inside her? Did they violate her that way? I want to know every detail, but at the same time I

241

want to shove my head in the sand and pretend like it never happened.

But it kills me—it fucking kills me—that she went through that for me. They could have all run, have left in the boat, without me, and Laney would never have needed to suffer those bastards' hands on her.

I'd have died for her to not have to live with this, and I'd have done so gratefully.

But she never let me have that choice.

She's so peaceful right now, her head on my lap, her hand tucked up under her cheek. Does she think everything is right between us now? No, fuck. How can she? How can anything be right? Even though we're away from those bastards, what they did to her will shape her now. She'll never be the same again.

I let my head fall back against the tree trunk and close my eyes.

I've never felt this way about another person before. Thoughts of her torture me. I can't think of anything else. I felt the same way before those assholes came into our lives, but then those thoughts were good, sexy, the way she made me feel. I obsessed over her, thinking about what it was like to be inside her, remembering the noises she made when I licked her clit, or the way her features tensed when she reached orgasm.

Now, I'm terrified I'll never be able to think of her that way again without picturing what those men did to her because of me.

My eyelids grow heavy, and my hands reach for Laney. One palm against her hair, the other on her shoulder. She's warm, her shoulder lifting and falling with her steady breathing, and her hair is soft.

The contact fills me with comfort, and I sink into it, lacing my fingers through the silky strands like she's a comfort blanket and I'm a small child who can't live without it.

———

When I wake, it's day once more, and Laney is still asleep in my lap, my brother and father curled in on either side of her.

They look so peaceful, I don't want to wake them, but I'm also aware that Smith and the others might still be after us, closing in. A part of me wants them to catch up so I can beat the living shit out of all of them, pummel my fist against their faces until they're nothing more than blood and flesh and chunks of bone. I don't even care about the harm they did to me. It's all about her.

Laney.

Her eyebrows furrow and she twitches, hard. A moan escapes her lips, and she jerks, like she's trying to shake me off.

"Laney, hey, it's okay. You're safe."

"No, please."

She jolts awake, sitting upright, throwing off Reed's arm, which was looped around her waist. She thrashes, as though she hasn't quite woken properly and is still trying to fight someone off.

"It's okay. You're safe," I tell her, though I don't know how true that is. She might be safe from those other men, but she still might die out here. We all might.

She blinks at me then closes her eyes again and takes a deep breath. She covers her face with her hands. "God, sorry."

"You don't have anything to be sorry about." Did I really mean that? If I did, then I needed to forgive her for not leaving me behind.

I see pain in her beautiful blue eyes, and I want to take it away, but I feel it as my own. I want to go back in time and force her to make different choices. If only I hadn't been hurt, things would have been so different.

My father and brother also stir and sit up. It's been cold overnight, and I hope our clothes are dry. I get up to check. They're slightly damp from the morning dew, but nothing like how wet they were yesterday. I take them down and toss my brother his shirt and pants.

"I wish we had something to eat," Darius says. "I'm starving."

Laney sighs. "I know. Me too. We might find some berries along the way."

I roll my eyes. "Fucking berries aren't going to do much."

She shoots me a look. "At least they'll be something."

Hunger and exhaustion has frayed all our tempers. I try to bite down on mine, knowing it won't do any good. Even during all our time at the cabin, we've never been as starved as this.

32
DARIUS

WE'VE DONE OUR BEST TO KEEP GOING, BUT OUR PACE HAS
slowed dramatically.

I think we've been walking for a couple of hours now, but I
have no idea what sort of distance we've covered. Are we ever
going to find civilization?

"I can't go any farther," Laney sobs. "I'm sorry. I can't. All I
want is to go to sleep and stay asleep."

"Let me help you," Cade says. "Here, lean on me."

He must be giving her the last of his strength.

"No, just leave me."

"We'll never do that, Cuckoo. You didn't leave me, remember? We stay together. All of us."

"Then we'll die together," she sniffs.

"But at least we'll be with each other in the end."

My heart is fucking breaking. Is this really how things are
going to end for us? Maybe it could be worse. We could have
died at the hands of Smith and his men. This might not be how
any of us would choose to go, but like Laney says, at least we'll
be together.

We haven't given up yet, though. Still, though painfully slowly, we keep going, sticking to the river.

I draw to a halt and strain my ears.

I can hear something. The last time I didn't speak up quickly enough—it almost got us all killed.

"Wait," I say, putting out a hand to stop Reed, who's walking beside me. "Something's changed."

"What is it?" my father asks.

I listen again, holding my breath. Then I exhale and shake my head. "I'm not totally sure. It's like a humming. High pitched."

"Like a person humming?" Laney checks.

"No, different than that."

"Is it like the waterfall?"

The waterfall had been like distant thunder. This is more like the world's largest mosquito. "No, it's different."

"Can you tell what direction it's coming from?" Cade asks.

Though distant, it seems to fill the forest, vibrating the air around the treetops.

I shake my head. "Not yet. Let's keep walking, see if it gets any louder."

We keep going. I'm on high alert now, trying to pinpoint the noise. It keeps trying to take shape in my mind. I definitely recognize it, but my brain can't seem to form the image. My utter exhaustion isn't helping—that, combined with the lack of food and water, has caused a brain fog that is preventing my thoughts from being coherent.

My heart suddenly lurches into my chest as the source of the sound comes to me. "I know what it is!"

I sense the others draw to a halt around me.

"What?" Cade asks.

"Chainsaws."

"Chainsaws?" he echoes. "If there are chainsaws, then there are people."

"Holy shit." Laney laughs. "If there are people, then we can get help."

Reed is more restrained. "Hang on a minute. We don't know what kind of people they are. Remember who we left behind? We don't know that whoever is using the chainsaw will be a friend."

We haven't seen hide nor hair of Smith and the others. I have no idea how far we've traveled from the cabin, but I can't imagine whoever's using the chainsaws will be connected to them in any way.

"We're starving," I say. "Literally starving. If we don't get help soon, we're going to die out here."

I'm not being dramatic. It's a fact.

"I agree," Cade says. "It's worth the risk."

"Worth the risk for Laney to get raped again?" Reed says, his tone harsh.

I flinch at his words.

I know he wants to protect her, how helpless he felt when he wasn't able to against Smith and Axel. But we will die. We need help.

"It's worth that risk, Reed," Laney tells him. "And besides, not everyone in the world is bad. There are people who will help us."

In the distance, there's a crack and a crash as a tree falls.

"It sounds like they're just loggers," I say. "They're not criminals. They can help us."

Cade clears his throat. "I think we have to take the risk. We're lucky to have made it this far. I don't think we're going to last much longer."

Though his struggle is clear in his hesitation, Reed eventually gives in. "Okay, let's go and introduce ourselves."

We keep walking, following the distant *brrrr* of the chain-saws and other machinery. There aren't only chainsaws being used. I can tell some of the equipment is far bigger—most likely skidders to drag the fallen logs from one spot to another and trucks for transportation.

"There are signs we're getting closer," Cade says, mostly for my benefit. "Clearings in the forest where they've already logged, and new trees that have been planted."

I don't need to see these things to know we're close. I can hear them, and smell them, too. The forest has taken on a heated, chemically scent. That of diesel and the friction of metal on wood. There's cigarette smoke, too, and a part of me—though it might be wishful thinking—believes I can even smell coffee.

I can't imagine what the loggers will think of us all emerging from the forest. We must look like zombies—clothes filthy and torn, faces bruised and bloodied, barely an ounce of body fat on us.

A shout comes from through the trees. A male voice I don't recognize. "Hey! Who goes there?"

A second voice joins him. "Jesus fucking Christ. What the fuck happened to you?"

That's a long story to tell.

Beside me, Laney is crying. I put my arm around her and pull her tight to my side. I kiss the top of her head. Her hair is dirty, but I don't even care. I'm sure I'm just as bad.

Reed steps in front of us all—I can tell by the position his voice comes from.

"We were in a plane crash. We've been surviving out in the wilderness for..." He hesitates, clearly unsure of how long we've been lost now. "Weeks," he finishes off.

The first male voice speaks again. "Wait one minute. Are you with that violinist?"

I find myself lifting a hand. "That would be me."

"Holy shit," he says. "I don't know much about that kind of music myself, I'm more a rock fan, but you've been all over the news and social media. It would have been pretty hard not to hear about you."

I wonder if we should tell them about Smith—warn them that dangerous men might be coming after us—but I decide not to complicate things. It needs to be the police we talk to, not some random loggers. Besides, there are going to be more than a couple of men working here, so Smith would be an idiot to try to take us on with so many witnesses. I also highly doubt they have any idea where we are. We've come such a long way, both by boat, and then being almost drowned in the waterfall, and then hiking the rest, that it seems almost impossible that they'd have been able to keep track of us.

"And now you've met me," I say. "And we'll all be really fucking grateful if you can help us."

33
Laney

I KEEP EXPECTING SOMETHING TO GO WRONG, FOR THE loggers to turn into serial killers or something, but they all seem more excited about meeting us than anything else. A buzz of curiosity surrounds them. This is probably the most thrilling thing that's happened here in some time.

"I'm Reed Riviera," Reed introduces himself. "These are my sons, Darius and Cade, and this is my stepdaughter, Laney Flores."

"I'm Brian," the second logger says. He claps his colleague on the shoulder. "And this here is Jonny."

"We need to get to a town or city," Reed tells them.

Jonny, the logger who first greeted us, purses his lips. "We can't get you folks to the city today, 'cause it's going to be dark soon, but we can call you in and get you airlifted out of here tomorrow."

"Tomorrow sounds good," Reed says. "We're all exhausted."

Cade blurts, "And starving. We need food and water. We haven't eaten in days."

Brian glances over his shoulder at his other colleagues, who are all starting to gather around to get a good look at the new arrivals. "Of course. There are solar showers in the bunkhouses as well, and we'll get you some clean clothes."

Reed offers him a smile. "Thanks, but first we need to eat."

I agree. Priorities. We're used to being grubby.

"Sure. Come this way."

The area is surrounded by the large log cabins Brian referred to as bunkhouses. One is a community area where they all eat and where the kitchen is located.

Word has gotten around fast about who we are and what's happened. I feel the stares of all the loggers as we make our way through their camp. They comment to each other, most likely marveling at who we are and how we're still alive.

"Sit," one of our rescuers tell us. "We'll bring you some food out from the kitchen."

The table is wooden, like the rest of the place, and huge, stretching down the length of the bunkhouse. Equally long benches run parallel on either side. We take up position at the end of the table, me and Reed on one side, Cade and Darius opposite us.

It feels strange to be sitting at a table, especially in our current state. Too civilized, somehow. I suddenly wonder how easy it's going to be to integrate back into normal society.

The loggers reappear with chopping boards full of food and plates for us to use.

"Eat as much as you want," Jonny says. "We can get more supplies."

I'm worried we're going to make ourselves sick, but after starving for so long, we can't help ourselves. I load my plate with slabs of thick bread with butter and cheese, and sliced tomatoes. I swear it's the nicest thing I've ever eaten. We crack open cans of soda as well and gulp them down. The sugar and caffeine go straight to my head. I feel like I'm drunk.

"We made it," Darius says, shaking his head. "I can't believe that we made it."

I reach over the table and grab his hand. "We did."

We grill the loggers for information, trying to work out exactly where we are.

It turns out Ottawa is our nearest city. It's over a hundred miles away, but it still feels like it's within reaching distance. This is the closest we've come to civilization in a very long time.

Once we've stuffed ourselves stupid, the loggers bring us a tall silver jug of hot liquid and cookies.

The smell instantly hits my senses.

"Oh, my God," I exclaim, "is that coffee? Real coffee?"

Brian chuckles. "Well, it's not good coffee, but it'll pass."

I don't care. It's the best coffee I've ever tasted.

They have radios here. I try to think if there is anyone I want to call back home to let them know I'm still alive, and fall short. Maybe I should tell my old boss at the restaurant, and some of my colleagues who I was friendlier with, but I don't have the energy for that now. There will be so many questions, and they're going to find out soon enough.

The thought of going back to society suddenly overwhelms me.

People will ask questions—lots of questions. The police will need to talk to us. An investigation will be done. They'll need to locate the shell of the plane and whatever remains they can find of the pilots and flight attendant. It worries me how close the plane is to the cabin. If they find the plane, will they also find Smith and the others? How much are we going to tell them?

When we're done with the food and drink, we're shown up to one of the bunkhouses.

"This one's empty right now," Brian tells us, "so make your-selves at home. It should have everything you need—toiletries and towels, and sheets on the bed. You'll find some clean clothes in the closet, too. We try to travel light when we're moving back and forth from a job."

It all sounds like heaven to me.

The bunkhouse doesn't have actual bunkbeds, but instead has about eight single beds all at intervals along the length of it. At the far end is the bathroom, which contains several showers and cubicles for the toilets.

"I know you're all going to want to get cleaned up and crash," Reed says, momentarily putting a dampener on our excitement, "but first we need to get our stories straight."

"Stories?" I say. "What stories? Surely we just tell the truth."

He draws his eyebrows together. "And give the location of the cabin? If that happens, Smith and his men will be found and rescued."

Darius drags his hand through his hair. "Not necessarily. They might start hiking out of the forest long before that happens."

I widen my eyes. "But if the police *do* pick them up, they'll arrest them, right? It's not like they'll go free and come and find us."

"Are you sure about that?" Cade asks.

I argue my point. "If the police have got our statements that Smith, Axel, and Zeke kidnapped us, held us at gunpoint, and assaulted me, I'd say that's a pretty good reason for putting them behind bars. Then there are all the guns that must still be at the cabin, and the remains of their colleague in the attic. I'm guessing those bastards will already have a record. The police might already be looking for them."

Reed chews his lower lip, clearly worried. "And they might

also have contacts on the outside who they'll send looking for us to shut us up. We have to be realistic about this. If they hike out of the forest, or the police find them, there's a chance they'll come after us. They'll be able to find us, too. The media storm is going to be huge when we reappear. The press are going to follow us around everywhere. People with their smart phones are going to photograph and film us, even if we don't want them to, and post our locations to their social media. If someone wants to find us, it won't be hard."

"Do you think we made a mistake by not killing them when we left?" Cade asks.

I close my eyes briefly. "Kill someone? That's a big deal, Cade. Taking a life, even if those lives are those of kidnapping rapists, changes a person."

"What they did to you..." He fades away, unable to even give voice to what happened, and swallows hard.

Had I wanted those men dead for what they did to me? Yes, absolutely. But there's a big difference between wanting someone dead and asking someone else to do the deed. I'd never want to put Reed or Cade or Darius through the trauma of murdering someone. Of taking a life.

"I would have killed them for you," Reed says, his teeth clenched tight.

"So would I," Cade agrees.

Darius nodded. "And me."

Cade clenches his fists. "Those motherfuckers didn't deserve to see another day for what they did to you. I wish I could have smashed their faces in with my bare hands."

"We should have shot them before we left," Reed says.

I appreciate their anger on my behalf, but I would never have expected them to do that.

"If we'd even tried," I tell them, "we might not have gotten away. We could all be dead now."

"Or worse," Darius says, "one of us might have been killed and the rest remained captive, and we'd have had to live with that."

We all fall silent as we contemplate that alternative reality.

Reed draws in a breath. "What are we saying, here? That we need to be as vague as we can about the location of both the plane and the cabin, so it reduces the chances of Smith and his men being rescued?"

Cade nods. "Makes sense to me."

I think of something. "What about the families of the pilots and the flight attendant? Don't they deserve to be able to recover their remains to put them to rest?"

Reed holds me in his gaze. "Yes, they do, but I'm not going to risk any of your lives for that to happen."

"If they find the plane," Darius says, "they'll find the cabin, and if they find the cabin, they'll find Smith and the others."

"Shit," I curse. "What do we tell the authorities? That we have no idea where we've been or how we've survived? They're not going to buy that."

"No." Reed shakes his head. "We can tell them about the cabin, but we're vague on the direction and distance. We've still come a huge way. We say we found the river by accident and that the plane didn't go down anywhere near it, and we got our water from a different source."

"Smith and the others might still come after us." The sense of relief I'd felt upon coming across the loggers has vanished. "They know they need to follow the river."

"Yes, but they don't have a boat anymore. We traveled farther than you think. It'll be much harder for them to make it, and winter is coming."

Harder, I think, *but not impossible.*

Reed looks around at us all. "Are we agreed, then?"

We all nod.

"Good," he says, "I'm going to have a word with whoever is scheduling our evacuation out of here, make sure I know exactly what's being organized and what they're saying. If we can avoid our names or descriptions going out over the radio, Smith or anyone he's associated with is less likely to find us."

He leaves the bunkhouse, and I do my best to shake off the unease that his words have left me with.

34

Laney

At least we have the bunkhouse to ourselves.

There's running water, and not only that, it's heated. Solar panels on the roof give us power, and there's a backup generator for when it's cloudy.

I go to the bathroom and turn on one of the showers and lean in, running my hand beneath the flow. "Oh, my God. It's hot. Perfectly hot."

I grin at Darius and Cade in excitement. I can hardly believe it. While the shower is nothing like five-star luxury, it feels that way to me. I've been wearing the same clothes for days, and I've never felt so grimy in my whole life.

Things might not be perfect, but they're hell of a lot better than they were only twenty-four hours ago. I haven't forgiven Cade for how he treated me in the forest when he found out about what Smith and Axel did to me, but right now it doesn't matter. It's something we'll deal with later. Right now, I just want to enjoy this. We deserve it.

Feeling no self-consciousness whatsoever, I strip off my filthy clothes and stand beneath the water. It drums on my head and shoulders, runs through my hair, taking with it the filth of the forest. After being so cold for so long, I finally feel myself warming up, the chill leaving my bones.

That's not the only thing getting heated in here.

"Is she naked?" Darius asks Cade. "Tell me she's naked."

Cade smirks. "Completely fucking naked."

Dax drags his t-shirt over his head, pulling his long hair with it so it vanishes for a moment inside the clothing, and then falls around his bare shoulders. "Fuck that. She doesn't get to be naked on her own."

"Hey," I only half protest. "There's not enough room for everyone."

"Bullshit. We'll make room."

His hands go to his jeans, and he yanks them off, too. He's already hard, and I put my hand out to him, taking his fingers in mine and pulling him into the shower.

"Well, that's not fair," Cade says, taking off his own t-shirt. "I want in, too."

Maybe I should tell him no, but I'm too happy to reject him right now.

Within seconds, he's naked, as well, and I find myself in a Cade and Darius sandwich, squashed between their two big bodies. Darius's erection is jammed into my spine, and Cade's is trapped between our stomachs.

We find the soap—a refillable bottle attached to the shower wall—and pump some into our palms. The men run their hands all over me, cupping my tits and squeezing my nipples, soaping down the curves of my ass. It feels so good, I'm in heaven.

"Is there shampoo?" I ask. "And conditioner?"

I'm not sure what use a group of loggers would have for conditioner, but Cade steps out quickly and checks in a medicine cabinet for me.

"Sure is. There's a few things here."

He hands a bottle of shampoo to Darius, who squirts some into his hand and then massages it through my hair. His strong fingers work my scalp, better than any professional I've ever come across, and my eyes roll with pleasure. When he's done, I tilt my head back to rinse out the shampoo, and he does the same with the conditioner, detangling my locks with his fingers. I'm feeling completely pampered.

Cade picks up one of the other bottles and smirks. "Wonder what they have this in here for?"

I look at the label. It's a bottle of baby oil.

I giggle. "I guess when the men are away from home for weeks on end, they need to make use of their hands."

Cade arches his eyebrow. "Or each other."

A flicker of arousal stirs at my core at the idea of two big loggers fucking each other in the shower.

Cade notices my blush. "You like that idea, huh?"

He tips some of the oil into his palm and touches himself, smoothing it along his huge cock until it's standing fully to attention, the ring straining at the end, as though it's begging to be touched. I put out my hand for some of the oil, and he obliges. I reach back for Darius and wrap my oiled hand around his length.

"Fuck, that feels good," he groans.

Darius bends at the knees and places his cock between my ass cheeks. He squeezes my ass cheeks together to make an oily tunnel for his dick and then rubs himself between them.

"God, you're so sexy." He kisses my shoulder. "So beautiful and perfect."

I don't feel perfect, not in the slightest, but I like hearing him say it.

Cade reaches between my thighs and pushes his finger inside me. "Is this okay?" he asks. "Me touching you like this?"

I'm wet and slippery and hot for them.

"Yes," I groan. "It feels good."

I don't want the memory of Smith and Axel to dominate my thoughts. It's like I'm trying to erase the memory of having those other men inside me by fucking my stepbrothers. I want Cade and Darius to flood me with themselves, to make me feel like it never happened. To claim me back as theirs.

"You take her pussy," Darius says to his brother. "I want her ass."

I blink. "What? At the same time?"

I wonder if they've done this before—been inside a girl at the same time as each other. It's not like their cocks are touching, so there's nothing really incestuous about it, though it does seem to walk the line.

"Wouldn't you like that, Cuckoo?" Cade says. "Feeling two cocks move inside you at the same time?"

I honestly have no idea.

"I don't know if I can."

It sounds like...too much.

"Don't worry," Darius assures me. "We'll be gentle with you."

Cade flashes a grin. "Well, he might be, but I intend to fuck you until you can't walk for a week."

We finish soaping up and rinsing ourselves down. I haven't been this clean in a long time, though from the way the brothers are looking at me, I won't stay clean for long.

They each take one of my hands, and together we step out of the shower. The men guide me over to one of the beds. We're all wet, and slippery with oil, but none of us care. We're clean and warm and safe, and that's all that matters.

35
CADE

I THROW MYSELF ONTO MY BACK ON ONE OF THE BEDS, AND then prop myself up on one elbow. I wrap my hand around my cock and slowly masturbate. The metal ring glints in the light overhead.

"Come and sit on my cock," I tell Laney.

I know the two of us still have some issues we need to talk through. There's tension between us that is different than we've had before. I hate that we're fighting, and that she probably thinks differently of me now. It kills me to think of her being touched by those other men, and I wish she'd never put herself in that position for me. I want to fuck any remnants of them right out of her.

Laney is wet and oily, her tan skin dripping. She straddles my hips, trapping my cock so it lies flat between my stomach and her pussy.

Farther down the bed, Darius also climbs on. He has to straddle my shins to get into the right position, which is fine as long as he doesn't lower himself down—I could do without my brother's balls landing on my legs.

I'm not focusing on him. Laney looks so fucking sexy, her small nipples dusky pink and hard, jutting out as though begging to be touched. I take in her beautiful torso, her stomach almost concave, her tits small and high. The gentle roundness of her hips. She is absolute fucking perfection.

She's also about to get my brother's cock in her ass.

We brought the oil with us, and Darius has it now. He opens the cap and dribbles some down over her asshole.

"You're not an anal virgin, are you?" he asks her.

Her cheeks pink up prettily, and she shakes her head. "No, your daddy likes fucking me that way."

I grin. "Does he, now...dirty fucker."

They shift positions slightly, and Laney's expression contorts, telling me that Dax's cock has met her asshole.

She sucks air over her teeth.

"Is this okay?" he asks her. "I can feel you stretching around me."

"Oh, it stings," she cries, her pretty features knotted.

"Just breathe," Dax tells her. "You can take me. You're doing so well."

She gasps and moans. "Oh, God. Oh, fuck."

He's pushing inside her. I wish I could see, wanting to watch how her asshole stretches around him, but I'm patient and wait my turn, though my cock bobs with anticipation.

This needs to be about Laney, about giving her the most mind-blowing orgasm of her life. Fuck it, why stop at one? I hope she has multiple Os while we're inside her.

"Fuck, you're so tight, Laney," Dax says from between gritted teeth. "Jesus."

"You're too big," she moans. "I don't know if I can take all of you."

"I'm nearly fully inside you. I'm almost there. Fuck, this is so hot."

She's making little animalistic mewls, her eyes squeezed shut. Her hips rock, so she grinds down on my cock beneath her pussy. She's so wet, and it feels incredible, but I want to be inside her.

Dax is fully embedded in her ass now, so he reaches around to play with her tits, cupping them in his palms and then squeezing her nipples. His hands are big enough to do both, his fingers, nimble from playing the violin, working her. He pulls away and lightly slaps one of her tits and then the other. She gives a strange little yelp, but she bites her lower lip. It's a pleasurable pain. Darius likes to slap and spank and smack. I'd almost forgotten that about him.

Her eyes flicker open, and her lips part. She blinks down at me, but I can tell she's struggling to focus with my brother's cock in her ass. She's going to struggle even harder in a minute when I'm inside her, too.

I give my hips a wiggle. "Come on, then, little sis. See if you can take us both."

"I don't know if I can. You're both too big."

"Yes, you can," I encourage her. "Your body is made for us. You can do it."

She only needs to lift up a fraction, bringing Dax with her, before her pussy is lined up with the head of my dick. I know how much she likes it when I rub my piercing over her clit, so I treat her to some of that before I try to enter her. I want her good and wet, practically gushing over me. If we can make her squirt, even better.

"I can feel when you do that, bro" Dax tells me. "Her ass clamps around me even harder."

"She's going to feel even tighter in a minute," I tell him.

I rub her again, paying extra attention to her clit. Her breathing is harsh, and she looks like she's going to unravel at any minute. That's fine by me. If she comes, we'll make her come for a second time.

"Are you ready?" I ask her.

She nods.

We're going to fuck any memory of those bastards right out of her.

I lift my hips and shunt the head of my cock inside her pussy.

She goes rigid, clearly feeling the stretch. "Oh, God, no, I can't. It's too much. You're too big."

"Yes, you can," I encourage her. "You can take it. You can take both of us."

"No, I'm going to lose my mind. I swear I will."

I want to see her unravel. I want to watch whatever guards she puts up completely shatter as she comes.

I slide deeper, and she whimpers again, but now, instead of pulling back, she sinks down on me.

I can tell we're both deep inside her.

"How does that feel?" I ask her, studying her face.

"So full," she gasps. "So fucking full."

"That's it, sweet girl. You're taking us so good. Your pussy feels so fucking perfect around my cock."

I thumb her clit and lift my hips so I'm balls deep inside her now. Darius has had the patience of a saint, holding still to give Laney the time to get used to the sensation of taking us both. We're both buried inside her now, a joined unit.

Darius pays attention to her nipples, pulling and tweaking the hard buds, while I work her clit. I can feel her inner muscles contract around me, and then she's the one who initiates our movement. She starts to rock, slowly and gently at first, and then building momentum.

"That's our good girl," Dax praises her. "Our sexy little sister."

"Do you like your big brothers fucking you?" I ask her.

She can barely speak. "Oh, yes. I do. Keep fucking me."

We go with her, allowing her to take the lead, until we find our rhythm.

Before long, we've lost what little control we have.

I grab her hips and pound into her hard from below. Dax has his chest pinned to her back, his hands on her tits, rutting into her ass. We're oily and damp, and sweaty and frantic, each of us climbing toward our release. The sounds of skin slapping and heaving breathing fills the room. My balls draw tight into my body, and I know I could let go at any moment, but I'm holding back for her.

"Oh, God. I'm coming, I'm coming," Laney cries.

Her whole body is a knot of tension, and then she shudders and shakes, her inner muscles convulsing around us. The noises she makes are the hottest things I've ever heard, and I imprint them to memory.

Behind her, Darius grunts, "Fuck," and jams himself deep, his jaw clenched and teeth bared as he releases himself inside her.

I let go, pleasure flooding through me, and, together, Darius and I cleanse her pussy and ass with our cum, washing away the taint of any other men.

It's raw and pure, and fucking beautiful. I know in that moment that no other woman will ever live up to her in my mind. She's ruined me now. All I want is her.

Without her, I might as well just turn to dust and blow away in the breeze.

36

Laney

I<small>T'S THE FOLLOWING MORNING, AND</small> I <small>DON'T THINK</small> I'<small>VE</small>
ever slept so well in my entire life.

Clean, and with a full belly, on a real bed with sheets, after
mind-blowing sex. How could anyone sleep badly after that?
Plus, we're getting out of here today.

Reed had returned to the bunkhouse shortly after the
insane orgasm I'd had with his sons. He must have understood
that all I'd needed was rest, because he just tucked me into one
of the single beds and placed a chaste kiss on my forehead. I'd
said, 'thank you, Daddy,' and he'd replied with 'you're welcome,
baby-girl,' which made me all warm inside. I know he takes
pleasure in looking after me, and I love how much he cares. Of
course, we're not real father and daughter—that would be weird
—but it's as though we fill that need in each other. I've never
had that before.

Though physically, I'm much improved, emotionally, I'm
struggling. The high of reaching safety and having food and
running water has ebbed away overnight. Now I'm left with the

knowledge that I'm going to have the time and space to process what's happened to me. The prospect is terrifying. I think the only thing that's allowed me to put it to the back of my mind is that we've been in a life-or-death situation. I haven't had that time because I've been too busy trying to survive.

Now I feel like a shell of a person, hollowed out, empty.

I'll do what needs to be done, go through the actions, because I know I need to in order to go back to normal society. I'm not doing it for myself, though. I'm doing it because I want the others to live their lives.

But do I still want to live mine?

I'm damaged. Even though it's only been a month, the thought of trying to go back to normal life is utterly overwhelming. How is it even going to work? Reed said he wanted me to stay with them, but Cade hurt me, and I'm sure Darius will want to go back to his life of touring and playing on stages around the world. He'll probably be even more famous now—the violinist who cheated death. They won't want me around to ruin things for them. Right now, all I want to do is climb into bed, pull the covers up over my head, and sleep for a month. It's not only that I'm exhausted—though I am—I want to go back to familiarity. I want to hide out. I don't want to deal with this anymore.

The guys all seem in a good mood, though, teasing each other and fooling around. They haven't noticed how quiet I am.

I take another shower—alone, this time—and then we get ready to go to the communal bunkhouse for breakfast. We're due to be airlifted out of the logging site in an hour.

The only clothes they had were men's, but I don't mind. The t-shirt is huge on me, hanging halfway down my thighs, and it swamps my arms to my elbows. They found me a pair of shorts as well, which I've had to cinch in with a belt.

"I think that's the most adorable I've ever seen you," Reed says.

"I look ridiculous."

"You look cute as hell."

I recognize the glint in his eye. That he still wants me even after everything warms me inside, but I'm still struggling with touch reminding me of what Smith and Axel did. I thought I could fuck the feeling away, to use Cade and Darius as a way of eradicating any memory of them from my body, but it hasn't worked.

"Let's go eat," Reed says.

"I'll be right there," I tell him.

He frowns. "You sure?"

"Absolutely. I won't be long."

I could do with a moment on my own.

Reed is clearly reluctant to leave me, but they all go down to the communal bunkhouse. When they're gone, I let out a sigh. I love them with all my heart, but I haven't had a moment alone in a long time. Maybe that's what I need—some space to process everything that's happened?

There's a chill in the air this morning, a sign of fall, and I grab a jacket that's way too big for me. As I turn, I discover someone standing in the cabin doorway.

"Laney, we need to talk."

My chest tightens at the sight of Cade standing there. His hair is longer now than when we first met, and he's all beardy. That, combined with his size and tattoos, makes him look incredibly sexy. I can't be distracted by his looks, though. Our relationship is on another level now. We've been through so much, but I don't know how I feel. He hurt me back in the forest, and after everything I've been through, I can't just forget what he said.

"No, we don't," I say. "Not right now."

I don't want to relive everything, all the hurt and disappointment.

"Laney?" His voice is soft.

"What is it, Cade?"

Maybe it had been a bad idea to get sex mixed in with everything when we still hadn't worked things out between us, but I'd been on a high yesterday, and I hadn't been thinking.

"I'm sorry," he says. "I'm so fucking sorry. I'm a stupid, selfish ass, and I understand that you may never forgive me for treating you like that, but if you can find it inside yourself to forgive me, I'll be yours forever."

"So, you break my fucking heart and reject me when I need you the most, and I'm supposed to roll over and forgive you because you changed your mind?"

"I'm sorry…" He sounds helpless, desperate, but instead of making me soften to him, it only hardens my heart.

"I got hurt, in the worst possible way, and instead of you comforting me and telling me how it would never change how you felt about me, you blamed me for it. You were so fucking selfish that you turned things around to make what they did to me to be about you."

He ducks his head. "Fuck, Laney…my head was messed up…I was going through some shit as well."

"And we should have come together, to support each other, not use it as a reason to push me away."

"It hurt, thinking of those fuckers touching you like that. Them being inside you. I didn't know how to deal with it."

I flare my nostrils. "No, you fucking didn't."

"I hated that you put yourself in that position because of me. I'd rather have died, Laney, and I meant that part. I still mean it now. If it means not another single person ever hurts you again for the rest of your life, I'll happily go to my death."

I make a sound somewhere between a laugh and a sob.

"And how do you think I'd carry on if you were dead? I would be hurt, devastatingly so."

His eyes are beseeching. "Does that mean you still love me?"

"Of course I love you. I've never stopped loving you, and that's what makes this so hard. I need to be able to trust you."

"You can," he insists.

But I can't bring myself to believe him. What if every time things get hard, he tries to hurt me again?

"I don't know, Cade. This has all been too much. How do I know that you won't push me away again the next time something happens that doesn't go the way you'd have wanted it?"

"I've learned my lesson."

I have to protect my heart. I've been through so much over the past few months—from losing my mom, to the plane crash, to being used and abused by Smith and his men. Now I need to figure out how I'm going to heal, and I don't know if Cade is good for me. I've always known he has a hard side. The way he'd treated me when we'd first met, even though he knew I'd just lost my only parent, highlighted that. He knew I was a young woman alone in the world, trying to blend in with a new family, and he hadn't given me so much as a kind word. Then the plane had crashed, and things had gotten even worse. If there hadn't been chemistry between us, would he have ever given me a chance? What if the plane had never gone down, and we'd landed in Canada without any hitch? What would our relationship be now? I'd been a distraction for him, and it wasn't as though there were tons of other women to choose from. If he'd still been able to pick up glamorous women, like the one from the concert hall on the first night we'd met, he probably wouldn't have even glanced my way.

"I don't know how to feel right now, Cade. You said your

head was fucked up in the cabin. Well, mine is fucked up now. I don't know if I can trust you with my heart."

"You can, I swear it. My heart is yours. Every single beat is for you. Don't shut me out now, Laney. Not after everything we've been through."

A part of me so desperately wants to give in to him, but I can't.

"I need some time, Cade. Time to heal. Time to think. Time to figure out what I want."

"And what about my brother? What about my dad, too?"

I can't look at him. "They weren't the ones who hurt me."

Realization flashes across his handsome features, quickly followed by hurt and then anger.

"So, you're going to carry on fucking them and leave me out in the cold. Is that how this is going to work?"

"I'm not going to talk to you about my relationship with them."

"You're cutting me out. This is exactly what Reed was worried about. That you'd end up coming between us."

"That's not what I'm doing."

"Isn't it? How am I supposed to be around you all, when you're all loved up with my father and brother, while I'm sitting around, desperate to get a kind look or word from you?"

"You know what, you should have thought about that before you got so fucking mad at me for saving your life!" I was angry again now.

He laces his hands behind his head. "I said I was sorry, Laney. What more do you fucking want from me?"

"To give me some time, some space. You say you'll die for me, but you won't do something as simple as that?"

"Because it would kill me not to be near you. Every second that passes where I can't hold you is like torture."

I want to tell him what it was like for me, having to

spread my legs for those men, the sort of torture I went through that he'll never understand. But I can't bring myself to say it. I can't relive that, even if it'll only be through my words. He has no idea how it feels to have someone inside you when you don't want them to be, how utterly defiling it is. How it makes you want to tear your own insides out, and rip off your own skin, and disintegrate into nothing. After going through that, the last thing I needed was someone making out that it was somehow my fault. That, if I'd made different choices, it wouldn't have happened to me. It was like someone blaming the girl because she wore the short dress, or had that extra drink, or tried to walk home too late at night.

"We need to eat before we're shipped out of here," I say, trying to focus on practical things.

But he hasn't finished.

"Do you think this is normal for me to feel this way about a girl? I've been with a lot of women—"

"Trying to make me feel better, are you?" I snap back.

"Listen to me. I've been with a lot of women, and not once have I met someone who's affected me the way you have. I've never given a single thought to how any of those women thought or felt, but with you, it's all I think about. You've taken over my heart and my head and my body. I don't think about anything else. My body craves a connection with you. How am I supposed to go through each day without you? I don't work without you, Laney."

"You're pressuring me. You think that's what I need, after what I went through? Another man laying claim to me?"

"I'm not just another man. Am I?"

He steps closer and tries to take my hand, but I pull out of his grip. I can't let him touch me, because I know if I do, I'll crumble.

"I love you," I tell him. "Knowing that needs to be enough for the moment."

He presses his lips together, his nostrils flaring as he shakes his head. "It's not. It's nowhere near enough."

"It's going to have to be."

I put my head down and push past him and step out into the open air. I'm aware of all the curious glances from the loggers. What must they think of us?

I'm welcomed with a warm smile from Reed.

"We were starting to worry where you'd gotten to," he says.

"Sorry. Just grabbing a jacket."

"And having a chat with Cade?"

I can't look at him. "Yeah, that, too."

"He loves you, you know."

I nod. "I love him, too."

I distract myself with breakfast. There's bacon and scrambled eggs—that most likely come from a powder, but what do I care—and butter and toast. There's hot coffee, too, and a concentrated orange juice.

After a few minutes, Cade comes and joins us, but he brings with it the tension from the bunkhouse.

Reed notices. He lowers his voice so we can't be overheard.

"We're getting out of here soon, and there are some things we need to remember. People can't know about what's happened between us all at the cabin—the nature of our relationship, I mean. They won't understand. I'm forty years old, and your stepfather, Laney, and the press and everyone else will vilify me if they find out."

"I understand. I won't say a word, I promise."

"But it's things like this, as well." He takes my hand from where I'd rested it on the inside of his thigh. "A stepdaughter wouldn't touch her stepfather like that."

Though I understand, his rejection still stings. "Shit, sorry."

"We have to be careful."

I want to say that we haven't done anything wrong, but I know how badly it'll reflect on the others—especially Reed. We need to be careful about how we act around each other, the easy, affectionate ways of touching hidden from the media. Reed needs to touch me only in the way he would his step-daughter. Cade and Darius need to think of me as their stepsister. And I need to do the same. No more kissing or holding hands. No slipping my arms around any of their waist and pressing my face to their chests. No more running my hands through their hair.

Even though they're right here with me, I miss them already. I hate that we won't be able to be ourselves around each other. I'm angry with Cade for being such a selfish asshole, but we'll work through it, I hope.

A niggling voice sounds inside my head. What if he just leaves? Goes and seeks solace in another woman's arms? A woman like the one in the short silver dress at the concert hall that night. I've always been worried about how our relationships will play out back in the real world, but what if the simple truth is that they won't?

We might have found safety, but what will happen between us now? It all feels so hard—too hard. All I want is peace, but will I find that if I'm questioning myself constantly, overanalyzing every move I make?

I make a decision.

"When we get back, I think I should go and stay at my trailer."

Reed stares at me. "You can't be serious. Why would you want to go back to that place?"

"I kept thinking that all I wanted was to be home and in my own bed, and that trailer is the only home, other than the cabin, that I've ever known. The bed might not be like the super soft king size ones you're used to, but I'm pretty sure it's going to feel like luxury compared to the cabin."

"But you hated that trailer. Your mom died inside it."

"I know. I'm not stupid."

"I'm trying to get my head around this, Laney. You want to go back to your trailer? Alone? To live?"

"I think I need some time, some space, a way of letting everything that's happened sink in."

Darius frowns at me. "You shouldn't be alone."

"I need to be. For a while, anyway. Don't you think it's better that way? No one will have any clue that anything happened between us that shouldn't have if we stay out of each other's way."

Reed shakes his head. "You can't mean that, Laney. After what you went through...it's not good to be alone."

"Perhaps it's exactly what I need. So much has happened, I'm struggling to get my head around it. Having the three of you around, and knowing we have to watch how we act...it's just going to make things even more complicated."

His expression is pinched and hurt, but he considers what I've said.

"Okay, Laney. If that's really what you want. I won't let you be without money, though. You don't need to struggle."

My struggles had nothing to do with finances, but I appreciate that he still wants to look after me.

"You don't have to pay for me. I'm eighteen now. I can take care of myself."

Perhaps I should get back to my job—if they'll have me. It would be better to stay busy instead of lying around the trailer all day. I think of how everyone will ask me questions, and the customers will whisper behind their hands, wondering if I'm the one they saw on the news or on their socials.

The weight of that possibility is so utterly unthinkable, it actually stops my breath for a moment, and I'm not sure I can draw another.

No work. No doing. No thinking. Just hiding.

I think of death like a dreamless sleep you never wake from, and, right now, the thought of that is so alluring it's almost impossible not to yearn for it. No more reliving what Smith and the others did to me. No more picturing the dead flight attendant' face each time I close my eyes. No more torturing myself with what may or may not happen between me, Reed, Cade, and Dax in the future.

Just peace.

"You don't have to struggle, Laney," Reed says.

"Don't I?"

I'm aware that he's still talking about money, but my mind is already elsewhere.

"No, you don't. Give me your bank details, and I'll make sure money is wired over."

I shake my head. "We don't need to talk about this now."

I think of my mom and wonder if she's even had a funeral. Would I have missed it, or have the authorities waited in the hope I'd be found again? I hope they've waited. It feels wrong that I never got to say a proper goodbye.

A sound catches my attention. I'm not the only one who hears it. Darius cocks his head, and both Reed and Cade look up to the sky.

It's the thrum of a helicopter.

My heart hitches. I can hardly believe it.

We're actually getting out of here.

We're going home.

Loved what you read? Don't miss out on the third and final book, Immoral Ties, on Amazon!

Want to read a dark cut scene that never made it into the final book? Click this link to download the scene and join my newsletter! You'll get all the latest news, free books, and I promise to never spam.

ACKNOWLEDGMENTS

Huge thank you to everyone who has read Immoral Steps and Immoral Games and have been sharing the books on social media and leaving reviews. I can't explain how happy it makes me to be scrolling through Facebook or Instagram and see my books pop up as recommendations in groups or on your stories. I've never been one of those authors who sees their books everywhere, so I'm loving the buzz you're all creating for this series!

As always, I have to also thank my fabulous team of editors and proofreaders—Lori Whitwam, Jessica Fraser, and Tammy Payne. I did have to include a 'I hope this book doesn't traumatise you' note when I sent this book off to each of you, and I'm glad you're all still in one piece!

Thank you, once again, to Lilibet James, for advance reading Immoral Games and giving me her thoughts on Darius's point of view. Your advice and opinions are invaluable.

Thanks to Wander Aguiar for another gorgeous photograph, and Daqri at Covers by Combs for the fantastic typography.

And finally thanks to Silla Webb for her stunning formatting. I love seeing these books in paperback and hardback on my shelf.

Until next time!

Marissa

ABOUT THE AUTHOR

about the author

Marissa Farrar has always been in love with being in love. But since she's been married for numerous years and has three young daughters, she's conducted her love affairs with multiple gorgeous men of the fictional persuasion.

The author of more than forty novels, she has written full time for the last eight years. She predominantly writes dark reverse harem romance, but also writes dark m/f, paranormal romance and fantasy as well.

If you want to know more about Marissa, then please visit her website at www.marissa-farrar.com. You can also find her at her Facebook page, www.facebook.com/marissa.farrar.author or follow her on TikTok @marissafarrarwrites.

She loves to hear from readers and can be emailed at marissafarrar@hotmail.co.uk. To stay updated on all new releases and sales, just sign up to her newsletter!

Other Dark Contemporary Books by the Author

The Limit Series:

Dark Contemporary Reverse Harem

Blurred Limits

Brutal Limit

Broken Limits

The Bad Blood Trilogy

Shattered Hearts

Broken Minds

Tattered Souls

The Monster Trilogy

Defaced

Denied

Delivered

Dark Codes: A Reverse Harem Series

Hacking Darkness

Unraveling Darkness

Decoding Darkness

Merging Darkness

For Him Trilogy

Raised for Him

Unbound for Him

Damaged for Him

The Mercenary Series

The Choice She Made

The Lie She Told

The Trust She Gave

The Trap She Faced

Standalone Novels

No Second Chances

Cut Too Deep

Survivor

Dirty Shots

Printed in Great Britain
by Amazon